SELECTED SHORT STORIES OF
WILLIAM FAULKNER

SELECTED
SHORT STORIES
OF
WILLIAM FAULKNER

THE MODERN LIBRARY

NEW YORK

This work was originally published in The Modern Library in 1962.

Jacket portrait by Hy Peskin, Life Magazine © Time Warner Inc.

LIBRARY OF CONGRESS CATALOGING-IN-PUBLICATION DATA
Faulkner, William, 1897–1962.
[Short stories. Selections]
Selected short stories of William Faulkner.
p.   cm.
ISBN 0-679-42478-4
I. Title.
PS3511.A86A6   1993
813´.52—dc20   92-51072

Modern Library website address: www.modernlibrary.com

Printed in the United States of America on acid-free paper

14 16 18 19 17 15

WILLIAM FAULKNER

William Faulkner was born in New Albany, Mississippi, on September 25, 1897. His family was rooted in local history: his great-grandfather, a Confederate colonel and state politician, was assassinated by a former partner in 1889, and his grandfather was a wealthy lawyer who owned a railroad. When Faulkner was five his parents moved to Oxford, Mississippi, where he received a desultory education in local schools, dropping out of high school in 1915. Rejected for pilot training in the U.S. Army, he passed himself off as British and joined the Canadian Royal Air Force in 1918, but the war ended before he saw any service. After the war, he took some classes at the University of Mississippi and worked for a time at the university post office. Mostly, however, he educated himself by reading promiscuously.

Faulkner had begun writing poems when he was a schoolboy, and in 1924 he published a poetry collection, *The Marble Faun,* at his own expense. His literary aspirations were fueled by his close friendship with Sherwood Anderson, whom he met during a stay in New Orleans. Faulkner's first novel, *Soldiers' Pay,* was published in 1926, followed a year later by *Mosquitoes,* a literary satire. His next book, *Flags in the Dust,* was heavily cut and rearranged at the publisher's insistence and appeared finally as *Sartoris* in 1929. In the meantime he had completed *The Sound and the Fury,* and when it appeared at the end of 1929 he had finished *Sanctuary* and was ready to begin writing *As I Lay Dying*. That same year he married Estelle Oldham, whom he had courted a decade earlier.

Although Faulkner gained literary acclaim from these and subsequent novels—*Light in August* (1932), *Pylon* (1935), *Absalom, Absalom!* (1936), *The Unvanquished* (1938), *The Wild Palms* (1939), *The Hamlet* (1940), and *Go Down, Moses* (1942) —and continued to publish stories regularly in magazines, he was unable to support himself solely by writing fiction. He worked as a screenwriter for MGM, Twentieth Century-Fox, and Warner Brothers, forming a close relationship with director Howard Hawks, with whom he worked on *To Have and Have Not, The Big Sleep,* and *Land of the Pharaohs,* among other films. In 1944 all but one of Faulkner's novels were out of print, and his personal life was at low ebb due in part to his chronic heavy drinking. During the war he had been discovered by Sartre and Camus and others in the French literary world. In the postwar period his reputation rebounded, as Malcolm Cowley's anthology *The Portable Faulkner* brought him fresh attention in America, and the immense esteem in which he was held in Europe consolidated his worldwide stature.

Faulkner wrote seventeen books set in the mythical Yoknapatawpha County, home of the Compson family of *The Sound and the Fury*. "No land in all fiction lives more vividly in its physical presence than this county of Faulkner's imagination," Robert Penn Warren wrote in an essay on Cowley's anthology. "The descendants of the old families, the descendants of bushwhackers and carpetbaggers, the swamp rats, the Negro cooks and farm hands, the bootleggers and gangsters, tenant farmers, college boys, county-seat lawyers, country storekeepers, peddlers—all are here in their fullness of life and their complicated interrelations." In 1950 Faulkner was awarded the Nobel Prize for Literature. In later books—*Intruder in the Dust* (1948), *Requiem for a Nun* (1951), *A Fable* (1954), *The Town* (1957), *The Mansion* (1959), and *The Reivers* (1962)—he continued to explore what he had called "the problems of the human heart in conflict with itself," but did so in the context of Yoknapatawpha's increasing connection with the modern world. He died of a heart attack on July 6, 1962.

Contents

BARN BURNING   1

TWO SOLDIERS   26

A ROSE FOR EMILY   47

DRY SEPTEMBER   60

THAT EVENING SUN   76

RED LEAVES   100

LO!   133

TURNABOUT   158

HONOR   197

THERE WAS A QUEEN   212

MOUNTAIN VICTORY   232

BEYOND   269

RACE AT MORNING   289

SELECTED SHORT STORIES OF
WILLIAM FAULKNER

Barn Burning

The store in which the Justice of the Peace's court was sitting smelled of cheese. The boy, crouched on his nail keg at the back of the crowded room, knew he smelled cheese, and more: from where he sat he could see the ranked shelves close-packed with the solid, squat, dynamic shapes of tin cans whose labels his stomach read, not from the lettering which meant nothing to his mind but from the scarlet devils and the silver curve of fish—this, the cheese which he knew he smelled and the hermetic meat which his intestines believes he smelled coming in intermittent gusts momentary and brief between the other constant one, the smell and sense just a little of fear because mostly of despair and grief, the old fierce pull of blood. He could not see the table where the Justice sat and before which his father and his father's enemy *(our enemy* he thought in that despair; *ourn! mine and hisn both! He's my father!)* stood, but he could hear them, the two of them that is, because his father had said no word yet:

"But what proof have you, Mr. Harris?"

"I told you. The hog got into my corn. I caught it up and sent it back to him. He had no fence that would hold it. I told him so, warned him. The next time I put the hog

1

in my pen. When he came to get it I gave him enough wire to patch up his pen. The next time I put the hog up and kept it. I rode down to his house and saw the wire I gave him still rolled on to the spool in his yard. I told him he could have the hog when he paid me a dollar pound fee. That evening a nigger came with the dollar and got the hog. He was a strange nigger. He said, 'He say to tell you wood and hay kin burn.' I said, 'What? ' 'That whut he say to tell you,' the nigger said. 'Wood and hay kin burn.' That night my barn burned. I got the stock out but I lost the barn."

"Where is the nigger? Have you got him?"

"He was a strange nigger, I tell you. I don't know what became of him."

"But that's not proof. Don't you see that's not proof?"

"Get that boy up here. He knows." For a moment the boy thought too that the man meant his older brother until Harris said, "Not him. The little one. The boy," and, crouching, small for his age, small and wiry like his father, in patched and faded jeans even too small for him, with straight, uncombed, brown hair and eyes gray and wild as storm scud, he saw the men between himself and the table part and become a lane of grim faces, at the end of which he saw the Justice, a shabby, collarless, graying man in spectacles, beckoning him. He felt no floor under his bare feet; he seemed to walk beneath the palpable weight of the grim turning faces. His father, stiff in his black Sunday coat donned not for the trial but for the moving, did not even look at him. *He aims for me to lie,* he thought, again with that frantic grief and despair. *And I will have to do hit.*

"What's your name, boy?" the Justice said.

"Colonel Sartoris Snopes," the boy whispered.

"Hey?" the Justice said. "Talk louder. Colonel Sartoris? I reckon anybody named for Colonel Sartoris in this country can't help but tell the truth, can they?" The boy said nothing. *Enemy! Enemy!* he thought; for a moment he could not even see, could not see that the Justice's face was kindly nor discern that his voice was troubled when he spoke to the man named Harris: "Do you want me to question this boy?" But he could hear, and during those subsequent long seconds while there was absolutely no sound in the crowded little room save that of quiet and intent breathing it was as if he had swung outward at the end of a grape vine, over a ravine, and at the top of the swing had been caught in a prolonged instant of mesmerized gravity, weightless in time.

"No!" Harris said violently, explosively. "Damnation! Send him out of here!" Now time, the fluid world, rushed beneath him again, the voices coming to him again through the smell of cheese and sealed meat, the fear and despair and the old grief of blood:

"This case is closed. I can't find against you, Snopes, but I can give you advice. Leave this country and don't come back to it."

His father spoke for the first time, his voice cold and harsh, level, without emphasis: "I aim to. I don't figure to stay in a country among people who . . ." he said something unprintable and vile, addressed to no one.

"That'll do," the Justice said. "Take your wagon and get out of this country before dark. Case dismissed."

His father turned, and he followed the stiff black coat, the wiry figure walking a little stiffly from where a Confederate provost's man's musket ball had taken him in the heel on a stolen horse thirty years ago, followed the two backs now, since his older brother had appeared from somewhere in the crowd, no taller than the father but thicker, chewing tobacco steadily, between the two lines of grim-faced men and out of the store and across the worn gallery and down the sagging steps and among the dogs and half-grown boys in the mild May dust, where as he passed a voice hissed:

"Barn burner!"

Again he could not see, whirling; there was a face in a red haze, moonlike, bigger than the full moon, the owner of it half again his size, he leaping in the red haze toward the face, feeling no blow, feeling no shock when his head struck the earth, scrabbling up and leaping again, feeling no blow this time either and tasting no blood, scrabbling up to see the other boy in full flight and himself already leaping into pursuit as his father's hand jerked him back, the harsh, cold voice speaking above him: "Go get in the wagon."

It stood in a grove of locusts and mulberries across the road. His two hulking sisters in their Sunday dresses and his mother and her sister in calico and sunbonnets were already in it, sitting on and among the sorry residue of the dozen and more movings which even the boy could remember—the battered stove, the broken beds and chairs, the clock inlaid with mother-of-pearl, which would not run, stopped at some fourteen minutes past two o'clock of a dead and forgotten day and time, which had been his mother's dowry. She was crying, though when she saw him she drew her sleeve across her face and began to descend from the wagon. "Get back," the father said.

"He's hurt. I got to get some water and wash his . . ."

"Get back in the wagon," his father said. He got in too, over the tail-gate. His father mounted to the seat where the older brother already sat and struck the gaunt mules two savage blows with the peeled willow, but without heat. It was not even sadistic; it was exactly that same quality which in later years would cause his descendants to over-run the engine before putting a motor car into motion, striking and reining back in the same movement. The wagon went on, the store with its quiet crowd of grimly watching men dropped behind; a curve in the road hid it. *Forever* he thought. *Maybe he's done satisfied now, now that he has* . . . stopping himself, not to say it aloud even to himself. His mother's hand touched his shoulder.

"Does hit hurt?" she said.

"Naw," he said. "Hit don't hurt. Lemme be."

"Can't you wipe some of the blood off before hit dries?"

"I'll wash tonight," he said. "Lemme be, I tell you."

The wagon went on. He did not know where they were going. None of them ever did or ever asked, because it was always somewhere, always a house of sorts waiting for them a day or two days or even three days away. Likely his father had already arranged to make a crop on another farm before he . . . Again he had to stop himself. He (the father) always did. There was something about his wolflike independence and even courage when the advantage was at least neutral which impressed strangers, as if they got from his latent ravening ferocity not so much a sense of dependability as a feeling that his ferocious conviction in the rightness of his own actions would be of advantage to all whose interest lay with his.

That night they camped, in a grove of oaks and

beeches where a spring ran. The nights were still cool and they had a fire against it, of a rail lifted from a nearby fence and cut into lengths—a small fire, neat, niggard almost, a shrewd fire; such fires were his father's habit and custom always, even in freezing weather. Older, the boy might have remarked this and wondered why not a big one; why should not a man who had not only seen the waste and extravagance of war, but who had in his blood an inherent voracious prodigality with material not his own, have burned everything in sight? Then he might have gone a step farther and thought that that was the reason: that niggard blaze was the living fruit of nights passed during those four years in the woods hiding from all men, blue or gray, with his strings of horses (captured horses, he called them). And older still, he might have divined the true reason: that the element of fire spoke to some deep mainspring of his father's being, as the element of steel or of powder spoke to other men, as the one weapon for the preservation of integrity, else breath were not worth the breathing, and hence to be regarded with respect and used with discretion.

But he did not think this now and he had seen those same niggard blazes all his life. He merely ate his supper beside it and was already half asleep over his iron plate when his father called him, and once more he followed the stiff back, the stiff and ruthless limp, up the slope and on to the starlit road where, turning, he could see his father against the stars but without face or depth—a shape black, flat, and bloodless as though cut from tin in the iron folds of the frockcoat which had not been made for him, the voice harsh like tin and without heat like tin:

"You were fixing to tell them. You would have told him." He didn't answer. His father struck him with the flat of his hand on the side of the head, hard but without heat, exactly as he had struck the two mules at the store, exactly as he would strike either of them with any stick in order to kill a horse fly, his voice still without heat or anger: "You're getting to be a man. You got to learn. You got to learn to stick to your own blood or you ain't going to have any blood to stick to you. Do you think either of them, any man there this morning, would? Don't you know all they wanted was a chance to get at me because they knew I had them beat? Eh?" Later, twenty years later, he was to tell himself, "If I had said they wanted only truth, justice, he would have hit me again." But now he said nothing. He was not crying. He just stood there. "Answer me," his father said.

"Yes," he whispered. His father turned.

"Get on to bed. We'll be there tomorrow."

Tomorrow they were there. In the early afternoon the wagon stopped before a paintless two-room house identical almost with the dozen others it had stopped before even in the boy's ten years, and again, as on the other dozen occasions, his mother and aunt got down and began to unload the wagon, although his two sisters and his father and brother had not moved.

"Likely hit ain't fitten for hawgs," one of the sisters said.

"Nevertheless, fit it will and you'll hog it and like it," his father said. "Get out of them chairs and help your Ma unload."

The two sisters got down, big, bovine, in a flutter of cheap ribbons; one of them drew from the jumbled wagon bed a battered lantern, the other a worn broom. His father handed the reins to the older son and began to climb stiffly over the wheel. "When they get unloaded, take the team to the barn and feed them." Then he said, and at first the boy thought he was still speaking to his brother: "Come with me."

"Me?" he said.

"Yes," his father said. "You."

"Abner," his mother said. His father paused and looked back—the harsh level stare beneath the shaggy, graying, irascible brows.

"I reckon I'll have a word with the man that aims to begin tomorrow owning me body and soul for the next eight months."

They went back up the road. A week ago—or before last night, that is—he would have asked where they were going, but not now. His father had struck him before last night but never before had he paused afterward to explain why; it was as if the blow and the following calm, outrageous voice still rang, repercussed, divulging nothing to him save the terrible handicap of being young, the light weight of his few years, just heavy enough to prevent his soaring free of the world as it seemed to be ordered but not heavy enough to keep him footed solid in it, to resist it and try to change the course of its events.

Presently he could see the grove of oaks and cedars and the other flowering trees and shrubs where the house would be, though not the house yet. They walked beside a fence massed with honeysuckle and Cherokee roses and came to a gate swinging open between two brick pillars, and now, beyond a sweep of drive, he saw the house for the first time and at that instant he forgot his father and the terror and despair both, and even when he remembered his father again (who had not stopped) the terror and despair did not return. Because, for all the twelve movings, they had sojourned until now in a poor country, a land of small farms and fields and houses, and he had never seen a house like this before. *Hit's big as a courthouse* he thought quietly, with a surge of peace and joy whose reason he could not have thought into words, being too young for that: *They are safe from him. People whose lives are a part of this peace and dignity are beyond his touch, he no more to them than a buzzing wasp: capable of stinging for a little moment but that's all; the spell of this peace and dignity rendering even the barns and stable and cribs which belong to it impervious to the puny flames he might contrive . . .* this, the peace and joy, ebbing for an instant as he looked again at the stiff black back, the stiff and implacable limp of the figure which was not dwarfed by the house, for the reason that it had never looked big anywhere and which now, against the serene columned backdrop, had more than ever that impervious quality of something cut ruthlessly from tin, depthless, as though, sidewise to the sun, it would cast no shadow. Watching him, the boy remarked the absolutely undeviating course which his father held and saw the stiff foot come squarely down in a pile of fresh droppings where a horse had stood in the drive and which his father could have avoided by a simple change of stride. But it ebbed only for a moment, though he could not have thought this into words either, walking on in the spell of the house, which he could even want but without envy, without sorrow, certainly never with that ravening and jealous rage which unknown to him walked in the ironlike black coat before him: *Maybe he will feel it too. Maybe it will even change him now from what maybe he couldn't help but be.*

They crossed the portico. Now he could hear his father's stiff foot as it came down on the boards with clocklike finality, a sound out of all proportion to the displacement of the body it bore and which was not dwarfed either by the white door before it, as though it had attained to a sort of vicious and ravening minimum not to be dwarfed by anything—the flat, wide, black hat, the formal coat of broadcloth which had once been black but which had now that friction-glazed greenish cast of the bodies of old house flies, the lifted sleeve which was too large, the lifted hand like a curled claw. The door opened so promptly that the boy knew the Negro must have been watching them all the time, an old man with neat grizzled hair, in a linen jacket, who stood barring the door with his body, saying, "Wipe yo foots, white man, fo you come in here. Major ain't home nohow."

"Get out of my way, nigger," his father said, without heat too, flinging the door back and the Negro also and entering, his hat still on his head. And now the boy saw the prints of the stiff foot on the doorsill and saw them appear on the pale rug behind the machinelike deliberation of the foot which seemed to bear (or transmit) twice the weight which the body compassed. The Negro was shouting "Miss Lula! Miss Lula!" somewhere behind them, then the boy, deluged as though by a warm wave by a suave turn of carpeted stair and a pendant glitter of chandeliers and a mute gleam of gold frames, heard the swift feet and saw her too, a lady—perhaps he had never seen her like before either—in a gray, smooth gown with lace at the throat and an apron tied at the waist and the

sleeves turned back, wiping cake or biscuit dough from
her hands with a towel as she came up the hall, looking
not at his father at all but at the tracks on the blond rug
with an expression of incredulous amazement.

"I tried," the Negro cried. "I tole him to . . ."

"Will you please go away?" she said in a shaking voice.
"Major de Spain is not at home. Will you please go
away?"

His father had not spoken again. He did not speak
again. He did not even look at her. He just stood stiff in
the center of the rug, in his hat, the shaggy iron-gray
brows twitching slightly above the pebble-colored eyes as
he appeared to examine the house with brief deliberation.
Then with the same deliberation he turned; the boy
watched him pivot on the good leg and saw the stiff foot
drag round the arc of the turning, leaving a final long and
fading smear. His father never looked at it, he never once
looked down at the rug. The Negro held the door. It
closed behind them, upon the hysteric and indistinguish-
able woman-wail. His father stopped at the top of the
steps and scraped his boot clean on the edge of it. At the
gate he stopped again. He stood for a moment, planted
stiffly on the stiff foot, looking back at the house. "Pretty
and white, ain't it?" he said. "That's sweat. Nigger sweat.
Maybe it ain't white enough yet to suit him. Maybe he
wants to mix some white sweat with it."

Two hours later the boy was chopping wood behind
the house within which his mother and aunt and the two
sisters (the mother and aunt, not the two girls, he knew
that; even at this distance and muffled by walls the flat
loud voices of the two girls emanated an incorrigible idle
inertia) were setting up the stove to prepare a meal, when

he heard the hooves and saw the linen-clad man on a fine sorrel mare, whom he recognized even before he saw the rolled rug in front of the Negro youth following on a fat bay carriage horse—a suffused, angry face vanishing, still at full gallop, beyond the corner of the house where his father and brother were sitting in the two tilted chairs; and a moment later, almost before he could have put the axe down, he heard the hooves again and watched the sorrel mare go back out of the yard, already galloping again. Then his father began to shout one of the sisters' names, who presently emerged backward from the kitchen door dragging the rolled rug along the ground by one end while the other sister walked behind it.

"If you ain't going to tote, go on and set up the wash pot," the first said.

"You, Sarty!" the second shouted. "Set up the wash pot!" His father appeared at the door, framed against that shabbiness, as he had been against that other bland perfection, impervious to either, the mother's anxious face at his shoulder.

"Go on," the father said. "Pick it up." The two sisters stooped, broad, lethargic; stooping, they presented an incredible expanse of pale cloth and a flutter of tawdry ribbons.

"If I thought enough of a rug to have to git hit all the way from France I wouldn't keep hit where folks coming in would have to tromp on hit," the first said. They raised the rug.

"Abner," the mother said. "Let me do it."

"You go back and git dinner," his father said. "I'll tend to this."

From the woodpile through the rest of the afternoon

the boy watched them, the rug spread flat in the dust beside the bubbling wash pot, the two sisters stooping over it with that profound and lethargic reluctance, while the father stood over them in turn, implacable and grim, driving them though never raising his voice again. He could smell the harsh homemade lye they were using; he saw his mother come to the door once and look toward them with an expression not anxious now but very like despair; he saw his father turn, and he fell to with the axe and saw from the corner of his eye his father raise from the ground a flattish fragment of field stone and examine it and return to the pot, and this time his mother actually spoke: "Abner. Abner. Please don't. Please, Abner."

Then he was done too. It was dusk; the whippoorwills had already begun. He could smell coffee from the room where they would presently eat the cold food remaining from the mid-afternoon meal, though when he entered the house he realized they were having coffee again probably because there was a fire on the hearth, before which the rug now lay spread over the backs of the two chairs. The tracks of his father's foot were gone. Where they had been were now long, water-cloudy scoriations resembling the sporadic course of a Lilliputian mowing machine.

It still hung there while they ate the cold food and then went to bed, scattered without order or claim up and down the two rooms, his mother in one bed, where his father would later lie, the older brother in the other, himself, the aunt, and the two sisters on pallets on the floor. But his father was not in bed yet. The last thing the boy remembered was the depthless, harsh silhouette of the hat and coat bending over the rug and it seemed to him that he had not even closed his eyes when the silhouette was standing over him, the fire almost dead behind it, the stiff foot prodding him awake. "Catch up the mule," his father said.

When he returned with the mule his father was standing in the black door, the rolled rug over his shoulder. "Ain't you going to ride?" he said.

"No. Give me your foot."

He bent his knee into his father's hand, the wiry, surprising power flowed smoothly, rising, he rising with it, on to the mule's bare back (they had owned a saddle once; the boy could remember it though not when or where) and with the same effortlessness his father swung the rug up in front of him. Now in the starlight they retraced the afternoon's path, up the dusty road rife with honeysuckle, through the gate and up the black tunnel of the drive to the lightless house, where he sat on the mule and felt the rough warp of the rug drag across his thighs and vanish.

"Don't you want me to help?" he whispered. His father did not answer and now he heard again that stiff foot striking the hollow portico with that wooden and clocklike deliberation, that outrageous overstatement of the weight it carried. The rug, hunched, not flung (the boy could tell that even in the darkness) from his father's shoulder, struck the angle of wall and floor with a sound unbelievably loud, thunderous, then the foot again, unhurried and enormous; a light came on in the house and the boy sat, tense, breathing steadily and quietly and just a little fast, though the foot itself did not increase its beat at all, descending the steps now; now the boy could see him.

"Don't you want to ride now?" he whispered. "We kin both ride now," the light within the house altering now, flaring up and sinking. *He's coming down the stairs now,* he thought. He had already ridden the mule up beside the horse block; presently his father was up behind him and he doubled the reins over and slashed the mule across the neck, but before the animal could begin to trot the hard, thin arm came round him, the hard, knotted hand jerking the mule back to a walk.

In the first red rays of the sun they were in the lot, putting plow gear on the mules. This time the sorrel mare was in the lot before he heard it at all, the rider collarless and even bareheaded, trembling, speaking in a shaking voice as the woman in the house had done, his father merely looking up once before stooping again to the hame he was buckling, so that the man on the mare spoke to his stooping back:

"You must realize you have ruined that rug. Wasn't there anybody here, any of your women . . ." He ceased, shaking, the boy watching him, the older brother leaning now in the stable door, chewing, blinking slowly and steadily at nothing apparently. "It cost a hundred dollars. But you never had a hundred dollars. You never will. So I'm going to charge you twenty bushels of corn against your crop. I'll add it in your contract and when you come to the commissary you can sign it. That won't keep Mrs. de Spain quiet but maybe it will teach you to wipe your feet off before you enter her house again."

Then he was gone. The boy looked at his father, who still had not spoken or even looked up again, who was now adjusting the logger-head in the hame.

"Pap," he said. His father looked at him—the inscrutable face, the shaggy brows beneath which the gray eyes glinted coldly. Suddenly the boy went toward him, fast, stopping as suddenly. "You done the best you could!" he cried. "If he wanted hit done different why didn't he wait and tell you how? He won't git no twenty bushels! He won't git none! We'll get hit and hide hit! I kin watch . . ."

"Did you put the cutter back in that straight stock like I told you?"

"No, sir," he said.

"Then go do it."

That was Wednesday. During the rest of that week he worked steadily, at what was within his scope and some which was beyond it, with an industry that did not need to be driven nor even commanded twice; he had this from his mother, with the difference that some at least of what he did he liked to do, such as splitting wood with the half-size axe which his mother and aunt had earned, or saved money somehow, to present him with at Christmas. In company with the two older women (and on one afternoon, even one of the sisters), he built pens for the shoat and the cow which were a part of his father's contract with the landlord, and one afternoon, his father being absent, gone somewhere on one of the mules, he went to the field.

They were running a middle buster now, his brother holding the plow straight while he handled the reins, and walking beside the straining mule, the rich black soil shearing cool and damp against his bare ankles, he thought *Maybe this is the end of it. Maybe even that twenty bushels that seems hard to have to pay for just a rug will be a cheap price for him to stop forever and always from being what he used to be;* thinking, dreaming now, so that his brother had to speak sharply to him to mind the mule: *Maybe he even won't collect the twenty bushels. Maybe it will all add up and balance and vanish—corn, rug, fire; the terror and grief, the being pulled two ways like between two teams of horses—gone, done with for ever and ever.*

Then it was Saturday; he looked up from beneath the mule he was harnessing and saw his father in the black coat and hat. "Not that," his father said. "The wagon gear." And then, two hours later, sitting in the wagon bed behind his father and brother on the seat, the wagon accomplished a final curve, and he saw the weathered paintless store with its tattered tobacco- and patent-medicine posters and the tethered wagons and saddle animals below the gallery. He mounted the gnawed steps behind his father and brother, and there again was the lane of quiet, watching faces for the three of them to walk through. He saw the man in spectacles sitting at the plank table and he did not need to be told this was a Justice of the Peace; he sent one glare of fierce, exultant, partisan defiance at the man in collar and cravat now, whom he had seen but twice before in his life, and that on a galloping horse, who now wore on his face an expression not of rage but of amazed unbelief which the boy could not have known was at the incredible circumstance of being sued by one of his own tenants, and came and stood against his father and cried at the Justice: "He ain't done it! He ain't burnt . . ."

"Go back to the wagon," his father said.

"Burnt?" the Justice said. "Do I understand this rug was burned too?"

"Does anybody here claim it was?" his father said. "Go back to the wagon." But he did not, he merely retreated to the rear of the room, crowded as that other had been, but not to sit down this time, instead, to stand pressing among the motionless bodies, listening to the voices:

"And you claim twenty bushels of corn is too high for the damage you did to the rug?"

"He brought the rug to me and said he wanted the tracks washed out of it. I washed the tracks out and took the rug back to him."

"But you didn't carry the rug back to him in the same condition it was in before you made the tracks on it."

His father did not answer, and now for perhaps half a minute there was no sound at all save that of breathing, the faint, steady suspiration of complete and intent listening.

"You decline to answer that, Mr. Snopes?" Again his father did not answer. "I'm going to find against you, Mr. Snopes. I'm going to find that you were responsible for the injury to Major de Spain's rug and hold you liable for it. But twenty bushels of corn seems a little high for a man in your circumstances to have to pay. Major de Spain claims it cost a hundred dollars. October corn will be worth about fifty cents. I figure that if Major de Spain can stand a ninety-five-dollar loss on something he paid cash for, you can stand a five-dollar loss you haven't earned yet. I hold you in damages to Major de Spain to the amount of ten bushels of corn over and above your contract with him, to be paid to him out of your crop at gathering time. Court adjourned."

It had taken no time hardly, the morning was but half begun. He thought they would return home and perhaps back to the field, since they were late, far behind all other farmers. But instead his father passed on behind the wagon, merely indicating with his hand for the older brother to follow with it, and crossed the road toward the blacksmith shop opposite, pressing on after his father, overtaking him, speaking, whispering up at the harsh, calm face beneath the weathered hat: "He won't git no ten bushels neither. He won't git one. We'll . . ." until his father glanced for an instant down at him, the face absolutely calm, the grizzled eyebrows tangled above the cold eyes, the voice almost pleasant, almost gentle:

"You think so? Well, we'll wait till October anyway."

The matter of the wagon—the setting of a spoke or two and the tightening of the tires—did not take long either, the business of the tires accomplished by driving the wagon into the spring branch behind the shop and letting it stand there, the mules nuzzling into the water from time to time, and the boy on the seat with the idle reins, looking up the slope and through the sooty tunnel of the shed where the slow hammer rang and where his father sat on an upended cypress bolt, easily, either talking or listening, still sitting there when the boy brought the dripping wagon up out of the branch and halted it before the door.

"Take them on to the shade and hitch," his father said. He did so and returned. His father and the smith and a third man squatting on his heels inside the door were talking, about crops and animals; the boy, squatting too in the ammoniac dust and hoof-parings and scales of rust, heard his father tell a long and unhurried story out of the time before the birth of the older brother even when he had been a professional horsetrader. And then his father came up beside him where he stood before a tattered last year's circus poster on the other side of the store, gazing rapt and quiet at the scarlet horses, the incredible poisings and convolutions of tulle and tights and the painted leers of comedians, and said, "It's time to eat."

But not at home. Squatting beside his brother against

the front wall, he watched his father emerge from the
store and produce from a paper sack a segment of cheese
and divide it carefully and deliberately into three with his
pocket knife and produce crackers from the same sack.
They all three squatted on the gallery and ate, slowly,
without talking; then in the store again, they drank from
a tin dipper tepid water smelling of the cedar bucket and
of living beech trees. And still they did not go home. It
was a horse lot this time, a tall rail fence upon and along
which men stood and sat and out of which one by one
horses were led, to be walked and trotted and then cantered back and forth along the road while the slow swapping and buying went on and the sun began to slant
westward, they—the three of them—watching and listening, the older brother with his muddy eyes and his steady,
inevitable tobacco, the father commenting now and then
on certain of the animals, to no one in particular.

It was after sundown when they reached home. They
ate supper by lamplight, then, sitting on the doorstep, the
boy watched the night fully accomplish, listening to the
whippoorwills and the frogs, when he heard his mother's
voice: "Abner! No! No! Oh, God. Oh, God. Abner!" and
he rose, whirled, and saw the altered light through the
door where a candle stub now burned in a bottle neck on
the table and his father, still in the hat and coat, at once
formal and burlesque as though dressed carefully for some
shabby and ceremonial violence, emptying the reservoir of
the lamp back into the five-gallon kerosene can from
which it had been filled, while the mother tugged at his
arm until he shifted the lamp to the other hand and flung
her back, not savagely or viciously, just hard, into the
wall, her hands flung out against the wall for balance, her

mouth open and in her face the same quality of hopeless despair as had been in her voice. Then his father saw him standing in the door.

"Go to the barn and get that can of oil we were oiling the wagon with," he said. The boy did not move. Then he could speak.

"What . . ." he cried. "What are you . . ."

"Go get that oil," his father said. "Go."

Then he was moving, running, outside the house, toward the stable: this the old habit, the old blood which he had not been permitted to choose for himself, which had been bequeathed him willy nilly and which had run for so long (and who knew where, battening on what of outrage and savagery and lust) before it came to him. *I could keep on,* he thought. *I could run on and on and never look back, never need to see his face again. Only I can't. I can't,* the rusted can in his hand now, the liquid sploshing in it as he ran back to the house and into it, into the sound of his mother's weeping in the next room, and handed the can to his father.

"Ain't you going to even send a nigger?" he cried. "At least you sent a nigger before!"

This time his father didn't strike him. The hand came even faster than the blow had, the same hand which had set the can on the table with almost excruciating care flashing from the can toward him too quick for him to follow it, gripping him by the back of his shirt and on to tiptoe before he had seen it quit the can, the face stooping at him in breathless and frozen ferocity, the cold, dead voice speaking over him to the older brother who leaned against the table, chewing with that steady, curious, side-wise motion of cows:

"Empty the can into the big one and go on. I'll catch up with you."

"Better tie him up to the bedpost," the brother said.

"Do like I told you," the father said. Then the boy was moving, his bunched shirt and the hard, bony hand between his shoulder-blades, his toes just touching the floor, across the room and into the other one, past the sisters sitting with spread heavy thighs in the two chairs over the cold hearth, and to where his mother and aunt sat side by side on the bed, the aunt's arms about his mother's shoulders.

"Hold him," the father said. The aunt made a startled movement. "Not you," the father said. "Lennie. Take hold of him. I want to see you do it." His mother took him by the wrist. "You'll hold him better than that. If he gets loose don't you know what he is going to do? He will go up yonder." He jerked his head toward the road. "Maybe I'd better tie him."

"I'll hold him," his mother whispered.

"See you do then." Then his father was gone, the stiff foot heavy and measured upon the boards, ceasing at last.

Then he began to struggle. His mother caught him in both arms, he jerking and wrenching at them. He would be stronger in the end, he knew that. But he had no time to wait for it. "Lemme go!" he cried. "I don't want to have to hit you!"

"Let him go!" the aunt said. "If he don't go, before God, I am going up there myself!"

"Don't you see I can't?" his mother cried. "Sarty! Sarty! No! No! Help me, Lizzie!"

Then he was free. His aunt grasped at him but it was too late. He whirled, running, his mother stumbled forward on to her knees behind him, crying to the nearer sister: "Catch him, Net! Catch him!" But that was too late too, the sister (the sisters were twins, born at the same time, yet either of them now gave the impression of being, encompassing as much living meat and volume and weight as any other two of the family) not yet having begun to rise from the chair, her head, face, alone merely turned, presenting to him in the flying instant an astonishing expanse of young female features untroubled by any surprise even, wearing only an expression of bovine interest. Then he was out of the room, out of the house, in the mild dust of the starlit road and the heavy rifeness of honeysuckle, the pale ribbon unspooling with terrific slowness under his running feet, reaching the gate at last and turning in, running, his heart and lungs drumming, on up the drive toward the lighted house, the lighted door. He did not knock, he burst in, sobbing for breath, incapable for the moment of speech; he saw the astonished face of the Negro in the linen jacket without knowing when the Negro had appeared.

"De Spain!" he cried, panted. "Where's . . ." then he saw the white man too emerging from a white door down the hall. "Barn!" he cried. "Barn!"

"What?" the white man said. "Barn?"

"Yes!" the boy cried. "Barn!"

"Catch him!" the white man shouted.

But it was too late this time too. The Negro grasped his shirt, but the entire sleeve, rotten with washing, carried away, and he was out that door too and in the drive again, and had actually never ceased to run even while he was screaming into the white man's face.

Behind him the white man was shouting, "My horse!

Fetch my horse!" and he thought for an instant of cutting across the park and climbing the fence into the road, but he did not know the park nor how high the vine-massed fence might be and he dared not risk it. So he ran on down the drive, blood and breath roaring; presently he was in the road again though he could not see it. He could not hear either: the galloping mare was almost upon him before he heard her, and even then he held his course, as if the very urgency of his wild grief and need must in a moment more find him wings, waiting until the ultimate instant to hurl himself aside and into the weed-choked roadside ditch as the horse thundered past and on, for an instant in furious silhouette against the stars, the tranquil early summer night sky which, even before the shape of the horse and rider vanished, strained abruptly and violently upward: a long, swirling roar incredible and soundless, blotting the stars, and he springing up and into the road again, running again, knowing it was too late yet still running even after he heard the shot and, an instant later, two shots, pausing now without knowing he had ceased to run, crying "Pap! Pap!", running again before he knew he had begun to run, stumbling, tripping over something and scrabbling up again without ceasing to run, looking backward over his shoulder at the glare as he got up, running on among the invisible trees, panting, sobbing, "Father! Father!"

At midnight he was sitting on the crest of a hill. He did not know it was midnight and he did not know how far he had come. But there was no glare behind him now and he sat now, his back toward what he had called home for four days anyhow, his face toward the dark woods which he would enter when breath was strong again, small, shaking steadily in the chill darkness, hugging himself into the remainder of his thin, rotten shirt, the grief and despair now no longer terror and fear but just grief and despair. *Father. My father,* he thought. "He was brave!" he cried suddenly, aloud but not loud, no more than a whisper: "He was! He was in the war! He was in Colonel Sartoris' cav'ry!" not knowing that his father had gone to that war a private in the fine old European sense, wearing no uniform, admitting the authority of and giving fidelity to no man or army or flag, going to war as Malbrouck himself did: for booty—it meant nothing and less than nothing to him if it were enemy booty or his own.

The slow constellations wheeled on. It would be dawn and then sun-up after a while and he would be hungry. But that would be tomorrow and now he was only cold, and walking would cure that. His breathing was easier now and he decided to get up and go on, and then he found that he had been asleep because he knew it was almost dawn, the night almost over. He could tell that from the whippoorwills. They were everywhere now among the dark trees below him, constant and inflectioned and ceaseless, so that, as the instant for giving over to the day birds drew nearer and nearer, there was no interval at all between them. He got up. He was a little stiff, but walking would cure that too as it would the cold, and soon there would be the sun. He went on down the hill, toward the dark woods within which the liquid silver voices of the birds called unceasing—the rapid and urgent beating of the urgent and quiring heart of the late spring night. He did not look back.

Two Soldiers

Me and Pete would go down to Old Man Killegrew's and listen to his radio. We would wait until after supper, after dark, and we would stand outside Old Man Killegrew's parlor window, and we could hear it because Old Man Killegrew's wife was deaf, and so he run the radio as loud as it would run, and so me and Pete could hear it plain as Old Man Killegrew's wife could, I reckon, even standing outside with the window closed.

And that night I said, "What? Japanese? What's a pearl harbor?" and Pete said, "Hush."

And so we stood there, it was cold, listening to the fellow in the radio talking, only I couldn't make no heads nor tails neither out of it. Then the fellow said that would be all for a while, and me and Pete walked back up the road to home, and Pete told me what it was. Because he was nigh twenty and he had done finished the Consolidated last June and he knowed a heap: about them Japanese dropping bombs on Pearl Harbor and that Pearl Harbor was across the water.

"Across what water?" I said. "Across that Government reservoy up at Oxford?"

"Naw," Pete said. "Across the big water. The Pacific Ocean."

We went home. Maw and pap was already asleep, and me and Pete laid in the bed, and I still couldn't understand where it was, and Pete told me again—the Pacific Ocean.

"What's the matter with you?" Pete said. "You're going on nine years old. You been in school now ever since September. Ain't you learned nothing yet?"

"I reckon we ain't got as fer as the Pacific Ocean yet," I said.

We was still sowing the vetch then that ought to been all finished by the fifteenth of November, because pap was still behind, just like he had been ever since me and Pete had knowed him. And we had firewood to git in, too, but every night me and Pete would go down to Old Man Killegrew's and stand outside his parlor window in the cold and listen to his radio; then we would come back home and lay in the bed and Pete would tell me what it was. That is, he would tell me for a while. Then he wouldn't tell me. It was like he didn't want to talk about it no more. He would tell me to shut up because he wanted to go to sleep, but he never wanted to go to sleep.

He would lay there, a heap stiller than if he was asleep, and it would be something, I could feel it coming out of him, like he was mad at me even, only I knowed he wasn't thinking about me, or like he was worried about something, and it wasn't that neither, because he never had nothing to worry about. He never got behind like pap, let alone stayed behind. Pap give him ten acres when he graduated from the Consolidated, and me and Pete both reckoned pap was durn glad to get shut of at least ten acres, less to have to worry with himself; and Pete had them ten acres all sowed to vetch and busted out and bedded for the winter, and so it wasn't that. But it was something. And still we would go down to Old Man Killegrew's every night and listen to his radio, and they was at it in the Philippines now, but General MacArthur was holding um. Then we would come back home and lay in the bed, and Pete wouldn't tell me nothing or talk at all. He would just lay there still as a ambush and when I would touch him, his side or his leg would feel hard and still as iron, until after a while I would go to sleep.

Then one night—it was the first time he had said nothing to me except to jump on me about not chopping enough wood at the wood tree where we was cutting—he said, "I got to go."

"Go where?" I said.

"To that war," Pete said.

"Before we even finish gettin' in the firewood?"

"Firewood, hell," Pete said.

"All right," I said. "When we going to start?"

But he wasn't even listening. He laid there, hard and still as iron in the dark. "I got to go," he said. "I jest ain't going to put up with no folks treating the Unity States that way."

"Yes," I said. "Firewood or no firewood, I reckon we got to go."

This time he heard me. He laid still again, but it was a different kind of still.

"You?" he said. "To a war?"

"You'll whup the big uns and I'll whup the little uns," I said.

Then he told me I couldn't go. At first I thought he just never wanted me tagging after him, like he wouldn't leave me go with him when he went sparking them girls of Tull's. Then he told me the Army wouldn't leave me go because I was too little, and then I knowed he really meant it and that I couldn't go nohow noways. And somehow I hadn't believed until then that he was going himself, but now I knowed he was and that he wasn't going to leave me go with him a-tall.

"I'll chop the wood and tote the water for you-all then!" I said. "You got to have wood and water!"

Anyway, he was listening to me now. He wasn't like iron now.

He turned onto his side and put his hand on my chest because it was me that was laying straight and hard on my back now.

"No," he said. "You got to stay here and help pap."

"Help him what?" I said. "He ain't never caught up nohow. He can't get no further behind. He can sholy take care of this little shirttail of a farm while me and you are whupping them Japanese. I got to go too. If you got to go, then so have I."

"No," Pete said. "Hush now. Hush." And he meant it, and I knowed he did. Only I made sho from his own mouth. I quit.

"So I just can't go then," I said.

"No," Pete said. "You just can't go. You're too little, in the first place, and in the second place——"

"All right," I said. "Then shut up and leave me go to sleep."

So he hushed then and laid back. And I laid there like I was already asleep, and pretty soon he was asleep and I knowed it was the wanting to go to the war that had worried him and kept him awake, and now that he had decided to go, he wasn't worried any more.

The next morning he told maw and pap. Maw was all right. She cried.

"No," she said, crying, "I don't want him to go. I would rather go myself in his place, if I could. I don't want to save the country. Them Japanese could take it and keep it, so long as they left me and my family and my children alone. But I remember my brother Marsh in that other war. He had to go to that one when he wasn't but nineteen, and our mother couldn't understand it then any more than I can now. But she told Marsh if he had to go, he had to go. And so, if Pete's got to go to this one, he's got to go to it. Jest don't ask me to understand why."

But pap was the one. He was the feller. "To the war?" he said. "Why, I just don't see a bit of use in that. You ain't old enough for the draft, and the country ain't being invaded. Our President in Washington, D.C., is watching the conditions and he will notify us. Besides, in that other war your ma just mentioned, I was drafted and sent clean to Texas and was held there nigh eight months until they finally quit fighting. It seems to me that that, along with your Uncle Marsh who received a actual wound on the battlefields of France, is enough for me and mine to have to do to protect the country, at least in my lifetime. Besides, what'll I do for help on the farm with you gone? It seems to be I'll get mighty far behind."

"You been behind as long as I can remember," Pete said. "Anyway, I'm going. I got to."

"Of course he's got to go," I said. "Them Japanese——"

"You hush your mouth!" maw said, crying. "Nobody's talking to you! Go and get me a armful of wood! That's what you can do!"

So I got the wood. And all the next day, while me and Pete and pap was getting in as much wood as we could in that time because Pete said how pap's idea of plenty of wood was one more stick laying against the wall that maw ain't put on the fire yet, maw was getting Pete ready to go. She washed and mended his clothes and cooked him a shoe box of vittles. And that night me and Pete laid in the bed and listened to her packing his grip and crying, until after a while Pete got up in his nightshirt and went back there, and I could hear them talking, until at last maw said, "You got to go, and so I want you to go. But I don't understand it, and I won't never, and so don't expect me to." And Pete come back and got into the bed again and laid again still and hard as iron on his back, and then he said, and he wasn't talking to me, he wasn't talking to nobody: "I got to go. I just got to."

"Sho you got to," I said. "Them Japanese——" He turned over hard, he kind of surged over onto his side, looking at me in the dark.

"Anyway, you're all right," he said. "I expected to have more trouble with you than with all the rest of them put together."

"I reckon I can't help it neither," I said. "But maybe it will run a few years longer and I can get there. Maybe someday I will jest walk in on you."

"I hope not," Pete said. "Folks don't go to wars for fun. A man don't leave his maw crying just for fun."

"Then why are you going?" I said.

"I got to," he said. "I just got to. Now you go on to sleep. I got to ketch that early bus in the morning."

"All right," I said. "I hear tell Memphis is a big place. How will you find where the Army's at?"

"I'll ask somebody where to go to join it," Pete said. "Go on to sleep now."

"Is that what you'll ask for? Where to join the Army?" I said.

"Yes," Pete said. He turned onto his back again. "Shut up and go to sleep."

We went to sleep. The next morning we et breakfast by lamplight because the bus would pass at six o'clock. Maw wasn't crying now. She jest looked grim and busy, putting breakfast on the table while we et it. Then she finished packing Pete's grip, except he never wanted to take no grip to the war, but maw said decent folks never went nowhere, not even to a war, without a change of clothes and something to tote them in. She put in the shoe box of fried chicken and biscuits and she put the Bible in, too, and then it was time to go. We didn't know until then that maw wasn't going to the bus. She jest brought Pete's cap and overcoat, and still she didn't cry no more, she jest stood with her hands on Pete's shoulders and she didn't move, but somehow, and jest holding Pete's shoulders, she looked as hard and fierce as when Pete had turned toward me in the bed last night and tole me that anyway I was all right.

"They could take the country and keep the country, so long as they never bothered me and mine," she said. Then she said, "Don't never forget who you are. You ain't rich and the rest of the world outside of French-man's Bend never heard of you. But your blood is good as any blood anywhere, and don't you never forget it."

Then she kissed him, and then we was out of the house, with pap toting Pete's grip whether Pete wanted him to or not. There wasn't no dawn even yet, not even after we had stood on the highway by the mailbox, a while. Then we seen the lights of the bus coming and I was watching the bus until it come up and Pete flagged it, and then, sho enough, there was daylight—it had started while I wasn't watching. And now me and Pete expected pap to say something else foolish, like he done before, about how Uncle Marsh getting wounded in France and that trip to Texas pap taken in 1918 ought to be enough to save the Unity States in 1942, but he never. He done all right too. He jest said, "Good-by, son. Always remember what your ma told you and write her whenever you find the time." Then he shaken Pete's hand, and Pete looked at me a minute and put his hand on my head and rubbed my head durn nigh hard enough to wring my neck off and jumped into the bus, and the feller wound the door shut and the bus began to hum, then it was moving, humming and grinding and whining louder and louder; it was going fast, with two little red lights behind it that never seemed to get no littler, but just seemed to be running together until pretty soon they would touch and jest be one light. But they never did, and then the bus was gone, and even like it was, I could have pretty nigh busted out crying, nigh to nine years old and all.

Me and pap went back to the house. All that day we worked at the wood tree, and so I never had no good chance until about middle of the afternoon. Then I taken my slingshot and I would have liked to took all my bird eggs, too, because Pete had give me his collection and he holp me with mine, and he would like to git the box out and look at them as good as I would, even if he was nigh twenty years old. But the box was too big to tote a long ways and have to worry with, so I just taken the shikepoke egg, because it was the best un, and wropped it up good into a matchbox and hid it and the slingshot under the corner of the barn. Then we et supper and went to bed, and I thought then how if I would 'a' had to stayed in that room and that bed like that even for one more night, I jest couldn't 'a' stood it. Then I could hear pap snoring, but I never heard no sound from maw, whether she was asleep or not, and I don't reckon she was. So I taken my shoes and drapped them out the window, and then I clumb out like I used to watch Pete do when he was still jest seventeen and pap held that he was too young yet to be tomcatting around at night, and wouldn't leave him out, and I put on my shoes and went to the barn and got the slingshot and the shikepoke egg and went to the highway.

It wasn't cold, it was jest durn confounded dark, and that highway stretched on in front of me like, without nobody using it, it had stretched out half again as fer just like a man does when he lays down, so that for a time it looked like full sun was going to ketch me before I had finished them twenty-two miles to Jefferson. But it didn't. Daybreak was jest starting when I walked up the hill into town. I could smell breakfast cooking in the cabins and I wished I had thought to brought me a cold biscuit, but that was too late now. And Pete had told me Memphis was a piece beyond Jefferson, but I never knowed it was no eighty miles. So I stood there on that empty square, with daylight coming and coming and the street lights still burning and that Law looking down at me, and me still eighty miles from Memphis, and it had took me all night to walk jest twenty-two miles, and so, by the time I got to Memphis at that rate, Pete would 'a' done already started for Pearl Harbor.

"Where do you come from?" the Law said.

And I told him again. "I got to git to Memphis. My brother's there."

"You mean you ain't got any folks around here?" the Law said. "Nobody but that brother? What are you doing way off down here and your brother in Memphis?"

And I told him again, "I got to git to Memphis. I ain't got no time to waste talking about it and I ain't got time to walk it. I got to git there today."

"Come on here," the Law said.

We went down another street. And there was the bus, just like when Pete got into it yestiddy morning, except there wasn't no lights on it now and it was empty. There was a regular bus dee-po like a railroad dee-po, with a ticket counter and a feller behind it, and the Law said, "Set down over there," and I set down on the bench, and the Law said, "I want to use your telephone," and he talked in the telephone a minute and put it down and said to the feller behind the ticket counter, "Keep your eye on him. I'll be back as soon as Mrs. Habersham can arrange to get herself up and dressed." He went out. I got up and went to the ticket counter.

"I want to go to Memphis," I said.

"You bet," the feller said. "You set down on the bench now. Mr. Foote will be back in a minute."

"I don't know no Mr. Foote," I said. "I want to ride that bus to Memphis."

"You got some money?" he said. "It'll cost you seventy-two cents."

I taken out the matchbox and unwropped the shike-poke egg. "I'll swap you this for a ticket to Memphis," I said.

"What's that?" he said.

"It's a shikepoke egg," I said. "You never seen one before. It's worth a dollar. I'll take seventy-two cents fer it."

"No," he said, "the fellers that own that bus insist on a cash basis. If I started swapping tickets for bird eggs and livestock and such, they would fire me. You go and set down on the bench now, like Mr. Foote——"

I started for the door, but he caught me, he put one hand on the ticket counter and jumped over it and caught up with me and reached his hand out to ketch my shirt. I whupped out my pocketknife and snapped it open.

"You put a hand on me and I'll cut it off," I said.

I tried to dodge him and run at the door, but he could move quicker than any grown man I ever see, quick as Pete almost. He cut me off and stood with his back against the door and one foot raised a little, and there wasn't no other way to get out. "Get back on that bench and stay there," he said.

And there wasn't no other way out. And he stood there with his back against the door. So I went back to the bench. And then it seemed like to me that dee-po was full of folks. There was that Law again, and there was two ladies in fur coats and their faces already painted. But they still looked like they had got up in a hurry and they still never liked it, a old one and a young one, looking down at me.

"He hasn't got a overcoat!" the old one said. "How in the world did he ever get down here by himself?"

"I ask you," the Law said. "I couldn't get nothing out of him except his brother is in Memphis and he wants to get back up there."

"That's right," I said. "I got to git to Memphis today."

"Of course you must," the old one said. "Are you sure you can find your brother when you get to Memphis?"

"I reckon I can," I said. "I ain't got but one and I have knowed him all my life. I reckon I will know him again when I see him."

The old one looked at me. "Somehow he doesn't look like he lives in Memphis," she said.

"He probably don't," the Law said. "You can't tell though. He might live anywhere, overhalls or not. This day and time they get scattered overnight from he—— hope to breakfast; boys and girls, too, almost before they can walk good. He might have been in Missouri or Texas either yestiddy, for all we know. But he don't seem to have any doubt his brother is in Memphis. All I know to do is send him up there and leave him look."

"Yes," the old one said.

The young one set down on the bench by me and opened a hand satchel and taken out a artermatic writing pen and some papers.

"Now, honey," the old one said, "we're going to see that you find your brother, but we must have a case history for our files first. We want to know your name and your brother's name and where you were born and when your parents died."

"I don't need no case history neither," I said. "All I want is to git to Memphis. I got to git there today."

"You see?" the Law said. He said it almost like he enjoyed it. "That's what I told you."

"You're lucky, at that, Mrs. Habersham," the bus feller said. "I don't think he's got a gun on him, but he can open that knife da——I mean, fast enough to suit any man."

But the old one just stood there looking at me.

"Well," she said. "Well. I really don't know what to do."

"I do," the bus feller said. "I'm going to give him a ticket out of my own pocket, as a measure of protecting the company against riot and bloodshed. And when Mr. Foote tells the city board about it, it will be a civic matter and they will not only reimburse me, they will give me a medal too. Hey, Mr. Foote?"

But never nobody paid him no mind. The old one still stood looking down at me. She said "Well," again. Then she taken a dollar from her purse and give it to the bus feller. "I suppose he will travel on a child's ticket, won't he?"

"Wellum," the bus feller said, "I just don't know what the regulations would be. Likely I will be fired for not crating him and marking the crate Poison. But I'll risk it."

Then they were gone. Then the Law come back with a sandwich and give it to me.

"You're sure you can find that brother?" he said.

"I ain't yet convinced why not," I said. "If I don't see Pete first, he'll see me. He knows me too."

Then the Law went out for good, too, and I et the sandwich. Then more folks come in and bought tickets, and then the bus feller said it was time to go, and I got into the bus just like Pete done, and we was gone.

I seen all the towns. I seen all of them. When the bus got to going good, I found out I was jest about wore out for sleep. But there was too much I hadn't never saw before. We run out of Jefferson and run past fields and woods, then we would run into another town and out of that un and past fields and woods again, and then into another town with stores and gins and water tanks, and we run along by the railroad for a spell and I seen the signal arm move, and then I seen the train and then some more towns, and I was jest about plumb wore out for sleep, but I couldn't risk it. Then Memphis begun. It seemed like, to me, it went on for miles. We would pass a patch of stores and I would think that was sholy it and the bus would even stop. But it wouldn't be Memphis yet and we would go on again past water tanks and smoke-stacks on top of the mills, and if they was gins and sawmills, I never knowed there was that many and I never seen any that big, and where they got enough cotton and logs to run um I don't know.

Then I see Memphis. I knowed I was right this time. It was standing up into the air. It looked like about a dozen whole towns bigger than Jefferson was set up on one edge in a field, standing up into the air higher than ara hill in all Yoknapatawpha County. Then we was in it, with the bus stopping ever' few feet, it seemed like to me, and cars rushing past on both sides of it and the street crowded with folks from ever'where in town that day, until I didn't see how there could 'a' been nobody left in Mis'sippi a-tall to even sell me a bus ticket, let alone write out no case histories. Then the bus stopped. It was another bus dee-po, a heap bigger than the one in Jefferson. And I said, "All right. Where do folks join the Army?"

"What?" the bus feller said.

And I said it again, "Where do folks join the Army?"

"Oh," he said. Then he told me how to get there. I was afraid at first I wouldn't ketch on how to do in a town big as Memphis. But I caught on all right. I never had to ask but twice more. Then I was there, and I was durn glad to git out of all them rushing cars and shoving folks and all that racket for a spell, and I thought, It won't be long now, and I thought how if there was any kind of a crowd there that had done already joined the Army, too, Pete would likely see me before I seen him. And so I walked into the room. And Pete wasn't there.

He wasn't even there. There was a soldier with a big arrerhead on his sleeve, writing, and two fellers standing in front of him, and there was some more folks there, I reckon. It seems to me I remember some more folks there.

I went to the table where the soldier was writing, and I said, "Where's Pete?" and he looked up and I said, "My brother. Pete Grier. Where is he?"

"What?" the soldier said. "Who?"

And I told him again. "He joined the Army yestiddy. He's going to Pearl Harbor. So am I. I want to ketch him. Where you all got him?" Now they were all looking at me, but I never paid them no mind. "Come on," I said. "Where is he?"

The soldier had quit writing. He had both hands spraddled out on the table. "Oh," he said. "You're going, too, hah?"

"Yes," I said. "They got to have wood and water. I can chop it and tote it. Come on. Where's Pete?"

The soldier stood up. "Who let you in here?" he said. "Go on. Beat it."

"Durn that," I said. "You tell me where Pete——"

I be dog if he couldn't move faster than the bus feller even. He never come over the table, he come around it, he was on me almost before I knowed it, so that I jest had time to jump back and whup out my pocketknife and snap it open and hit one lick, and he hollered and jumped back and grabbed one hand with the other and stood there cussing and hollering.

One of the other fellers grabbed me from behind, and I hit at him with the knife, but I couldn't reach him.

Then both of the fellers had me from behind, and then another soldier come out of a door at the back. He had on a belt with a britching strop over one shoulder.

"What the hell is this?" he said.

"That little son cut me with a knife!" the first soldier hollered. When he said that, I tried to get at him again, but both them fellers was holding me, two against one, and the soldier with the backing strop said, "Here, here. Put your knife up, feller. None of us are armed. A man don't knife-fight folks that are barehanded." I could begin to hear him then. He sounded jest like Pete talked to me. "Let him go," he said. They let me go. "Now what's all the trouble about?" And I told him. "I see," he said. "And you come up to see if he was all right before he left."

"No," I said. "I came to——"

But he had already turned to where the first soldier was wropping a handkerchief around his hand.

"Have you got him?" he said. The first soldier went back to the table and looked at some papers.

"Here he is," he said. "He enlisted yestiddy. He's in a detachment leaving this morning for Little Rock." He had a watch stropped on his arm. He looked at it. "The train leaves in about fifty minutes. If I know country boys, they're probably all down there at the station right now."

"Get him up here," the one with the backing strop said. "Phone the station. Tell the porter to get him a cab. And you come with me," he said.

It was another office behind that un, with jest a table and some chairs. We set there while the soldier smoked, and it wasn't long; I knowed Pete's feet soon as I heard them. Then the first soldier opened the door and Pete come in. He never had no soldier clothes on. He looked jest like he did when he got on the bus yestiddy morning, except it seemed to me like it was at least a week, so much had happened, and I had done had to do so much traveling. He come in and there he was, looking at me like he hadn't never left home, except that here we was in Memphis, on the way to Pearl Harbor.

"What in durnation are you doing here?" he said.

And I told him, "You got to have wood and water to cook with. I can chop it and tote it for you-all."

"No," Pete said. "You're going back home."

"No, Pete," I said. "I got to go too. I got to. It hurts my heart, Pete."

"No," Pete said. He looked at the soldier. "I jest don't know what could have happened to him, lootenant," he said. "He never drawed a knife on anybody before in his life." He looked at me. "What did you do it for?"

"I don't know," I said. "I jest had to. I jest had to git here. I jest had to find you."

"Well, don't you never do it again, you hear?" Pete said. "You put that knife in your pocket and you keep it there. If I ever again hear of you drawing it on anybody, I'm coming back from wherever I am at and whup the fire out of you. You hear me?"

"I would pure cut a throat if it would bring you back to stay," I said. "Pete," I said. "Pete."

"No," Pete said. Now his voice wasn't hard and quick no more, it was almost quiet, and I knowed now I wouldn't never change him. "You must go home. You must look after maw, and I am depending on you to look after my ten acres. I want you to go back home. Today. Do you hear?"

"I hear," I said.

"Can he get back home by himself?" the soldier said.

"He come up here by himself," Pete said.

"I can get back, I reckon," I said. "I don't live in but one place. I don't reckon it's moved."

Pete taken a dollar out of his pocket and give it to me. "That'll buy your bus ticket right to our mailbox," he said. "I want you to mind the lootenant. He'll send you to the bus. And you go back home and you take care of maw and look after my ten acres and keep that durn knife in your pocket. You hear me?"

"Yes, Pete," I said.

"All right," Pete said. "Now I got to go." He put his hand on my head again. But this time he never wrung my neck. He just laid his hand on my head a minute. And then I be dog if he didn't lean down and kiss me, and I heard his feet and then the door, and I never looked up and that was all, me setting there, rubbing the place where Pete kissed me and the soldier throwed back in his chair, looking out the window and coughing. He reached into his pocket and handed something to me without looking around. It was a piece of chewing gum.

"Much obliged," I said. "Well, I reckon I might as well start back. I got a right fer piece to go."

"Wait," the soldier said. Then he telephoned again and I said again I better start back, and he said again, "Wait. Remember what Pete told you."

So we waited, and then another lady come in, old, too,

in a fur coat, too, but she smelled all right, she never had no artermatic writing pen nor no case history neither. She come in and the soldier got up, and she looked around quick until she saw me, and come and put her hand on my shoulder light and quick and easy as maw herself might 'a' done it.

"Come on," she said. "Let's go home to dinner."

"Nome," I said. "I got to ketch the bus to Jefferson."

"I know. There's plenty of time. We'll go home and eat dinner first."

She had a car. And now we was right down in the middle of all them other cars. We was almost under the busses, and all them crowds of people on the street close enough to where I could have talked to them if I had knowed who they was. After a while she stopped the car. "Here we are," she said, and I looked at it, and if all that was her house, she sho had a big family. But all of it wasn't. We crossed a hall with trees growing in it and went into a little room without nothing in it but a nigger dressed up in a uniform a heap shinier than them soldiers had, and the nigger shut the door, and then I hollered, "Look out!" and grabbed, but it was all right; that whole little room jest went right on up and stopped and the door opened and we was in another hall, and the lady unlocked a door and we went in, and there was another soldier, a old feller, with a britching strop, too, and a silver-colored bird on each shoulder.

"Here we are," the lady said. "This is Colonel McKellogg. Now, what would you like for dinner?"

"I reckon I'll jest have some ham and eggs and coffee," I said.

She had done started to pick up the telephone. She stopped. "Coffee?" she said. "When did you start drinking coffee?"

"I don't know," I said. "I reckon it was before I could remember."

"You're about eight, aren't you?" she said.

"Nome," I said. "I'm eight and ten months. Going on eleven months."

She telephoned then. Then we set there and I told them how Pete had jest left that morning for Pearl Harbor and I had aimed to go with him, but I would have to go back home to take care of maw and look after Pete's ten acres, and she said how they had a little boy about my size, too, in a school in the East. Then a nigger, another one, in a short kind of shirttail coat, rolled a kind of wheelbarrer in. It had my ham and eggs and a glass of milk and a piece of pie, too, and I thought I was hungry. But when I taken the first bite I found out I couldn't swallow it, and I got up quick.

"I got to go," I said.

"Wait," she said.

"I got to go," I said.

"Just a minute," she said. "I've already telephoned for the car. It won't be but a minute now. Can't you drink the milk even? Or maybe some of your coffee?"

"Nome," I said. "I ain't hungry. I'll eat when I git home." Then the telephone rung. She never even answered it.

"There," she said. "There's the car." And we went back down in that 'ere little moving room with the dressed-up nigger. This time it was a big car with a soldier driving it. I got into the front with him. She give the soldier a dollar. "He might get hungry," she said. "Try to find a decent place for him."

"O.K., Mrs. McKellogg," the soldier said.

Then we was gone again. And now I could see Memphis good, bright in the sunshine, while we was swinging around it. And first thing I knowed, we was back on the same highway the bus run on this morning —the patches of stores and them big gins and sawmills, and Memphis running on for miles, it seemed like to me, before it begun to give out. Then we was running again between the fields and woods, running fast now, and except for that soldier, it was like I hadn't never been to Memphis a-tall. We was going fast now. At this rate, before I knowed it we would be home again, and I thought about me riding up to Frenchman's Bend in this big car with a soldier running it, and all of a sudden I begun to cry. I never knowed I was fixing to, and I couldn't stop it. I set there by that soldier, crying. We was going fast.

A Rose for Emily

When Miss Emily Grierson died, our whole town went to her funeral: the men through a sort of respectful affection for a fallen monument, the women mostly out of curiosity to see the inside of her house, which no one save an old man-servant—a combined gardener and cook—had seen in at least ten years.

It was a big, squarish frame house that had once been white, decorated with cupolas and spires and scrolled balconies in the heavily lightsome style of the seventies, set on what had once been our most select street. But garages and cotton gins had encroached and obliterated even the august names of that neighborhood; only Miss Emily's house was left, lifting its stubborn and coquettish decay above the cotton wagons and the gasoline pumps—an eyesore among eyesores. And now Miss Emily had gone to join the representatives of those august names where they lay in the cedar-bemused cemetery among the ranked and anonymous graves of Union and Confederate soldiers who fell at the battle of Jefferson.

Alive, Miss Emily had been a tradition, a duty, and a care; a sort of hereditary obligation upon the town, dating from that day in 1894 when Colonel Sartoris, the mayor—he who fathered the edict that no Negro woman should appear on the streets without an apron— remitted her taxes, the dispensation dating from the death of her father on into perpetuity. Not that Miss Emily would have accepted charity. Colonel Sartoris invented an involved tale to the effect that Miss Emily's father had loaned money to the town, which the town, as a matter of business, preferred this way of repaying. Only a man of Colonel Sartoris' generation and thought could have invented it, and only a woman could have believed it.

When the next generation, with its more modern ideas, became mayors and aldermen, this arrangement created some little dissatisfaction. On the first of the year they mailed her a tax notice. February came, and there was no reply. They wrote her a formal letter, asking her to call at the sheriff's office at her convenience. A week later the mayor wrote her himself, offering to call or to send his car for her, and received in reply a note on paper of an archaic shape, in a thin, flowing calligraphy in faded ink, to the effect that she no longer went out at all. The tax notice was also enclosed, without comment.

They called a special meeting of the Board of Aldermen. A deputation waited upon her, knocked at the door through which no visitor had passed since she ceased giving china-painting lessons eight or ten years earlier. They were admitted by the old Negro into a dim hall from which a stairway mounted into still more shadow. It smelled of dust and disuse—a close, dank smell. The Negro led them into the parlor. It was furnished in heavy, leather-covered furniture. When the Negro opened the blinds of one window, they could see that the leather was cracked; and when they sat down, a faint dust rose sluggishly about their thighs, spinning with slow motes in the single sun-ray. On a tarnished gilt easel before the fireplace stood a crayon portrait of Miss Emily's father.

They rose when she entered—a small, fat woman in black, with a thin gold chain descending to her waist and vanishing into her belt, leaning on an ebony cane with a tarnished gold head. Her skeleton was small and spare; perhaps that was why what would have been merely plumpness in another was obesity in her. She looked bloated, like a body long submerged in motionless water, and of that pallid hue. Her eyes, lost in the fatty ridges of her face, looked like two small pieces of coal pressed into a lump of dough as they moved from one face to another while the visitors stated their errand.

She did not ask them to sit. She just stood in the door and listened quietly until the spokesman came to a stumbling halt. Then they could hear the invisible watch ticking at the end of the gold chain.

Her voice was dry and cold. "I have no taxes in Jefferson. Colonel Sartoris explained it to me. Perhaps one of you can gain access to the city records and satisfy yourselves."

"But we have. We are the city authorities, Miss Emily. Didn't you get a notice from the sheriff, signed by him?"

"I received a paper, yes," Miss Emily said. "Perhaps he considers himself the sheriff . . . I have no taxes in Jefferson."

"But there is nothing on the books to show that, you see. We must go by the—"

"See Colonel Sartoris. I have no taxes in Jefferson."

"But, Miss Emily—"

"See Colonel Sartoris." (Colonel Sartoris had been dead

almost ten years.) "I have no taxes in Jefferson. Tobe!" The Negro appeared. "Show these gentlemen out."

II

So she vanquished them, horse and foot, just as she had vanquished their fathers thirty years before about the smell. That was two years after her father's death and a short time after her sweetheart—the one we believed would marry her—had deserted her. After her father's death she went out very little; after her sweetheart went away, people hardly saw her at all. A few of the ladies had the temerity to call, but were not received, and the only sign of life about the place was the Negro man—a young man then—going in and out with a market basket.

"Just as if a man—any man—could keep a kitchen properly," the ladies said; so they were not surprised when the smell developed. It was another link between the gross, teeming world and the high and mighty Griersons.

A neighbor, a woman, complained to the mayor, Judge Stevens, eighty years old.

"But what will you have me do about it, madam?" he said.

"Why, send her word to stop it," the woman said. "Isn't there a law?"

"I'm sure that won't be necessary," Judge Stevens said. "It's probably just a snake or a rat that nigger of hers killed in the yard. I'll speak to him about it."

The next day he received two more complaints, one from a man who came in diffident deprecation. "We really must do something about it, Judge. I'd be the last one in the world to bother Miss Emily, but we've got to do something." That night the Board of Aldermen met—three graybeards and one younger man, a member of the rising generation.

"It's simple enough," he said. "Send her word to have her place cleaned up. Give her a certain time to do it in, and if she don't . . ."

"Dammit, sir," Judge Stevens said, "will you accuse a lady to her face of smelling bad?"

So the next night, after midnight, four men crossed Miss Emily's lawn and slunk about the house like burglars, sniffing along the base of the brickwork and at the cellar openings while one of them performed a regular sowing motion with his hand out of a sack slung from his shoulder. They broke open the cellar door and sprinkled lime there, and in all the outbuildings. As they recrossed the lawn, a window that had been dark was lighted and Miss Emily sat in it, the light behind her, and her upright torso motionless as that of an idol. They crept quietly across the lawn and into the shadow of the locusts that lined the street. After a week or two the smell went away.

That was when people had begun to feel really sorry for her. People in our town, remembering how old lady Wyatt, her great-aunt, had gone completely crazy at last, believed that the Griersons held themselves a little too high for what they really were. None of the young men were quite good enough for Miss Emily and such. We had long thought of them as a tableau, Miss Emily a slender figure in white in the background, her father a spraddled silhouette in the foreground, his back to her and clutching a horsewhip, the two of them framed by the back-flung front door. So when she got to be thirty and was still single, we were not pleased exactly, but vindicated; even with insanity in the family she wouldn't have turned down all of her chances if they had really materialized.

When her father died, it got about that the house was all that was left to her; and in a way, people were glad. At last they could pity Miss Emily. Being left alone, and a pauper, she had become humanized. Now she too would know the old thrill and the old despair of a penny more or less.

The day after his death all the ladies prepared to call at the house and offer condolence and aid, as is our custom. Miss Emily met them at the door, dressed as usual and with no trace of grief on her face. She told them that her father was not dead. She did that for three days, with the ministers calling on her, and the doctors, trying to per-suade her to let them dispose of the body. Just as they were about to resort to law and force, she broke down, and they buried her father quickly.

We did not say she was crazy then. We believed she had to do that. We remembered all the young men her father had driven away, and we knew that with nothing left, she would have to cling to that which had robbed her, as people will.

III

She was sick for a long time. When we saw her again her hair was cut short, making her look like a girl, with a vague resemblance to those angels in colored church win-dows—sort of tragic and serene.

The town had just let the contracts for paving the side-walks, and in the summer after her father's death they began the work. The construction company came with niggers and mules and machinery, and a foreman named Homer Barron, a Yankee—a big, dark, ready man, with a big voice and eyes lighter than his face. The little boys would follow in groups to hear him cuss the niggers, and the niggers singing in time to the rise and fall of picks. Pretty soon he knew everybody in town. Whenever you heard a lot of laughing anywhere about the square, Homer Barron would be in the center of the group. Presently we began to see him and Miss Emily on Sunday afternoons driving in the yellow-wheeled buggy and the matched team of bays from the livery stable.

At first we were glad that Miss Emily would have an interest, because the ladies all said, "Of course a Grierson would not think seriously of a Northerner, a day laborer." But there were still others, older people, who said that even grief could not cause a real lady to forget *noblesse oblige*—without calling it *noblesse oblige*. They just said, "Poor Emily. Her kinsfolk should come to her." She had some kin in Alabama; but years ago her father had fallen out with them over the estate of old lady Wyatt, the crazy woman, and there was no communication between the two families. They had not even been represented at the funeral.

And as soon as the old people said, "Poor Emily," the whispering began. "Do you suppose it's really so?" they said to one another. "Of course it is. What else could . . ." This behind their hands; rustling of craned silk and satin behind jalousies closed upon the sun of Sunday afternoon as the thin, swift clop-clop-clop of the matched team passed: "Poor Emily."

She carried her head high enough—even when we believed that she was fallen. It was as if she demanded

more than ever the recognition of her dignity as the last
Grierson; as if it had wanted that touch of earthiness to
reaffirm her imperviousness. Like when she bought the
rat poison, the arsenic. That was over a year after they
had begun to say "Poor Emily," and while the two female
cousins were visiting her.

"I want some poison," she said to the druggist. She was
over thirty then, still a slight woman, though thinner than
usual, with cold, haughty black eyes in a face the flesh of
which was strained across the temples and about the eye-
sockets as you imagine a lighthousekeeper's face ought to
look. "I want some poison," she said.

"Yes, Miss Emily. What kind? For rats and such? I'd
recom—"

"I want the best you have. I don't care what kind."

The druggist named several. "They'll kill anything up
to an elephant. But what you want is—"

"Arsenic," Miss Emily said. "Is that a good one?"

"Is . . . arsenic? Yes, ma'am. But what you want—"

"I want arsenic."

The druggist looked down at her. She looked back at
him, erect, her face like a strained flag. "Why, of course,"
the druggist said. "If that's what you want. But the law
requires you to tell what you are going to use it for."

Miss Emily just stared at him, her head tilted back in
order to look him eye for eye, until he looked away and
went and got the arsenic and wrapped it up. The Negro
delivery boy brought her the package; the druggist didn't
come back. When she opened the package at home there
was written on the box, under the skull and bones: "For
rats."

IV

So the next day we all said, "She will kill herself"; and we said it would be the best thing. When she had first begun to be seen with Homer Barron, we had said, "She will marry him." Then we said, "She will persuade him yet," because Homer himself had remarked—he liked men, and it was known that he drank with the younger men in the Elks' Club—that he was not a marrying man. Later we said, "Poor Emily" behind the jalousies as they passed on Sunday afternoon in the glittering buggy, Miss Emily with her head high and Homer Barron with his hat cocked and a cigar in his teeth, reins and whip in a yellow glove.

Then some of the ladies began to say that it was a disgrace to the town and a bad example to the young people. The men did not want to interfere, but at last the ladies forced the Baptist minister—Miss Emily's people were Episcopal—to call upon her. He would never divulge what happened during that interview, but he refused to go back again. The next Sunday they again drove about the streets, and the following day the minister's wife wrote to Miss Emily's relations in Alabama.

So she had blood-kin under her roof again and we sat back to watch developments. At first nothing happened. Then we were sure that they were to be married. We learned that Miss Emily had been to the jeweler's and ordered a man's toilet set in silver, with the letters H. B. on each piece. Two days later we learned that she had bought a complete outfit of men's clothing, including a nightshirt, and we said, "They are married." We were really glad. We were glad because the two female cousins were even more Grierson than Miss Emily had ever been.

So we were not surprised when Homer Barron— the streets had been finished some time since—was gone. We were a little disappointed that there was not a public blowing-off, but we believed that he had gone on to prepare for Miss Emily's coming, or to give her a chance to get rid of the cousins. (By that time it was a cabal, and we were all Miss Emily's allies to help circumvent the cousins.) Sure enough, after another week they departed. And, as we had expected all along, within three days Homer Barron was back in town. A neighbor saw the Negro man admit him at the kitchen door at dusk one evening.

And that was the last we saw of Homer Barron. And of Miss Emily for some time. The Negro man went in and out with the market basket, but the front door remained closed. Now and then we would see her at a window for a moment, as the men did that night when they sprinkled the lime, but for almost six months she did not appear on the streets. Then we knew that this was to be expected too; as if that quality of her father which had thwarted her woman's life so many times had been too virulent and too furious to die.

When we next saw Miss Emily, she had grown fat and her hair was turning gray. During the next few years it grew grayer and grayer until it attained an even pepper-and-salt iron-gray, when it ceased turning. Up to the day of her death at seventy-four it was still that vigorous iron-gray, like the hair of an active man.

From that time on her front door remained closed, save for a period of six or seven years, when she was about forty, during which she gave lessons in china-painting.

She fitted up a studio in one of the downstairs rooms, where the daughters and granddaughters of Colonel Sartoris' contemporaries were sent to her with the same regularity and in the same spirit that they were sent to church on Sundays with a twenty-five-cent piece for the collection plate. Meanwhile her taxes had been remitted.

Then the newer generation became the backbone and the spirit of the town, and the painting pupils grew up and fell away and did not send their children to her with boxes of color and tedious brushes and pictures cut from the ladies' magazines. The front door closed upon the last one and remained closed for good. When the town got free postal delivery, Miss Emily alone refused to let them fasten the metal numbers above her door and attach a mailbox to it. She would not listen to them.

Daily, monthly, yearly we watched the Negro grow grayer and more stooped, going in and out with the market basket. Each December we sent her a tax notice, which would be returned by the post office a week later, unclaimed. Now and then we would see her in one of the downstairs windows—she had evidently shut up the top floor of the house—like the carven torso of an idol in a niche, looking or not looking at us, we could never tell which. Thus she passed from generation to generation—dear, inescapable, impervious, tranquil, and perverse.

And so she died. Fell ill in the house filled with dust and shadows, with only a doddering Negro man to wait on her. We did not even know she was sick; we had long since given up trying to get any information from the Negro. He talked to no one, probably not even to her, for his voice had grown harsh and rusty, as if from disuse.

She died in one of the downstairs rooms, in a heavy walnut bed with a curtain, her gray head propped on a pillow yellow and moldy with age and lack of sunlight.

V

The Negro met the first of the ladies at the front door and let them in, with their hushed, sibilant voices and their quick, curious glances, and then he disappeared. He walked right through the house and out the back and was not seen again.

The two female cousins came at once. They held the funeral on the second day, with the town coming to look at Miss Emily beneath a mass of bought flowers, with the crayon face of her father musing profoundly above the bier and the ladies sibilant and macabre; and the very old men—some in their brushed Confederate uniforms—on the porch and the lawn, talking of Miss Emily as if she had been a contemporary of theirs, believing that they had danced with her and courted her perhaps, confusing time with its mathematical progression, as the old do, to whom all the past is not a diminishing road but, instead, a huge meadow which no winter ever quite touches, divided from them now by the narrow bottle-neck of the most recent decade of years.

Already we knew that there was one room in that region above stairs which no one had seen in forty years, and which would have to be forced. They waited until Miss Emily was decently in the ground before they opened it.

The violence of breaking down the door seemed to fill this room with pervading dust. A thin, acrid pall as of the tomb seemed to lie everywhere upon this room decked and furnished as for a bridal: upon the valance curtains of faded rose color, upon the rose-shaded lights, upon the dressing table, upon the delicate array of crystal and the man's toilet things backed with tarnished silver, silver so tarnished that the monogram was obscured. Among them lay a collar and tie, as if they had just been removed, which, lifted, left upon the surface a·pale crescent in the dust. Upon a chair hung the suit, carefully folded; beneath it the two mute shoes and the discarded socks.

The man himself lay in the bed.

For a long while we just stood there, looking down at the profound and fleshless grin. The body had apparently once lain in the attitude of an embrace, but now the long sleep that outlasts love, that conquers even the grimace of love, had cuckolded him. What was left of him, rotted beneath what was left of the nightshirt, had become inextricable from the bed in which he lay; and upon him and upon the pillow beside him lay that even coating of the patient and biding dust.

Then we noticed that in the second pillow was the indentation of a head. One of us lifted something from it, and leaning forward, that faint and invisible dust dry and acrid in the nostrils, we saw a long strand of iron-gray hair.

Dry September

Through the bloody September twilight, aftermath of sixty-two rainless days, it had gone like a fire in dry grass—the rumor, the story, whatever it was. Something about Miss Minnie Cooper and a Negro. Attacked, insulted, frightened: none of them, gathered in the barber shop on that Saturday evening where the ceiling fan stirred, without freshening it, the vitiated air, sending back upon them, in recurrent surges of stale pomade and lotion, their own stale breath and odors, knew exactly what had happened.

"Except it wasn't Will Mayes," a barber said. He was a man of middle age; a thin, sand-colored man with a mild face, who was shaving a client. "I know Will Mayes. He's a good nigger. And I know Miss Minnie Cooper, too."

"What do you know about her?" a second barber said.

"Who is she?" the client said. "A young girl?"

"No," the barber said. "She's about forty, I reckon. She aint married. That's why I dont believe—"

"Believe, hell!" a hulking youth in a sweat-stained silk shirt said. "Wont you take a white woman's word before a nigger's?"

"I dont believe Will Mayes did it," the barber said. "I know Will Mayes."

"Maybe you know who did it, then. Maybe you already got him out of town, you damn niggerlover."

"I dont believe anybody did anything. I dont believe anything happened. I leave it to you fellows if them ladies that get old without getting married dont have notions that a man cant—"

"Then you are a hell of a white man," the client said. He moved under the cloth. The youth had sprung to his feet.

"You dont?" he said. "Do you accuse a white woman of lying?"

The barber held the razor poised above the half-risen client. He did not look around.

"It's this durn weather," another said. "It's enough to make a man do anything. Even to her."

Nobody laughed. The barber said in his mild, stubborn tone: "I aint accusing nobody of nothing. I just know and you fellows know how a woman that never—"

"You damn niggerlover!" the youth said.

"Shut up, Butch," another said. "We'll get the facts in plenty of time to act."

"Who is? Who's getting them?" the youth said. "Facts, hell! I—"

"You're a fine white man," the client said. "Aint you?" In his frothy beard he looked like a desert rat in moving pictures. "You can tell them, Jack," he said to the youth. "If there aint any white men in this town, you can count on me, even if I aint only a drummer and a stranger."

"That's right, boys," the barber said. "Find out the truth first. I know Will Mayes."

"Well, by God!" the youth shouted. "To think that a white man in this town—"

"Shut up, Butch," the second speaker said. "We got plenty of time."

The client sat up. He looked at the speaker. "Do you claim that anything excuses a nigger attacking a white woman? Do you mean to tell me you are a white man and you'll stand for it? You better go back North where you came from. The South dont want your kind here."

"North what?" the second said. "I was born and raised in this town."

"Well, by God!" the youth said. He looked about with a strained, baffled gaze, as if he was trying to remember what it was he wanted to say or to do. He drew his sleeve across his sweating face. "Damn if I'm going to let a white woman—"

"You tell them, Jack," the drummer said. "By God, if they—"

The screen door crashed open. A man stood in the floor, his feet apart and his heavy-set body poised easily. His white shirt was open at the throat; he wore a felt hat. His hot, bold glance swept the group. His name was McLendon. He had commanded troops at the front in France and had been decorated for valor.

"Well," he said, "are you going to sit there and let a black son rape a white woman on the streets of Jefferson?"

Butch sprang up again. The silk of his shirt clung flat to his heavy shoulders. At each armpit was a dark half-moon. "That's what I been telling them! That's what I—"

"Did it really happen?" a third said. "This aint the first man scare she ever had, like Hawkshaw says. Wasn't there something about a man on the kitchen roof, watching her undress, about a year ago?"

"What?" the client said. "What's that?" The barber had been slowly forcing him back into the chair; he arrested himself reclining, his head lifted, the barber still pressing him down.

McLendon whirled on the third speaker. "Happen? What the hell difference does it make? Are you going to let the black sons get away with it until one really does it?"

"That's what I'm telling them!" Butch shouted. He cursed, long and steady, pointless.

"Here, here," a fourth said. "Not so loud. Dont talk so loud."

"Sure," McLendon said; "no talking necessary at all. I've done my talking. Who's with me?" He poised on the balls of his feet, roving his gaze.

The barber held the drummer's face down, the razor poised. "Find out the facts first, boys. I know Willy Mayes. It wasn't him. Let's get the sheriff and do this thing right."

McLendon whirled upon him his furious, rigid face. The barber did not look away. They looked like men of different races. The other barbers had ceased also above their prone clients. "You mean to tell me," McLendon said, "that you'd take a nigger's word before a white woman's? Why, you damn niggerloving—"

The third speaker rose and grasped McLendon's arm; he too had been a soldier. "Now, now. Let's figure this thing out. Who knows anything about what really happened?"

"Figure out hell!" McLendon jerked his arm free. "All that're with me get up from there. The ones that aint—" He roved his gaze, dragging his sleeve across his face.

Three men rose. The drummer in the chair sat up. "Here," he said, jerking at the cloth about his neck; "get this rag off me. I'm with him. I dont live here, but by God, if our mothers and wives and sisters—" He smeared the cloth over his face and flung it to the floor. McLendon stood in the floor and cursed the others. Another rose and moved toward him. The remainder sat uncomfortable, not looking at one another, then one by one they rose and joined him.

The barber picked the cloth from the floor. He began to fold it neatly. "Boys, dont do that. Will Mayes never done it. I know."

"Come on," McLendon said. He whirled. From his hip pocket protruded the butt of a heavy automatic pistol. They went out. The screen door crashed behind them reverberant in the dead air.

The barber wiped the razor carefully and swiftly, and put it away, and ran to the rear, and took his hat from the wall. "I'll be back as soon as I can," he said to the other barbers. "I cant let—" He went out, running. The two other barbers followed him to the door and caught it on the rebound, leaning out and looking up the street after him. The air was flat and dead. It had a metallic taste at the base of the tongue.

"What can he do?" the first said. The second one was saying "Jees Christ, Jees Christ" under his breath. "I'd just as lief be Will Mayes as Hawk, if he gets McLendon riled."

"Jees Christ, Jees Christ," the second whispered.

"You reckon he really done it to her?" the first said.

II

She was thirty-eight or thirty-nine. She lived in a small frame house with her invalid mother and a thin, sallow, unflagging aunt, where each morning between ten and eleven she would appear on the porch in a lace-trimmed boudoir cap, to sit swinging in the porch swing until noon. After dinner she lay down for a while, until the afternoon began to cool. Then, in one of the three or four new voile dresses which she had each summer, she would go downtown to spend the afternoon in the stores with the other ladies, where they would handle the goods and haggle over the prices in cold, immediate voices, without any intention of buying.

She was of comfortable people—not the best in Jefferson, but good people enough—and she was still on the slender side of ordinary-looking, with a bright, faintly haggard manner and dress. When she was young she had had a slender nervous body and a sort of hard vivacity which had enabled her for a time to ride upon the crest of the town's social life as exemplified by the high school party and church social period of her contemporaries while still children enough to be unclass-conscious.

She was the last to realize that she was losing ground; that those among whom she had been a little brighter and louder flame than any other were beginning to learn the pleasure of snobbery—male—and retaliation — female. That was when her face began to wear that bright, haggard look. She still carried it to parties on shadowy porticoes and summer lawns, like a mask or a flag, with that bafflement of furious repudiation of truth in her eyes. One evening at a party she heard a boy and two girls, all schoolmates, talking. She never accepted another invitation.

She watched the girls with whom she had grown up as they married and got homes and children, but no man ever called on her steadily until the children of the other girls had been calling her "aunty" for several years, the while their mothers told them in bright voices about how popular Aunt Minnie had been as a girl. Then the town began to see her driving on Sunday afternoons with the cashier in the bank. He was a widower of about forty—a high-colored man, smelling always faintly of the barber shop or of whisky. He owned the first automobile in town, a red runabout; Minnie had the first motoring bonnet and veil the town ever saw. Then the town began to say: "Poor Minnie." "But she is old enough to take care of herself," others said. That was when she began to ask her old schoolmates that their children call her "cousin" instead of "aunty."

It was twelve years now since she had been relegated into adultery by public opinion, and eight years since the cashier had gone to a Memphis bank, returning for one day each Christmas, which he spent at an annual bachelors' party at a hunting club on the river. From behind their curtains the neighbors would see the party pass, and during the over-the-way Christmas day visiting they would tell her about him, about how well he looked, and how they heard that he was prospering in the city, watching with bright, secret eyes her haggard, bright face. Usually by that hour there would be the scent of whisky on her breath. It was supplied her by a youth, a clerk at the soda fountain: "Sure; I buy it for the old gal. I reckon she's entitled to a little fun."

Her mother kept to her room altogether now; the gaunt aunt ran the house. Against that background Minnie's bright dresses, her idle and empty days, had a quality of furious unreality. She went out in the evenings only with women now, neighbors, to the moving pictures. Each afternoon she dressed in one of the new dresses and went downtown alone, where her young "cousins" were already strolling in the late afternoons with their delicate, silken heads and thin, awkward arms and conscious hips, clinging to one another or shrieking and giggling with paired boys in the soda fountain when she passed and went on along the serried store fronts, in the doors of which the sitting and lounging men did not even follow her with their eyes any more.

III

The barber went swiftly up the street where the sparse lights, insect-swirled, glared in rigid and violent suspension in the lifeless air. The day had died in a pall of dust; above the darkened square, shrouded by the spent dust, the sky was as clear as the inside of a brass bell. Below the east was a rumor of the twice-waxed moon.

When he overtook them McLendon and three others were getting into a car parked in an alley. McLendon stooped his thick head, peering out beneath the top. "Changed your mind, did you?" he said. "Damn good thing; by God, tomorrow when this town hears about how you talked tonight—"

"Now, now," the other ex-soldier said. "Hawkshaw's all right. Come on Hawk; jump in."

"Will Mayes never done it, boys," the barber said. "If

anybody done it. Why, you all know well as I do there aint any town where they got better niggers than us. And you know how a lady will kind of think things about men when there aint any reason to, and Miss Minnie anyway—"

"Sure, sure," the soldier said. "We're just going to talk to him a little; that's all."

"Talk hell!" Butch said. "When we're through with the—"

"Shut up, for God's sake!" the soldier said. "Do you want everybody in town—"

"Tell them, by God!" McLendon said. "Tell every one of the sons that'll let a white woman—"

"Let's go; let's go: here's the other car." The second car slid squealing out of a cloud of dust at the alley mouth. McLendon started his car and took the lead. Dust lay like fog in the street. The street lights hung nimbused as in water. They drove on out of town.

A rutted lane turned at right angles. Dust hung above it too, and above all the land. The dark bulk of the ice plant, where the Negro Mayes was night watchman, rose against the sky. "Better stop here, hadn't we?" the soldier said. McLendon did not reply. He hurled the car up and slammed to a stop, the headlights glaring on the blank wall.

"Listen here, boys," the barber said; "if he's here, dont that prove he never done it? Dont it? If it was him, he would run. Dont you see he would?" The second car came up and stopped. McLendon got down; Butch sprang down beside him. "Listen, boys," the barber said.

"Cut the lights off!" McLendon said. The breathless dark rushed down. There was no sound in it save their lungs as they sought air in the parched dust in which for two months they had lived; then the diminishing crunch of McLendon's and Butch's feet, and a moment late McLendon's voice:

"Will! . . . Will!"

Below the east the wan hemorrhage of the moon increased. It heaved above the ridge, silvering the air, the dust, so that they seemed to breathe, live, in a bowl of molten lead. There was no sound of nightbird nor insect, no sound save their breathing and a faint ticking of contracting metal about the cars. Where their bodies touched one another they seemed to sweat dryly, for no more moisture came. "Christ!" a voice said; "let's get out of here."

But they didn't move until vague noises began to grow out of the darkness ahead; then they got out and waited tensely in the breathless dark. There was another sound: a blow, a hissing expulsion of breath and McLendon cursing in undertone. They stood a moment longer, then they ran forward. They ran in a stumbling clump, as though they were fleeing something. "Kill him, kill the son," a voice whispered. McLendon flung them back.

"Not here," he said. "Get him into the car." "Kill him, kill the black son!" the voice murmured. They dragged the Negro to the car. The barber had waited beside the car. He could feel himself sweating and he knew he was going to be sick at the stomach.

"What is it, captains?" the Negro said. "I aint done nothing. 'Fore God, Mr John." Someone produced handcuffs. They worked busily about the Negro as though he were a post, quiet, intent, getting in one another's way. He submitted to the handcuffs, looking swiftly and constantly from dim face to dim face. "Who's here, captains?" he said, leaning to peer into the faces until they could feel his breath and smell his sweaty reek. He spoke a name or two. "What you all say I done, Mr John?"

McLendon jerked the car door open. "Get in!" he said.

The Negro did not move. "What you all going to do with me, Mr John? I aint done nothing. White folks, captains, I aint done nothing: I swear 'fore God." He called another name.

"Get in!" McLendon said. He struck the Negro. The others expelled their breath in a dry hissing and struck him with random blows and he whirled and cursed them, and swept his manacled hands across their faces and slashed the barber upon the mouth, and the barber struck him also. "Get him in there," McLendon said. They pushed at him. He ceased struggling and got in and sat quietly as the others took their places. He sat between the barber and the soldier, drawing his limbs in so as not to touch them, his eyes going swiftly and constantly from face to face. Butch clung to the running board. The car moved on. The barber nursed his mouth with his handkerchief.

"What's the matter, Hawk?" the soldier said.

"Nothing," the barber said. They regained the highroad and turned away from town. The second car dropped back out of the dust. They went on, gaining speed; the final fringe of houses dropped behind.

"Goddamn, he stinks!" the soldier said.

"We'll fix that," the drummer in front beside McLendon said. On the running board Butch cursed into the hot rush of air. The barber leaned suddenly forward and touched McLendon's arm.

"Let me out, John," he said.

"Jump out, niggerlover," McLendon said without turning his head. He drove swiftly. Behind them the sourceless lights of the second car glared in the dust. Presently McLendon turned into a narrow road. It was rutted with disuse. It led back to an abandoned brick kiln—a series of reddish mounds and weed- and vine-choked vats without bottom. It had been used for pasture once, until one day the owner missed one of his mules. Although he prodded carefully in the vats with a long pole, he could not even find the bottom of them.

"John," the barber said.

"Jump out, then," McLendon said, hurling the car along the ruts. Beside the barber the Negro spoke:

"Mr Henry."

The barber sat forward. The narrow tunnel of the road rushed up and past. Their motion was like an extinct furnace blast: cooler, but utterly dead. The car bounded from rut to rut.

"Mr Henry," the Negro said.

The barber began to tug furiously at the door. "Look out, there!" the soldier said, but the barber had already kicked the door open and swung onto the running board. The soldier leaned across the Negro and grasped at him, but he had already jumped. The car went on without checking speed.

The impetus hurled him crashing through dust-sheathed weeds, into the ditch. Dust puffed about him, and in a thin, vicious crackling of sapless stems he lay choking and retching until the second car passed and died away. Then he rose and limped on until he reached the highroad and turned toward town, brushing at his clothes with his hands. The moon was higher, riding high and clear of the dust at last, and after a while the town began to glare beneath the dust. He went on, limping. Presently he heard cars and the glow of them grew in the dust behind him and he left the road and crouched again in the weeds until they passed. McLendon's car came last now. There were four people in it and Butch was not on the running board.

They went on; the dust swallowed them; the glare and the sound died away. The dust of them hung for a while, but soon the eternal dust absorbed it again. The barber climbed back onto the road and limped on toward town.

IV

As she dressed for supper on that Saturday evening, her own flesh felt like fever. Her hands trembled among the hooks and eyes, and her eyes had a feverish look, and her hair swirled crisp and crackling under the comb. While she was still dressing the friends called for her and sat while she donned her sheerest underthings and stockings and a new voile dress. "Do you feel strong enough to go out?" they said, their eyes bright too, with a dark glitter. "When you have had time to get over the shock, you must tell us what happened. What he said and did; everything."

In the leafed darkness, as they walked toward the square, she began to breathe deeply, something like a swimmer preparing to dive, until she ceased trembling, the four of them walking slowly because of the terrible heat and out of solicitude for her. But as they neared the square she began to tremble again, walking with her head up, her hands clenched at her sides, their voices about her murmurous, also with that feverish, glittering quality of their eyes.

They entered the square, she in the center of the group, fragile in her fresh dress. She was trembling worse. She walked slower and slower, as children eat ice cream, her head up and her eyes bright in the haggard banner of her face, passing the hotel and the coatless drummers in chairs along the curb looking around at her: "That's the one: see? The one in pink in the middle." "Is that her? What did they do with the nigger? Did they—?" "Sure. He's all right." "All right, is he?" "Sure. He went on a little trip." Then the drug store, where even the young men lounging in the doorway tipped their hats and followed with their eyes the motion of her hips and legs when she passed.

They went on, passing the lifted hats of the gentlemen, the suddenly ceased voices, deferent, protective. "Do you see?" the friends said. Their voices sounded like long, hovering sighs of hissing exultation. "There's not a Negro on the square. Not one."

They reached the picture show. It was like a miniature fairyland with its lighted lobby and colored lithographs of life caught in its terrible and beautiful mutations. Her lips began to tingle. In the dark, when the picture began, it would be all right; she could hold back the laughing so it would not waste away so fast and so soon. So she hurried on before the turning faces, the undertones of low astonishment, and they took their accustomed places where she could see the aisle against the silver glare and the young men and girls coming in two and two against it.

The lights flicked away; the screen glowed silver, and

soon life began to unfold, beautiful and passionate and sad, while still the young men and girls entered, scented and sibilant in the half dark, their paired backs in silhouette delicate and sleek, their slim, quick bodies awkward, divinely young, while beyond them the silver dream accumulated, inevitably on and on. She began to laugh. In trying to suppress it, it made more noise than ever; heads began to turn. Still laughing, her friends raised her and led her out, and she stood at the curb, laughing on a high, sustained note, until the taxi came up and they helped her in.

They removed the pink voile and the sheer underthings and the stockings, and put her to bed, and cracked ice for her temples, and sent for the doctor. He was hard to locate, so they ministered to her with hushed ejaculations, renewing the ice and fanning her. While the ice was fresh and cold she stopped laughing and lay still for a time, moaning only a little. But soon the laughing welled again and her voice rose screaming.

"Shhhhhhhhhhh! Shhhhhhhhhhhhhhh!" they said, freshening the icepack, smoothing her hair, examining it for gray; "poor girl!" Then to one another: "Do you suppose anything really happened?" their eyes darkly aglitter, secret and passionate. "Shhhhhhhhhh! Poor girl! Poor Minnie!"

V

It was midnight when McLendon drove up to his neat new house. It was trim and fresh as a birdcage and almost as small, with its clean, green-and-white paint. He locked the car and mounted the porch and entered. His wife rose from a chair beside the reading lamp. McLendon stopped in the floor and stared at her until she looked down.

"Look at that clock," he said, lifting his arm, pointing. She stood before him, her face lowered, a magazine in her hands. Her face was pale, strained, and weary-looking. "Haven't I told you about sitting up like this, waiting to see when I come in?"

"John," she said. She laid the magazine down. Poised on the balls of his feet, he glared at her with his hot eyes, his sweating face.

"Didn't I tell you?" He went toward her. She looked up then. He caught her shoulder. She stood passive, looking at him.

"Dont, John. I couldn't sleep . . . The heat; something. Please, John. You're hurting me."

"Didn't I tell you?" He released her and half struck, half flung her across the chair, and she lay there and watched him quietly as he left the room.

He went on through the house, ripping off his shirt, and on the dark, screened porch at the rear he stood and mopped his head and shoulders with the shirt and flung it away. He took the pistol from his hip and laid it on the table beside the bed, and sat on the bed and removed his shoes, and rose and slipped his trousers off. He was sweating again already, and he stooped and hunted furiously for the shirt. At last he found it and wiped his body again, and, with his body pressed against the dusty screen, he stood panting. There was no movement, no sound, not even an insect. The dark world seemed to lie stricken beneath the cold moon and the lidless stars.

That Evening Sun

Monday is no different from any other weekday in Jefferson now. The streets are paved now, and the telephone and electric companies are cutting down more and more of the shade trees—the water oaks, the maples and locusts and elms—to make room for iron poles bearing clusters of bloated and ghostly and bloodless grapes, and we have a city laundry which makes the rounds on Monday morning, gathering the bundles of clothes into bright-colored, specially-made motor cars: the soiled wearing of a whole week now flees apparitionlike behind alert and irritable electric horns, with a long diminishing noise of rubber and asphalt like tearing silk, and even the Negro women who still take in white people's washing after the old custom, fetch and deliver it in automobiles.

But fifteen years ago, on Monday morning the quiet, dusty, shady streets would be full of Negro women with, balanced on their steady, turbaned heads, bundles of clothes tied up in sheets, almost as large as cotton bales, carried so without touch of hand between the kitchen door of the white house and the blackened washpot beside a cabin door in Negro Hollow.

Nancy would set her bundle on the top of her head, then upon the bundle in turn she would set the black

76

straw sailor hat which she wore winter and summer. She was tall, with a high, sad face sunken a little where her teeth were missing. Sometimes we would go a part of the way down the lane and across the pasture with her, to watch the balanced bundle and the hat that never bobbed nor wavered, even when she walked down into the ditch and up the other side and stooped through the fence. She would go down on her hands and knees and crawl through the gap, her head rigid, uptilted, the bundle steady as a rock or a balloon, and rise to her feet again and go on.

Sometimes the husbands of the washing women would fetch and deliver the clothes, but Jesus never did that for Nancy, even before father told him to stay away from our house, even when Dilsey was sick and Nancy would come to cook for us.

And then about half the time we'd have to go down the lane to Nancy's cabin and tell her to come on and cook breakfast. We would stop at the ditch, because father told us to not have anything to do with Jesus—he was a short black man, with a razor scar down his face—and we would throw rocks at Nancy's house until she came to the door, leaning her head around it without any clothes on.

"What yawl mean, chunking my house?" Nancy said. "What you little devils mean?"

"Father says for you to come on and get breakfast, Caddy said. "Father says it's over a half an hour now, and you've got to come this minute."

"I aint studying no breakfast," Nancy said. "I going to get my sleep out."

"I bet you're drunk," Jason said. "Father says you're drunk. Are you drunk, Nancy?"

"Who says I is?" Nancy said. "I got to get my sleep out. I aint studying no breakfast."

So after a while we quit chunking the cabin and went back home. When she finally came, it was too late for me to go to school. So we thought it was whisky until that day they arrested her again and they were taking her to jail and they passed Mr Stovall. He was the cashier in the bank and a deacon in the Baptist church, and Nancy began to say:

"When you going to pay me, white man? When you going to pay me, white man? It's been three times now since you paid me a cent—" Mr Stovall knocked her down, but she kept on saying, "When you going to pay me, white man? It's been three times now since—" until Mr Stovall kicked her in the mouth with his heel and the marshal caught Mr Stovall back, and Nancy lying in the street, laughing. She turned her head and spat out some blood and teeth and said, "It's been three times now since he paid me a cent."

That was how she lost her teeth, and all that day they told about Nancy and Mr Stovall, and all that night the ones that passed the jail could hear Nancy singing and yelling. They could see her hands holding to the window bars, and a lot of them stopped along the fence, listening to her and to the jailer trying to make her stop. She didn't shut up until almost daylight, when the jailer began to hear a bumping and scraping upstairs and he went up there and found Nancy hanging from the window bar. He said that it was cocaine and not whisky, because no nigger would try to commit suicide unless he was full of cocaine, because a nigger full of cocaine wasn't a nigger any longer.

The jailer cut her down and revived her; then he beat her, whipped her. She had hung herself with her dress. She had fixed it all right, but when they arrested her she didn't have on anything except a dress and so she didn't have anything to tie her hands with and she couldn't make her hands let go of the window ledge. So the jailer heard the noise and ran up there and found Nancy hanging from the window, stark naked, her belly already swelling out a little, like a little balloon.

When Dilsey was sick in her cabin and Nancy was cooking for us, we could see her apron swelling out; that was before father told Jesus to stay away from the house. Jesus was in the kitchen, sitting behind the stove, with his razor scar on his black face like a piece of dirty string. He said it was a watermelon that Nancy had under her dress.

"It never come off of your vine, though," Nancy said.

"Off of what vine?" Caddy said.

"I can cut down the vine it did come off of," Jesus said.

"What makes you want to talk like that before these chillen?" Nancy said. "Whyn't you go on to work? You done et. You want Mr Jason to catch you hanging around his kitchen, talking that way before these chillen?"

"Talking what way?" Caddy said. "What vine?"

"I cant hang around white man's kitchen," Jesus said. "But white man can hang around mine. White man can come in my house, but I cant stop him. When white man want to come in my house, I aint got no house. I cant stop him, but he cant kick me outen it. He cant do that."

Dilsey was still sick in her cabin. Father told Jesus to stay off our place. Dilsey was still sick. It was a long time. We were in the library after supper.

"Isn't Nancy through in the kitchen yet?" mother said. "It seems to me that she has had plenty of time to have finished the dishes."

"Let Quentin go and see," father said. "Go and see if Nancy is through, Quentin. Tell her she can go on home."

I went to the kitchen. Nancy was through. The dishes were put away and the fire was out. Nancy was sitting in a chair, close to the cold stove. She looked at me.

"Mother wants to know if you are through," I said.

"Yes," Nancy said. She looked at me. "I done finished." She looked at me.

"What is it?" I said. "What is it?"

"I aint nothing but a nigger," Nancy said. "It aint none of my fault."

She looked at me, sitting in the chair before the cold stove, the sailor hat on her head. I went back to the library. It was the cold stove and all, when you think of a kitchen being warm and busy and cheerful. And with a cold stove and the dishes all put away, and nobody wanting to eat at that hour.

"Is she through?" mother said.

"Yessum," I said.

"What is she doing?" mother said.

"She's not doing anything. She's through."

"I'll go and see," father said.

"Maybe she's waiting for Jesus to come and take her home," Caddy said.

"Jesus is gone," I said. Nancy told us how one morning she woke up and Jesus was gone.

"He quit me," Nancy said. "Done gone to Memphis, I reckon. Dodging them city *po*-lice for a while, I reckon."

"And a good riddance," father said. "I hope he stays there."

"Nancy's scaired of the dark," Jason said.

"So are you," Caddy said.

"I'm not," Jason said.

"Scairy cat," Caddy said.

"I'm not," Jason said.

"You, Candace!" mother said. Father came back.

"I am going to walk down the lane with Nancy," he said. "She says that Jesus is back."

"Has she seen him?" mother said.

"No. Some Negro sent her word that he was back in town. I wont be long."

"You'll leave me alone, to take Nancy home?" mother said. "Is her safety more precious to you than mine?"

"I wont be long," father said.

"You'll leave these children unprotected, with that Negro about?"

"I'm going too," Caddy said. "Let me go, father."

"What would he do with them, if he were unfortunate enough to have them?" father said.

"I want to go, too," Jason said.

"Jason!" mother said. She was speaking to father. You could tell that by the way she said the name. Like she believed that all day father had been trying to think of doing the thing she wouldn't like the most, and that she knew all the time that after a while he would think of it. I stayed quiet, because father and I both knew that mother would want him to make me stay with her if she just thought of it in time. So father didn't look at me. I was the oldest. I was nine and Caddy was seven and Jason was five.

"Nonsense," father said. "We wont be long."

Nancy had her hat on. We came to the lane. "Jesus always been good to me," Nancy said. "Whenever he had two dollars, one of them was mine." We walked in the lane. "If I can just get through the lane," Nancy said, "I be all right then."

The lane was always dark. "This is where Jason got scared on Hallowe'en," Caddy said.

"I didn't," Jason said.

"Cant Aunt Rachel do anything with him?" father said. Aunt Rachel was old. She lived in a cabin beyond Nancy's, by herself. She had white hair and she smoked a pipe in the door, all day long; she didn't work any more. They said she was Jesus' mother. Sometimes she said she was and sometimes she said she wasn't any kin to Jesus.

"Yes, you did," Caddy said. "You were scairder then Frony. You were scairder than T. P. even. Scairder than niggers."

"Cant nobody do nothing with him," Nancy said. "He say I done woke up the devil in him and aint but one thing going to lay it down again."

"Well, he's gone now," father said. "There's nothing for you to be afraid of now. And if you'd just let white men alone."

"Let what white men alone?" Caddy said. "How let them alone?"

"He aint gone nowhere," Nancy said. "I can feel him. I can feel him now, in this lane. He hearing us talk, every word, hid somewhere, waiting. I aint seen him, and I aint going to see him again but once more, with that razor in his mouth. That razor on that string down his back, inside his shirt. And then I aint going to be even surprised."

"I wasn't scaired," Jason said.

"If you'd behave yourself, you'd have kept out of this," father said. "But it's all right now. He's probably in St. Louis now. Probably got another wife by now and forgot all about you."

"If he has, I better not find out about it," Nancy said. "I'd stand there right over them, and every time he wropped her, I'd cut that arm off. I'd cut his head off and I'd slit her belly and I'd shove—"

"Hush," father said.

"Slit whose belly, Nancy?" Caddy said.

"I wasn't scaired," Jason said. "I'd walk right down this lane by myself."

"Yah," Caddy said. "You wouldn't dare to put your foot down in it if we were not here too."

II

Dilsey was still sick, so we took Nancy home every night until mother said, "How much longer is this going on? I to be left alone in this big house while you take home a frightened Negro?"

We fixed a pallet in the kitchen for Nancy. One night we waked up, hearing the sound. It was not singing and it was not crying, coming up the dark stairs. There was a light in mother's room and we heard father going down the hall, down the back stairs, and Caddy and I went into the hall. The floor was cold. Our toes curled away from it while we listened to the sound. It was like singing and it wasn't like singing, like the sounds that Negroes make.

Then it stopped and we heard father going down the back stairs, and we went to the head of the stairs. Then the sound began again, in the stairway, not loud, and we could see Nancy's eyes halfway up the stairs, against the wall. They looked like cat's eyes do, like a big cat against the wall, watching us. When we came down the steps to where she was, she quit making the sound again, and we stood there until father came back up from the kitchen, with his pistol in his hand. He went back down with Nancy and they came back with Nancy's pallet.

We spread the pallet in our room. After the light in mother's room went off, we could see Nancy's eyes again. "Nancy," Caddy whispered, "are you asleep, Nancy?"

Nancy whispered something. It was oh or no, I dont know which. Like nobody had made it, like it came from nowhere and went nowhere, until it was like Nancy was not there at all; that I had looked so hard at her eyes on the stairs that they had got printed on my eyeballs, like the sun does when you have closed your eyes and there is no sun. "Jesus," Nancy whispered. "Jesus."

"Was it Jesus?" Caddy said. "Did he try to come into the kitchen?"

"Jesus," Nancy said. Like this: Jeeeeeeeeeeeeeeesus, until the sound went out, like a match or a candle does.

"It's the other Jesus she means," I said.

"Can you see us, Nancy?" Caddy whispered. "Can you see our eyes too?"

"I aint nothing but a nigger," Nancy said. "God knows. God knows."

"What did you see down there in the kitchen?" Caddy whispered. "What tried to get in?"

"God knows," Nancy said. We could see her eyes. "God knows."

Dilsey got well. She cooked dinner. "You'd better stay in bed a day or two longer," father said.

"What for?" Dilsey said. "If I had been a day later, this place would be to rack and ruin. Get on out of here now, and let me get my kitchen straight again."

Dilsey cooked supper too. And that night, just before dark, Nancy came into the kitchen.

"How do you know he's back?" Dilsey said. "You aint seen him."

"Jesus is a nigger," Jason said.

"I can feel him," Nancy said. "I can feel him laying yonder in the ditch."

"Tonight?" Dilsey said. "Is he there tonight?"

"Dilsey's a nigger too," Jason said.

"You try to eat something," Dilsey said.

"I dont want nothing," Nancy said.

"I aint a nigger," Jason said.

"Drink some coffee," Dilsey said. She poured a cup of coffee for Nancy. "Do you know he's out there tonight? How come you know it's tonight?"

"I know," Nancy said. "He's there, waiting. I know. I done lived with him too long. I know what he is fixing to do fore he know it himself."

"Drink some coffee," Dilsey said. Nancy held the cup to her mouth and blew into the cup. Her mouth pursed out like a spreading adder's, like a rubber mouth, like she had blown all the color out of her lips with blowing the coffee.

"I aint a nigger," Jason said. "Are you a nigger, Nancy?"

"I hellborn, child," Nancy said. "I wont be nothing soon. I going back where I come from soon."

III

She began to drink the coffee. While she was drinking, holding the cup in both hands, she began to make the sound again. She made the sound into the cup and the coffee sploshed out onto her hands and her dress. Her eyes looked at us and she sat there, her elbows on her knees, holding the cup in both hands, looking at us across the wet cup, making the sound. "Look at Nancy," Jason said. "Nancy cant cook for us now. Dilsey's got well now."

"You hush up," Dilsey said. Nancy held the cup in both hands, looking at us, making the sound, like there were two of them: one looking at us and the other making the sound. "Whyn't you let Mr Jason telefoam the marshal?" Dilsey said. Nancy stopped then, holding the cup in her long brown hands. She tried to drink some coffee again, but it sploshed out of the cup, onto her hands and her dress, and she put the cup down. Jason watched her.

"I cant swallow it," Nancy said. "I swallows but it wont go down me."

"You go down to the cabin," Dilsey said. "Frony will fix you a pallet and I'll be there soon."

"Wont no nigger stop him," Nancy said.

"I aint a nigger," Jason said. "Am I, Dilsey?"

"I reckon not," Dilsey said. She looked at Nancy. "I dont reckon so. What you going to do, then?"

Nancy looked at us. Her eyes went fast, like she was afraid there wasn't time to look, without hardly moving at all. She looked at us, at all three of us at one time. "You member that night I stayed in yawls' room?" she said. She told about how we waked up early the next morning, and played. We had to play quiet, on her pallet, until father woke up and it was time to get breakfast. "Go and ask your maw to let me stay here tonight," Nancy said. "I wont need no pallet. We can play some more."

Caddy asked mother. Jason went too. "I cant have Negroes sleeping in the bedrooms," mother said. Jason cried. He cried until mother said he couldn't have any dessert for three days if he didn't stop. Then Jason said he would stop if Dilsey would make a chocolate cake. Father was there.

"Why dont you do something about it?" mother said. "What do we have officers for?"

"Why is Nancy afraid of Jesus?" Caddy said. "Are you afraid of father, mother?"

"What could the officers do?" father said. "If Nancy hasn't seen him, how could the officers find him?"

"Then why is she afraid?" mother said.

"She says he is there. She says she knows he is there tonight."

"Yet we pay taxes," mother said. "I must wait here alone in this big house while you take a Negro woman home."

"You know that I am not lying outside with a razor," father said.

"I'll stop if Dilsey will make a chocolate cake," Jason said. Mother told us to go out and father said he didn't know if Jason would get a chocolate cake or not, but he knew what Jason was going to get in about a minute. We went back to the kitchen and told Nancy.

"Father said for you to go home and lock the door, and you'll be all right," Caddy said. "All right from what, Nancy? Is Jesus mad at you?" Nancy was holding the coffee cup in her hands again, her elbows on her knees and her hands holding the cup between her knees. She was looking into the cup. "What have you done that made Jesus mad?" Caddy said. Nancy let the cup go. It didn't break on the floor, but the coffee spilled out, and Nancy sat there with her hands still making the shape of the cup. She began to make the sound again, not loud. Not singing and not unsinging. We watched her.

"Here," Dilsey said. "You quit that, now. You get aholt of yourself. You wait here. I going to get Versh to walk home with you." Dilsey went out.

We looked at Nancy. Her shoulders kept shaking, but she quit making the sound. We watched her. "What's Jesus going to do to you?" Caddy said. "He went away."

Nancy looked at us. "We had fun that night I stayed in yawls' room, didn't we?"

"I didn't," Jason said. "I didn't have any fun."

"You were asleep in mother's room," Caddy said. "You were not there."

"Let's go down to my house and have some more fun," Nancy said.

"Mother wont let us," I said. "It's too late now."

"Dont bother her," Nancy said. "We can tell her in the morning. She wont mind."

"She wouldn't let us," I said.

"Dont ask her now," Nancy said. "Dont bother her now."

"She didn't say we couldn't go," Caddy said.

"We didn't ask," I said.

"If you go, I'll tell," Jason said.

"We'll have fun," Nancy said. "They wont mind, just to my house. I been working for yawl a long time. They won't mind."

"I'm not afraid to go," Caddy said. "Jason is the one that's afraid. He'll tell."

"I'm not," Jason said.

"Yes, you are," Caddy said. "You'll tell."

"I won't tell," Jason said. "I'm not afraid."

"Jason aint afraid to go with me," Nancy said. "Is you, Jason?"

"Jason is going to tell," Caddy said. The lane was dark. We passed the pasture gate. "I bet if something was to jump out from behind that gate, Jason would holler."

"I wouldn't," Jason said. We walked down the lane. Nancy was talking loud.

"What are you talking so loud for, Nancy?" Caddy said.

"Who; me?" Nancy said. "Listen at Quentin and Caddy and Jason saying I'm talking loud."

"You talk like there was five of us here," Caddy said. "You talk like father was here too."

"Who; me talking loud, Mr Jason?" Nancy said.

"Nancy called Jason 'Mister,' " Caddy said.

"Listen how Caddy and Quentin and Jason talk," Nancy said.

"We're not talking loud," Caddy said. "You're the one that's talking like father—"

"Hush," Nancy said; "hush, Mr Jason."

"Nancy called Jason 'Mister' aguh—"

"Hush," Nancy said. She was talking loud when we

crossed the ditch and stooped through the fence where she used to stoop through with the clothes on her head. Then we came to her house. We were going fast then. She opened the door. The smell of the house was like the lamp and the smell of Nancy was like the wick, like they were waiting for one another to begin to smell. She lit the lamp and closed the door and put the bar up. Then she quit talking loud, looking at us.

"What're we going to do?" Caddy said.

"What do yawl want to do?" Nancy said.

"You said we would have some fun," Caddy said.

There was something about Nancy's house; something you could smell besides Nancy and the house. Jason smelled it, even. "I dont want to stay here," he said. "I want to go home."

"Go home, then," Caddy said.

"I dont want to go by myself," Jason said.

"We're going to have some fun," Nancy said.

"How?" Caddy said.

Nancy stood by the door. She was looking at us, only it was like she had emptied her eyes, like she had quit using them. "What do you want to do?" she said.

"Tell us a story," Caddy said. "Can you tell a story?"

"Yes," Nancy said.

"Tell it," Caddy said. We looked at Nancy. "You dont know any stories."

"Yes," Nancy said. "Yes, I do."

She came and sat in a chair before the hearth. There was a little fire there. Nancy built it up, when it was already hot inside. She built a good blaze. She told a story. She talked like her eyes looked, like her eyes watching us and her voice talking to us did not belong to her.

Like she was living somewhere else, waiting somewhere else. She was outside the cabin. Her voice was inside and the shape of her, the Nancy that could stoop under a barbed wire fence with a bundle of clothes balanced on her head as though without weight, like a balloon, was there. But that was all. "And so this here queen come walking up to the ditch, where that bad man was hiding. She was walking up to the ditch, and she say, 'If I can just get past this here ditch,' was what she say . . ."

"What ditch?" Caddy said. "A ditch like that one out there? Why did a queen want to go into a ditch?"

"To get to her house," Nancy said. She looked at us. "She had to cross the ditch to get into her house quick and bar the door."

"Why did she want to go home and bar the door?" Caddy said.

IV

Nancy looked at us. She quit talking. She looked at us. Jason's legs stuck straight out of his pants where he sat on Nancy's lap. "I dont think that's a good story," he said. "I want to go home."

"Maybe we had better," Caddy said. She got up from the floor. "I bet they are looking for us right now." She went toward the door.

"No," Nancy said. "Dont open it." She got up quick and passed Caddy. She didn't touch the door, the wooden bar.

"Why not?" Caddy said.

"Come back to the lamp," Nancy said. "We'll have fun. You dont have to go."

"We ought to go," Caddy said. "Unless we have a lot of fun." She and Nancy came back to the fire, the lamp.

"I want to go home," Jason said. "I'm going to tell."

"I know another story," Nancy said. She stood close to the lamp. She looked at Caddy, like when your eyes look up at a stick balanced on your nose. She had to look down to see Caddy, but her eyes looked like that, like when you are balancing a stick.

"I wont listen to it," Jason said. "I'll bang on the floor."

"It's a good one," Nancy said. "It's better than the other one."

"What's it about?" Caddy said. Nancy was standing by the lamp. Her hand was on the lamp, against the light, long and brown.

"Your hand is on that hot globe," Caddy said. "Don't it feel hot to your hand?"

Nancy looked at her hand on the lamp chimney. She took her hand away, slow. She stood there, looking at Caddy, wringing her long hand as though it were tied to her wrist with a string.

"Let's do something else," Caddy said.

"I want to go home," Jason said.

"I got some popcorn," Nancy said. She looked at Caddy and then at Jason and then at me and then at Caddy again. "I got some popcorn."

"I don't like popcorn," Jason said. "I'd rather have candy."

Nancy looked at Jason. "You can hold the popper." She was still wringing her hand; it was long and limp and brown.

"All right," Jason said. "I'll stay a while if I can do

that. Caddy cant hold it. I'll want to go home again if Caddy holds the popper."

Nancy built up the fire. "Look at Nancy putting her hands in the fire," Caddy said. "What's the matter with you, Nancy?"

"I got popcorn," Nancy said. "I got some." She took the popper from under the bed. It was broken. Jason began to cry.

"Now we cant have any popcorn," he said.

"We ought to go home, anyway," Caddy said. "Come on, Quentin."

"Wait," Nancy said; "wait. I can fix it. Dont you want to help me fix it?"

"I dont think I want any," Caddy said. "It's too late now."

"You help me, Jason," Nancy said. "Dont you want to help me?"

"No," Jason said. "I want to go home."

"Hush," Nancy said; "hush. Watch. Watch me. I can fix it so Jason can hold it and pop the corn." She got a piece of wire and fixed the popper.

"It wont hold good," Caddy said.

"Yes, it will," Nancy said. "Yawl watch. Yawl help me shell some corn."

The popcorn was under the bed too. We shelled it into the popper and Nancy helped Jason hold the popper over the fire.

"It's not popping," Jason said. "I want to go home."

"You wait," Nancy said. "It'll begin to pop. We'll have fun then." She was sitting close to the fire. The lamp was turned up so high it was beginning to smoke.

"Why dont you turn it down some?" I said.

"It's all right," Nancy said. "I'll clean it. Yawl wait. The popcorn will start in a minute."

"I dont believe it's going to start," Caddy said. "We ought to start home, anyway. They'll be worried."

"No," Nancy said. "It's going to pop. Dilsey will tell um yawl with me. I been working for yawl long time. They won't mind if yawl at my house. You wait, now. It'll start popping any minute now."

Then Jason got some smoke in his eyes and he began to cry. He dropped the popper into the fire. Nancy got a wet rag and wiped Jason's face, but he didn't stop crying.

"Hush," she said. "Hush." But he didn't hush. Caddy took the popper out of the fire.

"It's burned up," she said. "You'll have to get some more popcorn, Nancy."

"Did you put all of it in?" Nancy said.

"Yes," Caddy said. Nancy looked at Caddy. Then she took the popper and opened it and poured the cinders into her apron and began to sort the grains, her hands long and brown, and we watching her.

"Haven't you got any more?" Caddy said.

"Yes," Nancy said; "yes. Look. This here aint burnt. All we need to do is—"

"I want to go home," Jason said. "I'm going to tell."

"Hush," Caddy said. We all listened. Nancy's head was already turned toward the barred door, her eyes filled with red lamplight. "Somebody is coming," Caddy said.

Then Nancy began to make that sound again, not loud, sitting there above the fire, her long hands dangling between her knees; all of a sudden water began to come out on her face in big drops, running down her face, carrying in each one a little turning ball of firelight like a spark until it dropped off her chin. "She's not crying," I said.

"I aint crying," Nancy said. Her eyes were closed. "I aint crying. Who is it?"

"I dont know," Caddy said. She went to the door and looked out. "We've got to go now," she said. "Here comes father."

"I'm going to tell," Jason said. "Yawl made me come."

The water still ran down Nancy's face. She turned in her chair. "Listen. Tell him. Tell him we going to have fun. Tell him I take good care of yawl until in the morning. Tell him to let me come home with yawl and sleep on the floor. Tell him I wont need no pallet. We'll have fun. You member last time how we had so much fun?"

"I didn't have fun," Jason said. "You hurt me. You put smoke in my eyes. I'm going to tell."

V

Father came in. He looked at us. Nancy did not get up.

"Tell him," she said.

"Caddy made us come down here," Jason said. "I didn't want to."

Father came to the fire. Nancy looked up at him. "Cant you go to Aunt Rachel's and stay?" he said. Nancy looked up at father, her hands between her knees. "He's not here," father said. "I would have seen him. There's not a soul in sight."

"He in the ditch," Nancy said. "He waiting in the ditch yonder."

"Nonsense," father said. He looked at Nancy. "Do you know he's there?"

"I got the sign," Nancy said.

"What sign?"

"I got it. It was on the table when I come in. It was a hogbone, with blood meat still on it, laying by the lamp. He out there. When yawl walk out that door, I gone."

"Gone where, Nancy?" Caddy said.

"I'm not a tattletale," Jason said.

"Nonsense," father said.

"He out there," Nancy said. "He looking through that window this minute, waiting for yawl to go. Then I gone."

"Nonsense," father said. "Lock up your house and we'll take you on to Aunt Rachel's."

" 'Twont do no good," Nancy said. She didn't look at father now, but he looked down at her, at her long, limp, moving hands. "Putting it off wont do no good."

"Then what do you want to do?" father said.

"I dont know," Nancy said. "I cant do nothing. Just put it off. And that don't do no good. I reckon it belong to me. I reckon what I going to get aint no more than mine."

"Get what?" Caddy said. "What's yours?"

"Nothing," father said. "You all must get to bed."

"Caddy made me come," Jason said.

"Go on to Aunt Rachel's," father said.

"It wont do no good," Nancy said. She sat before the fire, her elbows on her knees, her long hands between her knees. "When even your own kitchen wouldn't do no good. When even if I was sleeping on the floor in the room with your chillen, and the next morning there I am, and blood—"

"Hush," father said. "Lock the door and put out the lamp and go to bed."

"I scared of the dark," Nancy said. "I scared for it to happen in the dark."

"You mean you're going to sit right here with the lamp lighted?" father said. Then Nancy began to make the sound again, sitting before the fire, her long hands between her knees. "Ah, damnation," father said. "Come along, chillen. It's past bedtime."

"When yawl go home, I gone," Nancy said. She talked quieter now, and her face looked quiet, like her hands. "Anyway, I got my coffin money saved up with Mr. Lovelady." Mr. Lovelady was a short, dirty man who collected the Negro insurance, coming around to the cabins or the kitchens every Saturday morning, to collect fifteen cents. He and his wife lived at the hotel. One morning his wife committed suicide. They had a child, a little girl. He and the child went away. After a week or two he came back alone. We would see him going along the lanes and the back streets on Saturday mornings.

"Nonsense," father said. "You'll be the first thing I'll see in the kitchen tomorrow morning."

"You'll see what you'll see, I reckon," Nancy said. "But it will take the Lord to say what that will be."

VI

We left her sitting before the fire.

"Come and put the bar up," father said. But she didn't

move. She didn't look at us again, sitting quietly there between the lamp and the fire. From some distance down the lane we could look back and see her through the open door.

"What, father?" Caddy said. "What's going to happen?"

"Nothing," father said. Jason was on father's back, so Jason was the tallest of all of us. We went down into the ditch. I looked at it, quiet. I couldn't see much where the moonlight and the shadows tangled.

"If Jesus is hid here, he can see us, cant he?" Caddy said.

"He's not there," father said. "He went away a long time ago."

"You made me come," Jason said, high; against the sky it looked like father had two heads, a little one and a big one. "I didn't want to."

We went up out of the ditch. We could still see Nancy's house and the open door, but we couldn't see Nancy now, sitting before the fire with the door open, because she was tired. "I just done got tired," she said. "I just a nigger. It aint no fault of mine."

But we could hear her, because she began just after we came up out of the ditch, the sound that was not singing and not unsinging. "Who will do our washing now, father?" I said.

"I'm not a nigger," Jason said, high and close above father's head.

"You're worse," Caddy said, "you are a tattletale. If something was to jump out, you'd be scairder than a nigger."

"I wouldn't," Jason said.
"You'd cry," Caddy said.
"Caddy," father said.
"I wouldn't!" Jason said.
"Scairy cat," Caddy said.
"Candace!" father said.

Red Leaves

The two Indians crossed the plantation toward the slave quarters. Neat with whitewash, of baked soft brick, the two rows of houses in which lived the slaves belonging to the clan, faced one another across the mild shade of the lane marked and scored with naked feet and with a few home-made toys mute in the dust. There was no sign of life.

"I know what we will find," the first Indian said.

"What we will not find," the second said. Although it was noon, the lane was vacant, the doors of the cabins empty and quiet; no cooking smoke rose from any of the chinked and plastered chimneys.

"Yes. It happened like this when the father of him who is now the Man, died."

"You mean, of him who was the Man."

"Yao."

The first Indian's name was Three Basket. He was perhaps sixty. They were both squat men, a little solid, burgher-like; paunchy, with big heads, big, broad, dust-colored faces of a certain blurred serenity like carved heads on a ruined wall in Siam or Sumatra, looming out of a mist. The sun had done it, the violent sun, the violent shade. Their hair looked like sedge grass on burnt-over land. Clamped through one ear Three Basket wore an enameled snuffbox.

"I have said all the time that this is not the good way. In the old days there were no quarters, no Negroes. A man's time was his own then. He had time. Now he must spend most of it finding work for them who prefer sweating to do."

"They are like horses and dogs."

"They are like nothing in this sensible world. Nothing contents them save sweat. They are worse than the white people."

"It is not as though the Man himself had to find work for them to do."

"You said it. I do not like slavery. It is not the good way. In the old days, there was the good way. But not now."

"You do not remember the old way either."

"I have listened to them who do. And I have tried this way. Man was not made to sweat."

"That's so. See what it has done to their flesh."

"Yes. Black. It has a bitter taste, too."

"You have eaten of it?"

"Once. I was young then, and more hardy in the appetite than now. Now it is different with me."

"Yes. They are too valuable to eat now."

"There is a bitter taste to the flesh which I do not like."

"They are too valuable to eat, anyway, when the white men will give horses for them."

They entered the lane. The mute, meager toys—the fetish-shaped objects made of wood and rags and feathers—lay in the dust about the patinaed doorsteps, among bones and broken gourd dishes. But there was no sound from any cabin, no face in any door; had not been since yesterday, when Issetibbeha died. But they already knew what they would find.

It was in the central cabin, a house a little larger than the others, where at certain phases of the moon the Negroes would gather to begin their ceremonies before removing after nightfall to the creek bottom, where they kept the drums. In this room they kept the minor accessories, the cryptic ornaments, the ceremonial records which consisted of sticks daubed with red clay in symbols. It had a hearth in the center of the floor, beneath a hole in the roof, with a few cold wood ashes and a suspended iron pot. The window shutters were closed; when the two Indians entered, after the abashless sunlight they could distinguish nothing with the eyes save a movement, shadow, out of which eyeballs rolled, so that the place appeared to be full of Negroes. The two Indians stood in the doorway.

"Yao," Basket said. "I said this is not the good way."

"I don't think I want to be here," the second said.

"That is black man's fear which you smell. It does not smell as ours does."

"I don't think I want to be here."

"Your fear has an odor too."

"Maybe it is Issetibbeha which we smell."

"Yao. He knows. He knows what we will find here. He knew when he died what we should find here today." Out of the rank twilight of the room the eyes, the smell, of Negroes rolled about them. "I am Three Basket, whom you know," Basket said into the room. "We are come from the Man. He whom we seek is gone?" The Negroes said nothing. The smell of them, of their bodies, seemed to ebb and flux in the still hot air. They seemed to be musing as one upon something remote, inscrutable. They were like a single octopus. They were like the roots of a huge tree uncovered, the earth broken momentarily upon the writhen, thick, fetid tangle of its lightless and outraged life. "Come," Basket said. "You know our errand. Is he whom we seek gone?"

"They are thinking something," the second said. "I do not want to be here."

"They are knowing something," Basket said.

"They are hiding him, you think?"

"No. He is gone. He has been gone since last night. It happened like this before, when the grandfather of him who is now the Man died. It took us three days to catch him. For three days Doom lay above the ground, saying 'I see my horse and my dog. But I do not see my slave. What have you done with him that you will not permit me to lie quiet?' "

"They do not like to die."

"Yao. They cling. It makes trouble for us, always. A people without honor and without decorum. Always a trouble."

"I do not like it here."

"Nor do I. But then, they are savages; they cannot be expected to regard usage. That is why I say that this way is a bad way."

"Yao. They cling. They would even rather work in the sun than to enter the earth with a chief. But he is gone."

The Negroes had said nothing, made no sound. The white eyeballs rolled, wild, subdued; the smell was rank, violent. "Yes, they fear," the second said. "What shall we do now?"

"Let us go and talk with the Man."

"Will Moketubbe listen?"

"What can he do? He will not like to. But he is the Man now."

"Yao. He is the Man. He can wear the shoes with the red heels all the time now." They turned and went out. There was no door in the door frame. There were no doors in any of the cabins.

"He did that anyway," Basket said.

"Behind Issetibbeha's back. But now they are his shoes, since he is the Man."

"Yao. Issetibbeha did not like it. I have heard. I know that he said to Moketubbe: 'When you are the Man, the shoes will be yours. But until then, they are my shoes.' But now Moketubbe is the Man; he can wear them."

"Yao," the second said. "He is the Man now. He used to wear the shoes behind Issetibbeha's back, and it was not known if Issetibbeha knew this or not. And then Issetibbeha became dead, who was not old, and the shoes are Moketubbe's, since he is the Man now. What do you think of that?"

"I don't think about it," Basket said. "Do you?"

"No," the second said.

"Good," Basket said. "You are wise."

II

The house sat on a knoll, surrounded by oak trees. The front of it was one story in height, composed of the deck house of a steamboat which had gone ashore and which Doom, Issetibbeha's father, had dismantled with his slaves and hauled on cypress rollers twelve miles home

overland. It took them five months. His house consisted
at the time of one brick wall. He set the steamboat broadside on to the wall, where now the chipped and flaked
gilding of the rococo cornices arched in faint splendor
above the gilt lettering of the stateroom names above the
jalousied doors.

Doom had been born merely a subchief, a Mingo, one
of three children on the mother's side of the family. He
made a journey—he was a young man then and New
Orleans was a European city—from north Mississippi to
New Orleans by keel boat, where he met the Chevalier
Sœur Blonde de Vitry, a man whose social position, on
its face, was as equivocal as Doom's own. In New
Orleans, among the gamblers and cutthroats of the river
front, Doom, under the tutelage of his patron, passed as
the chief, the Man, the hereditary owner of that land
which belonged to the male side of the family; it was the
Chevalier de Vitry who called him *du homme,* and hence
Doom.

They were seen everywhere together—the Indian, the
squat man with a bold, inscrutable, underbred face, and
the Parisian, the expatriate, the friend, it was said, of
Carondelet and the intimate of General Wilkinson. Then
they disappeared, the two of them, vanishing from their
old equivocal haunts and leaving behind them the legend
of the sums which Doom was believed to have won, and
some tale about a young woman, daughter of a fairly well-
to-do West Indian family, the son and brother of whom
sought Doom with a pistol about his old haunts for some
time after his disappearance.

Six months later the young woman herself disappeared,
boarding the St. Louis packet, which put in one night at a

wood landing on the north Mississippi side, where the woman, accompanied by a Negro maid, got off. Four Indians met her with a horse and wagon, and they traveled for three days, slowly, since she was already big with child, to the plantation, where she found that Doom was now chief. He never told her how he accomplished it, save that his uncle and his cousin had died suddenly. At that time the house consisted of a brick wall built by shiftless slaves, against which was propped a thatched lean-to divided into rooms and littered with bones and refuse, set in the center of ten thousand acres of matchless parklike forest where deer grazed like domestic cattle. Doom and the woman were married there a short time before Issetibbeha was born, by a combination itinerant minister and slave trader who arrived on a mule, to the saddle of which was lashed a cotton umbrella and a three-gallon demijohn of whisky. After that, Doom began to acquire more slaves and to cultivate some of his land, as the white people did. But he never had enough for them to do. In utter idleness the majority of them led lives transplanted whole out of African jungles, save on the occasions when, entertaining guests, Doom coursed them with dogs.

When Doom died, Issetibbeha, his son, was nineteen. He became proprietor of the land and of the quintupled herd of blacks for which he had no use at all. Though the title of Man rested with him, there was a hierarchy of cousins and uncles who ruled the clan and who finally gathered in squatting conclave over the Negro question, squatting profoundly beneath the golden names above the doors of the steamboat.

"We cannot eat them," one said.

"Why not?"

"There are too many of them."

"That's true," a third said. "Once we started, we should have to eat them all. And that much flesh diet is not good for man."

"Perhaps they will be like deer flesh. That cannot hurt you."

"We might kill a few of them and not eat them," Issetibbeha said.

They looked at him for a while. "What for?" one said.

"That is true," a second said. "We cannot do that. They are too valuable; remember all the bother they have caused us, finding things for them to do. We must do as the white men do."

"How is that?" Issetibbeha said.

"Raise more Negroes by clearing more land to make corn to feed them, then sell them. We will clear the land and plant it with food and raise Negroes and sell them to the white men for money."

"But what will we do with this money?" a third said.

They thought for a while.

"We will see," the first said. They squatted, profound, grave.

"It means work," the third said.

"Let the Negroes do it," the first said.

"Yao. Let them. To sweat is bad. It is damp. It opens the pores."

"And then the night air enters."

"Yao. Let the Negroes do it. They appear to like sweating."

So they cleared the land with the Negroes and planted it in grain. Up to that time the slaves had lived in a huge pen with a lean-to roof over one corner, like a pen for pigs. But now they began to build quarters, cabins, putting the young Negroes in the cabins in pairs to mate; five years later Issetibbeha sold forty head to a Memphis trader, and he took the money and went abroad upon it, his maternal uncle from New Orleans conducting the trip. At that time the Chevalier Sœur Blonde de Vitry was an old man in Paris, in a toupee and a corset, with a careful toothless old face fixed in a grimace quizzical and profoundly tragic. He borrowed three hundred dollars from Issetibbeha and in return he introduced him into certain circles; a year later Issetibbeha returned home with a gilt bed, a pair of girandoles by whose light it was said that Pompadour arranged her hair while Louis smirked at his mirrored face across her powdered shoulder, and a pair of slippers with red heels. They were too small for him, since he had not worn shoes at all until he reached New Orleans on his way abroad.

He brought the slippers home in tissue paper and kept them in the remaining pocket of a pair of saddlebags filled with cedar shavings, save when he took them out on occasion for his son, Moketubbe, to play with. At three years of age Moketubbe had a broad, flat, Mongolian face that appeared to exist in a complete and unfathomable lethargy, until confronted by the slippers.

Moketubbe's mother was a comely girl whom Issetibbeha had seen one day working in her shift in a melon patch. He stopped and watched her for a while—the broad, solid thighs, the sound back, the serene face. He was on his way to the creek to fish that day, but he didn't go any farther; perhaps while he stood there watching the unaware girl he may have remembered his own mother, the city woman, the fugitive with her fans

and laces and her Negro blood, and all the tawdry shabbiness of that sorry affair. Within the year Moketubbe
was born; even at three he could not get his feet into the
slippers. Watching him in the still, hot afternoons as he
struggled with the slippers with a certain monstrous
repudiation of fact, Issetibbeha laughed quietly to himself. He laughed at Moketubbe and the shoes for several
years, because Moketubbe did not give up trying to put
them on until he was sixteen. Then he quit. Or
Issetibbeha thought he had. But he had merely quit trying in Issetibbeha's presence. Issetibbeha's newest wife
told him that Moketubbe had stolen and hidden the
shoes. Issetibbeha quit laughing then, and he sent the
woman away, so that he was alone. "Yao," he said. "I too
like being alive, it seems." He sent for Moketubbe. "I
give them to you," he said.

Moketubbe was twenty-five then, unmarried.
Issetibbeha was not tall, but he was taller by six inches
than his son and almost a hundred pounds lighter. Moketubbe was already diseased with flesh, with a pale, broad,
inert face and dropsical hands and feet. "They are yours
now," Issetibbeha said, watching him. Moketubbe had
looked at him once when he entered, a glance brief, dis-
creet, veiled.

"Thanks," he said.

Issetibbeha looked at him. He could never tell if Moketubbe saw anything, looked at anything. "Why will it not
be the same if I give the slippers to you?"

"Thanks," Moketubbe said. Issetibbeha was using
snuff at the time; a white man had shown him how to put
the powder into his lip and scour it against his teeth with
a twig of gum or of alphea.

"Well," he said, "a man cannot live forever." He looked at his son, then his gaze went blank in turn, unseeing, and he mused for an instant. You could not tell what he was thinking, save that he said half aloud: "Yao. But Doom's uncle had no shoes with red heels." He looked at his son again, fat, inert. "Beneath all that, a man might think of doing anything and it not be known until too late." He sat in a splint chair hammocked with deer thongs. "He cannot even get them on; he and I are both frustrated by the same gross meat which he wears. He cannot even get them on. But is that my fault?"

He lived for five years longer, then he died. He was sick one night, and though the doctor came in a skunk-skin vest and burned sticks, he died before noon.

That was yesterday; the grave was dug, and for twelve hours now the People had been coming in wagons and carriages and on horseback and afoot, to eat the baked dog and the succotash and the yams cooked in ashes and to attend the funeral.

III

"It will be three days," Basket said, as he and the other Indian returned to the house. "It will be three days and the food will not be enough; I have seen it before."

The second Indian's name was Louis Berry. "He will smell too, in this weather."

"Yao. They are nothing but a trouble and a care."

"Maybe it will not take three days."

"They run far. Yao. We will smell this Man before he enters the earth. You watch and see if I am not right."

They approached the house.

"He can wear the shoes now," Berry said. "He can wear them now in man's sight."

"He cannot wear them for a while yet," Basket said. Berry looked at him. "He will lead the hunt."

"Moketubbe?" Berry said. "Do you think he will? A man to whom even talking is travail?"

"What else can he do? It is his own father who will soon begin to smell."

"That is true," Berry said. "There is even yet a price he must pay for the shoes. Yao. He has truly bought them. What do you think?"

"What do you think?"

"What do you think?"

"I think nothing."

"Nor do I. Issetibbeha will not need the shoes now. Let Moketubbe have them; Issetibbeha will not care."

"Yao. Man must die."

"Yao. Let him; there is still the Man."

The bark roof of the porch was supported by peeled cypress poles, high above the texas of the steamboat, shading an unfloored banquette where on the trodden earth mules and horses were tethered in bad weather. On the forward end of the steamboat's deck sat an old man and two women. One of the women was dressing a fowl, the other was shelling corn. The old man was talking. He was barefoot, in a long linen frock coat and a beaver hat.

"This world is going to the dogs," he said. "It is being ruined by white men. We got along fine for years and years, before the white men foisted their Negroes upon us. In the old days the old men sat in the shade and ate stewed deer's flesh and corn and smoked tobacco and talked of honor and grave affairs; now what do we do?

Even the old wear themselves into the grave taking care of them that like sweating." When Basket and Berry crossed the deck he ceased and looked up at them. His eyes were querulous, bleared; his face was myriad with tiny wrinkles. "He is fled also," he said.

"Yes," Berry said, "he is gone."

"I knew it. I told them so. It will take three weeks, like when Doom died. You watch and see."

"It was three days, not three weeks," Berry said.

"Were you there?"

"No," Berry said. "But I have heard."

"Well, I was there," the old man said. "For three whole weeks, through the swamps and the briars—" They went on and left him talking.

What had been the saloon of the steamboat was now a shell, rotting slowly; the polished mahogany, the carving glinting momentarily and fading through the mold in figures cabalistic and profound; the gutted windows were like cataracted eyes. It contained a few sacks of seed or grain, and the fore part of the running gear of a barouche, to the axle of which two C-springs rusted in graceful curves, supporting nothing. In one corner a fox cub ran steadily and soundlessly up and down a willow cage; three scrawny gamecocks moved in the dust, and the place was pocked and marked with their dried droppings.

They passed through the brick wall and entered a big room of chinked logs. It contained the hinder part of the barouche, and the dismantled body lying on its side, the window slatted over with willow withes, through which protruded the heads, the still, beady, outraged eyes and frayed combs of still more game chickens. It was floored with packed clay; in one corner leaned a crude plow and two hand-hewn boat paddles. From the ceiling, suspended by four deer thongs, hung the gilt bed which Issetibbeha had fetched from Paris. It had neither mattress nor springs, the frame crisscrossed now by a neat hammocking of thongs.

Issetibbeha had tried to have his newest wife, the young one, sleep in the bed. He was congenitally short of breath himself, and he passed the nights half reclining in his splint chair. He would see her to bed and, later, wakeful, sleeping as he did but three or four hours a night, he would sit in the darkness and simulate slumber and listen to her sneak infinitesimally from the gilt and ribboned bed, to lie on a quilt pallet on the floor until just before daylight. Then she would enter the bed quietly again and in turn simulate slumber, while in the darkness beside her Issetibbeha quietly laughed and laughed.

The girandoles were lashed by thongs to two sticks propped in a corner where a ten-gallon whisky keg lay also. There was a clay hearth; facing it, in the splint chair, Moketubbe sat. He was maybe an inch better than five feet tall, and he weighed two hundred and fifty pounds. He wore a broadcloth coat and no shirt, his round, smooth copper balloon of belly swelling above the bottom piece of a suit of linen underwear. On his feet were the slippers with the red heels. Behind his chair stood a stripling with a punkah-like fan made of fringed paper. Moketubbe sat motionless, with his broad, yellow face with its closed eyes and flat nostrils, his flipperlike arms extended. On his face was an expression profound, tragic, and inert. He did not open his eyes when Basket and Berry came in.

"He has worn them since daylight?" Basket said.

"Since daylight," the stripling said. The fan did not cease. "You can see."

"Yao," Basket said. "We can see." Moketubbe did not move. He looked like an effigy, like a Malay god in frock coat, drawers, naked chest, the trivial scarlet-heeled shoes.

"I wouldn't disturb him, if I were you," the stripling said.

"Not if I were you," Basket said. He and Berry squatted. The stripling moved the fan steadily. "O Man," Basket said, "listen." Moketubbe did not move. "He is gone," Basket said.

"I told you so," the stripling said. "I knew he would flee. I told you."

"Yao," Basket said. "You are not the first to tell us afterward what we should have known before. Why is it that some of you wise men took no steps yesterday to prevent this?"

"He does not wish to die," Berry said.

"Why should he not wish it?" Basket said.

"Because he must die some day is no reason," the stripling said. "That would not convince me either, old man."

"Hold your tongue," Berry said.

"For twenty years," Basket said, "while others of his race sweat in the fields, he served the Man in the shade. Why should he not wish to die, since he did not wish to sweat?"

"And it will be quick," Berry said. "It will not take long."

"Catch him and tell him that," the stripling said.

"Hush," Berry said. They squatted, watching Moketubbe's face. He might have been dead himself. It was as though he were cased so in flesh that even breathing took place too deep within him to show.

"Listen, O Man," Basket said. "Issetibbeha is dead. He waits. His dog and his horse we have. But his slave has fled. The one who held the pot for him, who ate of his food, from his dish, is fled. Issetibbeha waits."

"Yao," Berry said.

"This is not the first time," Basket said. "This happened when Doom, thy grandfather, lay waiting at the door of the earth. He lay waiting three days, saying, 'Where is my Negro?' And Issetibbeha, thy father, answered, 'I will find him. Rest; I will bring him to you so that you may begin the journey.' "

"Yao," Berry said.

Moketubbe had not moved, had not opened his eyes.

"For three days Issetibbeha hunted in the bottom," Basket said. "He did not even return home for food, until the Negro was with him; then he said to Doom, his father, 'Here is thy dog, thy horse, thy Negro; rest.' Issetibbeha, who is dead since yesterday, said it. And now Issetibbeha's Negro is fled. His horse and his dog wait with him, but his Negro is fled."

"Yao," Berry said.

Moketubbe had not moved. His eyes were closed; upon his supine monstrous shape there was a colossal inertia, something profoundly immobile, beyond and impervious to flesh. They watched his face, squatting.

"When thy father was newly the Man, this happened," Basket said. "And it was Issetibbeha who brought back the slave to where his father waited to enter the earth." Moketubbe's face had not moved, his eyes had not moved. After a while Basket said, "Remove the shoes."

The stripling removed the shoes. Moketubbe began to pant, his bare chest moving deep, as though he were rising from beyond his unfathomed flesh back into life, like up from the water, the sea. But his eyes had not opened yet.

Berry said, "He will lead the hunt."

"Yao," Basket said. "He is the Man. He will lead the hunt."

IV

All that day the Negro, Issetibbeha's body servant, hidden in the barn, watched Issetibbeha's dying. He was forty, a Guinea man. He had a flat nose, a close, small head; the inside corners of his eyes showed red a little, and his prominent gums were a pale bluish red above his square, broad teeth. He had been taken at fourteen by a trader off Kamerun, before his teeth had been filed. He had been Issetibbeha's body servant for twenty-three years.

On the day before, the day on which Issetibbeha lay sick, he returned to the quarters at dusk. In that unhurried hour the smoke of the cooking fires blew slowly across the street from door to door, carrying into the opposite one the smell of the identical meat and bread. The women tended them; the men were gathered at the head of the lane, watching him as he came down the slope from the house, putting his naked feet down carefully in a strange dusk. To the waiting men his eyeballs were a little luminous.

"Issetibbeha is not dead yet," the headman said.

"Not dead," the body servant said. "Who not dead?"

In the dusk they had faces like his, the different ages, the thoughts sealed inscrutable behind faces like the death masks of apes. The smell of the fires, the cooking, blew sharp and slow across the strange dusk, as from another world, above the lane and the pickaninnies naked in the dust.

"If he lives past sundown, he will live until daybreak," one said.

"Who says?"

"Talk says."

"Yao. Talk says. We know but one thing." They looked at the body servant as he stood among them, his eyeballs a little luminous. He was breathing slow and deep. His chest was bare; he was sweating a little. "He knows. He knows it."

"Let us let the drums talk."

"Yao. Let the drums tell it."

The drums began after dark. They kept them hidden in the creek bottom. They were made of hollowed cypress knees, and the Negroes kept them hidden; why, none knew. They were buried in the mud on the bank of a slough; a lad of fourteen guarded them. He was undersized, and a mute; he squatted in the mud there all day, clouded over with mosquitoes, naked save for the mud with which he coated himself against the mosquitoes, and about his neck a fiber bag containing a pig's rib to which black shreds of flesh still adhered, and two scaly barks on a wire. He slobbered onto his clutched knees, drooling; now and then Indians came noiselessly out of the bushes behind him and stood there and contemplated him for a while and went away, and he never knew it.

From the loft of the stable where he lay hidden until

dark and after, the Negro could hear the drums. They were three miles away, but he could hear them as though they were in the barn itself below him, thudding and thudding. It was as though he could see the fire too, and the black limbs turning into and out of the flames in copper gleams. Only there would be no fire. There would be no more light there than where he lay in the dusty loft, with the whispering arpeggios of rat feet along the warm and immemorial ax-squared rafters. The only fire there would be the smudge against mosquitoes where the women with nursing children crouched, their heavy sluggish breasts nippled full and smooth into the mouths of men children; contemplative, oblivious of the drumming, since a fire would signify life.

There was a fire in the steamboat, where Issetibbeha lay dying among his wives, beneath the lashed girandoles and the suspended bed. He could see the smoke, and just before sunset he saw the doctor come out, in a waistcoat made of skunk skins, and set fire to two clay-daubed sticks at the bows of the boat deck. "So he is not dead yet," the Negro said into the whispering gloom of the loft, answering himself; he could hear the two voices, himself and himself:

"Who not dead?"

"You are dead."

"Yao, I am dead," he said quietly. He wished to be where the drums were. He imagined himself springing out of the bushes, leaping among the drums on his bare, lean, greasy, invisible limbs. But he could not do that, because man leaped past life, into where death was; he dashed into death and did not die, because when death took a man, it took him just this side of the end of living. It was when death overran him from behind, still in life. The thin whisper of rat feet died in fainting gusts along the rafters. Once he had eaten rat. He was a boy then, but just come to America. They had lived ninety days in a three-foot-high 'tween-deck in tropic latitudes, hearing from topside the drunken New England captain intoning aloud from a book which he did not recognize for ten years afterward to be the Bible. Squatting in the stable so, he had watched the rat, civilized, by association with man reft of its inherent cunning of limb and eye; he had caught it without difficulty, with scarce a movement of his hand, and he ate it slowly, wondering how any of the rats had escaped so long. At that time he was still wearing the single white garment which the trader, a deacon in the Unitarian church, had given him, and he spoke then only his native tongue.

He was naked now, save for a pair of dungaree pants bought by Indians from white men, and an amulet slung on a thong about his hips. The amulet consisted of one half of a mother-of-pearl lorgnon which Issetibbeha had brought back from Paris, and the skull of a cottonmouth moccasin. He had killed the snake himself and eaten it, save the poison head. He lay in the loft, watching the house, the steamboat, listening to the drums, thinking of himself among the drums.

He lay there all night. The next morning he saw the doctor come out, in his skunk vest, and get on his mule and ride away, and he became quite still and watched the final dust from beneath the mule's delicate feet die away, and then he found that he was still breathing and it seemed strange to him that he still breathed air, still needed air. Then he lay and watched quietly, waiting to move, his eyeballs a little luminous, but with a quiet light, and his breathing light and regular, and saw Louis Berry come out and look at the sky. It was good light then, and already five Indians squatted in their Sunday clothes along the steamboat deck; by noon there were twenty-five there. That afternoon they dug the trench in which the meat would be baked, and the yams; by that time there were almost a hundred guests—decorous, quiet, patient in their stiff European finery—and he watched Berry lead Issetibbeha's mare from the stable and tie her to a tree, and then he watched Berry emerge from the house with the old hound which lay beside Issetibbeha's chair. He tied the hound to the tree too, and it sat there, looking gravely about at the faces. Then it began to howl. It was still howling at sundown, when the Negro climbed down the back wall of the barn and entered the spring branch, where it was already dusk. He began to run then. He could hear the hound howling behind him, and near the spring, already running, he passed another Negro. The two men, the one motionless and the other running, looked for an instant at each other as though across an actual boundary between two different worlds. He ran on into full darkness, mouth closed, fists doubled, his broad nostrils bellowing steadily.

He ran on in the darkness. He knew the country well, because he had hunted it often with Issetibbeha, following on his mule the course of the fox or the cat beside Issetibbeha's mare; he knew it as well as did the men who would pursue him. He saw them for the first time shortly before sunset of the second day. He had run thirty miles then, up the creek bottom, before doubling back; lying in a pawpaw thicket he saw the pursuit for the first time.

There were two of them, in shirts and straw hats, carrying their neatly rolled trousers under their arms, and they
had no weapons. They were middle-aged, paunchy, and
they could not have moved very fast anyway; it would be
twelve hours before they could return to where he lay
watching them. "So I will have until midnight to rest," he
said. He was near enough to the plantation to smell the
cooking fires, and he thought how he ought to be hungry, since he had not eaten in thirty hours. "But it is more
important to rest," he told himself. He continued to tell
himself that, lying in the pawpaw thicket, because the
effort of resting, the need and the haste to rest, made his
heart thud the same as the running had done. It was as
though he had forgot how to rest, as though the six hours
were not long enough to do it in, to remember again how
to do it.

As soon as dark came he moved again. He had thought
to keep going steadily and quietly through the night, since
there was nowhere for him to go, but as soon as he moved
he began to run at top speed, breasting his panting chest,
his broad-flaring nostrils through the choked and whipping darkness. He ran for an hour, lost by then, without
direction, when suddenly he stopped, and after a time his
thudding heart unraveled from the sound of the drums.
By the sound they were not two miles away; he followed
the sound until he could smell the smudge fire and taste
the acrid smoke. When he stood among them the drums
did not cease; only the headman came to him where he
stood in the drifting smudge, panting, his nostrils flaring
and pulsing, the hushed glare of his ceaseless eyeballs in
his mud-daubed face as though they were worked from
lungs.

"We have expected thee," the headman said. "Go, now."

"Go?"

"Eat, and go. The dead may not consort with the living; thou knowest that."

"Yao. I know that." They did not look at one another. The drums had not ceased.

"Wilt thou eat?" the headman said.

"I am not hungry. I caught a rabbit this afternoon, and ate while I lay hidden."

"Take some cooked meat with thee, then."

He accepted the cooked meat, wrapped in leaves, and entered the creek bottom again; after a while the sound of the drums ceased. He walked steadily until daybreak. "I have twelve hours," he said. "Maybe more, since the trail was followed by night." He squatted and ate the meat and wiped his hands on his thighs. Then he rose and removed the dungaree pants and squatted again beside a slough and coated himself with mud—face, arms, body and legs—and squatted again, clasping his knees, his head bowed. When it was light enough to see, he moved back into the swamp and squatted again and went to sleep so. He did not dream at all. It was well that he moved, for, waking suddenly in broad daylight and the high sun, he saw the two Indians. They still carried their neatly rolled trousers; they stood opposite the place where he lay hidden, paunchy, thick, soft-looking, a little ludicrous in their straw hats and shirt tails.

"This is wearying work," one said.

"I'd rather be at home in the shade myself," the other said. "But there is the Man waiting at the door to the earth."

"Yao." They looked quietly about; stooping, one of them removed from his shirt tail a clot of cockleburs. "Damn that Negro," he said.

"Yao. When have they ever been anything but a trial and a care to us?"

In the early afternoon, from the top of a tree, the Negro looked down into the plantation. He could see Issetibbeha's body in a hammock between the two trees where the horse and the dog were tethered, and the concourse about the steamboat was filled with wagons and horses and mules, with carts and saddle-horses, while in bright clumps the women and the smaller children and the old men squatted about the long trench where the smoke from the barbecuing meat blew slow and thick. The men and the big boys would all be down there in the creek bottom behind him, on the trail, their Sunday clothes rolled carefully up and wedged into tree crotches. There was a clump of men near the door to the house, to the saloon of the steamboat, though, and he watched them, and after a while he saw them bring Moketubbe out in a litter made of buckskin and persimmon poles; high hidden in his leafed nook the Negro, the quarry, looked quietly down upon his irrevocable doom with an expression as profound as Moketubbe's own. "Yao," he said quietly. "He will go then. That man whose body has been dead for fifteen years, he will go also."

In the middle of the afternoon he came face to face with an Indian. They were both on a footlog across a slough—the Negro gaunt, lean, hard, tireless and desperate; the Indian thick, soft-looking, the apparent embodiment of the ultimate and the supreme reluctance and inertia. The Indian made no move, no sound; he stood on the log and watched the Negro plunge into the slough and swim ashore and crash away into the undergrowth.

Just before sunset he lay behind a down log. Up the log in slow procession moved a line of ants. He caught them and ate them slowly, with a kind of detachment, like that of a dinner guest eating salted nuts from a dish. They too had a salt taste, engendering a salivary reaction out of all proportion. He ate them slowly, watching the unbroken line move up the log and into oblivious doom with a steady and terrific undeviation. He had eaten nothing else all day; in his caked mud mask his eyes rolled in reddened rims. At sunset, creeping along the creek bank toward where he had spotted a frog, a cottonmouth moccasin slashed him suddenly across the forearm with a thick, sluggish blow. It struck clumsily, leaving two long slashes across his arm like two razor slashes, and half sprawled with its own momentum and rage, it appeared for the moment utterly helpless with its own awkwardness and choleric anger. "Olé, grandfather," the Negro said. He touched its head and watched it slash him again across his arm, and again, with thick, raking, awkward blows. "It's that I do not wish to die," he said. Then he said it again—"It's that I do not wish to die"—in a quiet tone, of slow and low amaze, as though it were something that, until the words had said themselves, he found that he had not known, or had not known the depth and extent of his desire.

V

Moketubbe took the slippers with him. He could not wear them very long while in motion, not even in the litter where he was slung reclining, so they rested upon a square of fawnskin upon his lap—the cracked, frail slippers a little shapeless now, with their scaled patent-leather surfaces and buckleless tongues and scarlet heels, lying upon the supine obese shape just barely alive, carried through swamp and brier by swinging relays of men who bore steadily all day long the crime and its object, on the business of the slain. To Moketubbe it must have been as though, himself immortal, he were being carried rapidly through hell by doomed spirits which, alive, had contemplated his disaster, and, dead, were oblivious partners to his damnation.

After resting for a while, the litter propped in the center of the squatting circle and Moketubbe motionless in it, with closed eyes and his face at once peaceful for the instant and filled with inescapable foreknowledge, he could wear the slippers for a while. The stripling put them on him, forcing his big, tender, dropsical feet into them; whereupon into his face came again that expression tragic, passive and profoundly attentive, which dyspeptics wear. Then they went on. He made no move, no sound, inert in the rhythmic litter out of some reserve of inertia, or maybe of some kingly virtue such as courage or fortitude. After a time they set the litter down and looked at him, at the yellow face like that of an idol, beaded over with sweat. Then Three Basket or Had-Two-Fathers would say: "Take them off. Honor has been served." They would remove the shoes. Moketubbe's face would not alter, but only then would his breathing become perceptible, going in and out of his pale lips with a faint ah-ah-ah sound, and they would squat again while the couriers and the runners came up.

"Not yet?"

"Not yet. He is going east. By sunset he will reach Mouth of Tippah. Then he will turn back. We may take him tomorrow."

"Let us hope so. It will not be too soon."

"Yao. It has been three days now."

"When Doom died, it took only three days."

"But that was an old man. This one is young."

"Yao. A good race. If he is taken tomorrow, I will win a horse."

"May you win it."

"Yao. This work is not pleasant."

That was the day on which the food gave out at the plantation. The guests returned home and came back the next day with more food, enough for a week longer. On that day Issetibbeha began to smell; they could smell him for a long way up and down the bottom when it got hot toward noon and the wind blew. But they didn't capture the Negro on that day, nor on the next. It was about dusk on the sixth day when the couriers came up to the litter; they had found blood. "He has injured himself."

"Not bad, I hope," Basket said. "We cannot send with Issetibbeha one who will be of no service to him."

"Nor whom Issetibbeha himself will have to nurse and care for," Berry said.

"We do not know," the courier said. "He has hidden himself. He has crept back into the swamp. We have left pickets."

They trotted with the litter now. The place where the Negro had crept into the swamp was an hour away. In the hurry and excitement they had forgotten that Moketubbe still wore the slippers; when they reached the place Moketubbe had fainted. They removed the slippers and brought him to.

With dark, they formed a circle about the swamp. They squatted, clouded over with gnats and mosquitoes; the evening star burned low and close down the west, and the constellations began to wheel overhead. "We will give him time," they said. "Tomorrow is just another name for today."

"Yao. Let him have time." Then they ceased, and gazed as one into the darkness where the swamp lay. After a while the noise ceased, and soon the courier came out of the darkness.

"He tried to break out."

"But you turned him back?"

"He turned back. We feared for a moment, the three of us. We could smell him creeping in the darkness, and we could smell something else, which we did not know. That was why we feared, until he told us. He said to slay him there, since it would be dark and he would not have to see the face when it came. But it was not that which we smelled; he told us what it was. A snake had struck him. That was two days ago. The arm swelled, and it smelled bad. But it was not that which we smelled then, because the swelling had gone down and his arm was no larger than that of a child. He showed us. We felt the arm, all of us did; it was no larger than that of a child. He said to give him a hatchet so he could chop the arm off. But tomorrow is today also."

"Yao. Tomorrow is today."

"We feared for a while. Then he went back into the swamp."

"That is good."

"Yao. We feared. Shall I tell the Man?"

"I will see," Basket said. He went away. The courier squatted, telling again about the Negro. Basket returned. "The Man says that it is good. Return to your post."

The courier crept away. They squatted about the litter; now and then they slept. Sometime after midnight the Negro waked them. He began to shout and talk to himself, his voice coming sharp and sudden out of the darkness, then he fell silent. Dawn came; a white crane flapped slowly across the jonquil sky. Basket was awake. "Let us go now," he said. "It is today."

Two Indians entered the swamp, their movements noisy. Before they reached the Negro they stopped, because he began to sing. They could see him, naked and mud-caked, sitting on a log, singing. They squatted silently a short distance away, until he finished. He was chanting something in his own language, his face lifted to the rising sun. His voice was clear, full, with a quality wild and sad. "Let him have time," the Indians said, squatting, patient, waiting. He ceased and they approached. He looked back and up at them through the cracked mud mask. His eyes were bloodshot, his lips cracked upon his square short teeth. The mask of mud appeared to be loose on his face, as if he might have lost flesh since he put it there; he held his left arm close to his breast. From the elbow down it was caked and shapeless with black mud. They could smell him, a rank smell. He watched them quietly until one touched him on the arm. "Come," the Indian said. "You ran well. Do not be ashamed."

VI

As they neared the plantation in the tainted bright morning, the Negro's eyes began to roll a little, like those of a horse. The smoke from the cooking pit blew low along the earth and upon the squatting and waiting guests about the yard and upon the steamboat deck, in their bright, stiff, harsh finery; the women, the children, the old men. They had sent couriers along the bottom, and another on ahead, and Issetibbeha's body had already been removed to where the grave waited, along with the horse and the dog, though they could still smell him in death about the house where he had lived in life. The guests were beginning to move toward the grave when the bearers of Moketubbe's litter mounted the slope.

The Negro was the tallest there, his high, close, mud-caked head looming above them all. He was breathing hard, as though the desperate effort of the six suspended and desperate days had catapulted upon him at once; although they walked slowly, his naked scarred chest rose and fell above the close-clutched left arm. He looked this way and that continuously, as if he were not seeing, as though sight never quite caught up with the looking. His mouth was open a little upon his big white teeth; he began to pant. The already moving guests halted, pausing, looking back, some with pieces of meat in their hands, as the Negro looked about at their faces with his wild, restrained, unceasing eyes.

"Will you eat first?" Basket said. He had to say it twice.

"Yes," the Negro said. "That's it. I want to eat."

The throng had begun to press back toward the center; the word passed to the outermost: "He will eat first."

They reached the steamboat. "Sit down," Basket said. The Negro sat on the edge of the deck. He was still panting, his chest rising and falling, his head ceaseless with its white eyeballs, turning from side to side. It was as if the inability to see came from within, from hopelessness, not from absence of vision. They brought food and watched quietly as he tried to eat it. He put the food into his mouth and chewed it, but chewing, the half-masticated matter began to emerge from the corners of his mouth and to drool down his chin, onto his chest, and after a while he stopped chewing and sat there, naked, covered with dried mud, the plate on his knees, and his mouth filled with a mass of chewed food, open, his eyes wide and unceasing, panting and panting. They watched him, patient, implacable, waiting.

"Come," Basket said at last.

"It's water I want," the Negro said. "I want water."

The well was a little way down the slope toward the quarters. The slope lay dappled with the shadows of noon, of that peaceful hour when, Issetibbeha napping in his chair and waiting for the noon meal and the long afternoon to sleep in, the Negro, the body servant, would be free. He would sit in the kitchen door then, talking with the women who prepared the food. Beyond the kitchen the lane between the quarters would be quiet, peaceful, with the women talking to one another across the lane and the smoke of the dinner fires blowing upon the pickaninnies like ebony toys in the dust.

"Come," Basket said.

The Negro walked among them, taller than any. The guests were moving on toward where Issetibbeha and the horse and the dog waited. The Negro walked with his high ceaseless head, his panting chest. "Come," Basket said. "You wanted water."

"Yes," the Negro said. "Yes." He looked back at the house, then down to the quarters, where today no fire burned, no face showed in any door, no pickaninny in the dust, panting. "It struck me here, raking me across this arm; once, twice, three times. I said, 'Olé, grandfather.' "

"Come now," Basket said. The Negro was still going through the motion of walking, his knee action high, his head high, as though he were on a treadmill. His eyeballs had a wild, restrained glare, like those of a horse. "You wanted water," Basket said. "Here it is."

There was a gourd in the well. They dipped it full and gave it to the Negro, and they watched him try to drink. His eyes had not ceased as he tilted the gourd slowly against his caked face. They could watch his throat working and the bright water cascading from either side of the gourd, down his chin and breast. Then the water stopped. "Come," Basket said.

"Wait," the Negro said. He dipped the gourd again and tilted it against his face, beneath his ceaseless eyes. Again they watched his throat working and the unswallowed water sheathing broken and myriad down his chin, channeling his caked chest. They waited, patient, grave, decorous, implacable; clansman and guest and kin. Then the water ceased, though still the empty gourd tilted higher and higher, and still his black throat aped the vain motion of his frustrated swallowing. A piece of water-loosened mud carried away from his chest and broke at his muddy feet, and in the empty gourd they could hear his breath: ah-ah-ah.

"Come," Basket said, taking the gourd from the Negro and hanging it back in the well.

Lo!

The President stood motionless at the door of the Dressing Room, fully dressed save for his boots. It was half-past six in the morning and it was snowing; already he had stood for an hour at the window, watching the snow. Now he stood just inside the door to the corridor, utterly motionless in his stockings, stooped a little from his lean height as though listening, on his face an expression of humorless concern, since humor had departed from his situation and his view of it almost three weeks before. Hanging from his hand, low against his flank, was a hand mirror of elegant French design, such as should have been lying upon a lady's dressing table: certainly at this hour of a February day.

At last he put his hand on the knob and opened the door infinitesimally; beneath his hand the door crept by inches and without any sound; still with that infinitesimal silence he put his eye to the crack and saw, lying upon the deep, rich pile of the corridor carpet, a bone. It was a cooked bone, a rib; to it still adhered close shreds of flesh holding in mute and overlapping half-moons the marks of human teeth. Now that the door was open he could hear the voices too. Still without any sound, with that infinite care, he raised and advanced the mirror. For an instant he caught his own reflection in it and he paused for a time and with a kind of cold unbelief he examined his own face—the face of the shrewd and courageous fighter, of that well-nigh infallible expert in the anticipation of and controlling of man and his doings, overlaid now with the baffled helplessness of a child. Then he slanted the glass a little further until he could see the corridor reflected in it. Squatting and facing one another across the carpet as across a stream of water were two men. He did not know the faces, though he knew the Face, since he had looked upon it by day and dreamed upon it by night for three weeks now. It was a squat face, dark, a little flat, a little Mongol; secret, decorous, impenetrable, and grave. He had seen it repeated until he had given up trying to count it or even estimate it; even now, though he could see the two men squatting before him and could hear the two quiet voices, it seemed to him that in some idiotic moment out of attenuated sleeplessness and strain he looked upon a single man facing himself in a mirror.

They wore beaver hats and new frock coats; save for the minor detail of collars and waistcoats they were impeccably dressed—though a little early—for a forenoon of the time, down to the waist. But from here down credulity, all sense of fitness and decorum, was outraged. At a glance one would have said that they had come intact out of Pickwickian England, save that the tight, light-colored smallclothes ended not in Hessian boots nor in any boots at all, but in dark, naked feet. On the floor beside each one lay a neatly rolled bundle of dark cloth; beside each bundle in turn, mute toe and toe and heel and heel, as though occupied by invisible sentries facing one another across the corridor, sat two pairs of new boots. From a basket woven of whiteoak withes beside one of the squatting men there shot suddenly the snakelike head and neck of a gamecock, which glared at the faint flash of the mirror with a round, yellow, outraged eye. It was from these that the voices came, pleasant, decorous, quiet:

"That rooster hasn't done you much good up here."

"That's true. Still, who knows? Besides, I certainly couldn't have left him at home, with those damned lazy Indians. I wouldn't find a feather left. You know that. But it is a nuisance, having to lug this cage around with me day and night."

"This whole business is a nuisance, if you ask me."

"You said it. Squatting here outside this door all night long, without a gun or anything. Suppose bad men tried to get in during the night: what could we do? If anyone would want to get in. I don't."

"Nobody does. It's for honor."

"Whose honor? Yours? Mine? Frank Weddel's?"

"White man's honor. You don't understand white people. They are like children: you have to handle them careful because you never know what they are going to do next. So if it's the rule for guests to squat all night long in the cold outside this man's door, we'll just have to do it. Besides, hadn't you rather be in here than out yonder in the snow in one of those damn tents?"

"You said it. What a climate. What a country. I wouldn't have this town if they gave it to me."

"Of course you wouldn't. But that's white men: no accounting for taste. So as long as we are here, we'll have to try to act like these people believe that Indians ought to act. Because you never know until afterward just what you have done to insult or scare them. Like this having to talk white talk all the time. . . ."

The President withdrew the mirror and closed the door quietly. Once more he stood silent and motionless in the middle of the room, his head bent, musing, baffled yet indomitable: indomitable since this was not the first time that he had faced odds; baffled since he faced not an enemy in the open field, but was besieged within his very high and lonely office by them to whom he was, by legal if not divine appointment, father. In the iron silence of the winter dawn he seemed, clairvoyant of walls, to be ubiquitous and one with the waking of the stately House. Invisible and in a kind of musing horror he seemed to be of each group of his Southern guests—that one squatting without the door, that larger one like so many figures carved of stone in the very rotunda itself of this concrete and visible apotheosis of the youthful Nation's pride—in their new beavers and frock coats and woolen drawers. With their neatly rolled pantaloons under their arms and their virgin shoes in the other hand; dark, timeless, decorous and serene beneath the astonished faces and golden braid, the swords and ribbons and stars, of European diplomats.

The President said quietly, "Damn. Damn. Damn." He moved and crossed the room, pausing to take up his boots from where they sat beside a chair, and approached the opposite door. Again he paused and opened this door too quietly and carefully, out of the three weeks' habit of expectant fatalism, though there was only his wife beyond it, sleeping peacefully in bed. He crossed this room in turn, carrying his boots, pausing to replace the hand glass on the dressing table, among its companion pieces of the set which the new French Republic had presented to a predecessor, and tiptoed on and into the anteroom, where a man in a long cloak looked up and then rose, also in his stockings. They looked at one another soberly. "All clear?" the President said in a low tone.

"Yes, General."

"Good. Did you . . ." The other produced a second long, plain cloak. "Good, good," the President said. He swung the cloak about him before the other could move. "Now the . . ." This time the other anticipated him; the President drew the hat well down over his face. They left the room on tiptoe, carrying their boots in their hands.

The back stairway was cold; their stockinged toes curled away from the treads, their vaporized breath wisped about their heads. They descended quietly and sat on the bottom step and put on their boots.

Outside it still snowed; invisible against snow-colored sky and snow-colored earth, the flakes seemed to materialize with violent and silent abruptness against the dark orifice of the stables. Each bush and shrub resembled a white balloon whose dark shroud lines descended, light and immobile, to the white earth. Interspersed among these in turn and with a certain regularity were a dozen vaguely tent-shaped mounds, from the ridge of each of which a small column of smoke rose into the windless snow, as if the snow itself were in a state of peaceful combustion. The President looked at these, once, grimly. "Get along," he said. The other, his head lowered and his cloak held closely about his face, scuttled on and ducked into the stable. Perish the day when these two words were applied to the soldier chief of a party and a nation, yet the President was so close behind him that their breaths made one cloud. And perish the day when the word *flight* were so applied, yet they had hardly vanished into the stable when they emerged, mounted now and already at a canter, and so across the lawn and past the snow-hidden tents and toward the gates which gave upon that Avenue in embryo yet but which in time would be the stage upon which each four years would parade the proud panoply of the young Nation's lusty man's estate for the admiration and envy and astonishment of the weary world. At the moment, though, the gates were occupied by those more immediate than splendid augurs of the future.

"Look out," the other man said, reining back. They reined aside—the President drew the cloak about his face—and allowed the party to enter: the squat, broad, dark men dark against the snow, the beaver hats, the formal coats, the solid legs clad from thigh to ankle in woolen drawers. Among them moved three horses on whose backs were lashed the carcasses of six deer. They passed on, passing the two horsemen without a glance.

"Damn, damn, damn," the President said; then aloud: "You found good hunting."

One of the group glanced at him, briefly. He said courteously, pleasantly, without inflection, going on: "So so."

The horses moved again. "I didn't see any guns," the other man said.

"Yes," the President said grimly. "I must look into this, too. I gave strict orders. . . ." He said fretfully, "Damn. Damn. Do they carry their pantaloons when they go hunting too, do you know?"

The Secretary was at breakfast, though he was not eating. Surrounded by untasted dishes he sat, in his dressing gown and unshaven; his expression too was harried as he perused the paper which lay upon his empty plate. Before the fire were two men—one a horseman with unmelted snow still upon his cloak, seated on a wooden settle, the other standing, obviously the secretary to the Secretary. The horseman rose as the President and his companion entered. "Sit down, sit down," the President said. He approached the table, slipping off the cloak, which the secretary came forward and took. "Give us some breakfast," the President said. "We don't dare go home." He sat down; the Secretary served him in person. "What is it now?" the President said.

"Do you ask?" the Secretary said. He took up the paper again and glared at it. "From Pennsylvania, this time." He struck the paper. "Maryland, New York, and now Pennsylvania; apparently the only thing that can stop them is the temperature of the water in the Potomac River." He spoke in a harsh, irascible voice. "Complaint, complaint, complaint: here is a farmer near Gettysburg. His Negro slave was in the barn, milking by lantern light after dark, when—the Negro doubtless thought about two hundred, since the farmer estimated them at ten or twelve—springing suddenly out of the darkness in plug hats and carrying knives and naked from the waist down. Result, item: One barn and loft of hay and cow destroyed when the lantern was kicked over; item: one able-bodied slave last seen departing from the scene at a high rate of speed, headed for the forest, and doubtless now dead of fear or by the agency of wild beasts. Debit the Government of the United States: for barn and hay, one hundred dollars; for cow, fifteen dollars; for Negro slave, two hundred dollars. He demands it in gold."

"Is that so?" the President said, eating swiftly. "I suppose the Negro and the cow took them to be ghosts of Hessian soldiers."

"I wonder if they thought the cow was a deer," the horseman said.

"Yes," the President said. "That's something else I want. . . ."

"Who wouldn't take them for anything on earth or under it?" the Secretary said. "The entire Atlantic seaboard north of the Potomac River overrun by creatures in beaver hats and frock coats and woolen drawers, frightening women and children, setting fire to barns and running off slaves, killing deer. . . ."

"Yes," the President said. "I want to say a word about that, myself. I met a party of them returning as I came out. They had six deer. I thought I gave strict orders that they were not to be permitted guns."

Again it was the horseman who spoke. "They don't use guns."

"What?" the President said. "But I saw myself . . ."

"No, sir. They use knives. They track the deer down and slip up on them and cut their throats."

"What?" the President said.

"All right, sir. I seen one of the deer. It never had a mark on it except its throat cut up to the neckbone with one lick."

Again the President said, "Damn. Damn. Damn." Then the President ceased and the Soldier cursed steadily for a while. The others listened, gravely, their faces carefully averted, save the Secretary, who had taken up another paper. "If you could just persuade them to keep their pantaloons on," the President said. "At least about the House. . . ."

The Secretary started back, his hair upcrested like an outraged iron-gray cockatoo. "I, sir? *I* persuade them?"

"Why not? Aren't they subject to your Department? I'm just the President. Confound it, it's got to where my wife no longer dares leave her bedroom, let alone receive lady guests. How am I to explain to the French Ambassador, for instance, why his wife no longer dares call upon my wife because the corridors and the very entrance to the House are blocked by half-naked Chickasaw Indians asleep on the floor or gnawing at half-raw ribs of meat? And I, myself, having to hide away from my own table and beg breakfast, while the official representative of the Government has nothing to do but . . ."

". . . but explain again each morning to the Treasury," the Secretary said in shrill rage, "why another Dutch farmer in Pennsylvania or New York must have three hundred dollars in gold in payment for the destruction of his farm and livestock, and explain to the State Department that the capital is not being besieged by demons from hell itself, and explain to the War Department why twelve brand-new army tents must be ventilated at the top with butcher knives. . . ."

"I noticed that, too," the President said mildly. "I had forgot it."

"Ha. Your Excellency noted it," the Secretary said fiercely. "Your Excellency saw it and then forgot it. I have neither seen it nor been permitted to forget it. And now Your Excellency wonders why I do not persuade them to wear their pantaloons."

"It does seem like they would," the President said fretfully. "The other garments seem to please them well enough. But there's no accounting for taste." He ate again. The Secretary looked at him, about to speak. Then he did not. As he watched the oblivious President a curious, secret expression came into his face; his gray and irate crest settled slowly, as if it were deflating itself. When he spoke now his tone was bland, smooth; now the other three men were watching the President with curious, covert expressions.

"Yes," the Secretary said, "there's no accounting for taste. Though it does seem that when one has been presented with a costume as a mark of both honor and esteem, let alone decorum, and by the chief of a well, tribe . . ."

"That's what I thought," the President said innocently. Then he ceased chewing and said "Eh?" sharply, looking up. The three lesser men looked quickly away, but the Secretary continued to watch the President with that bland, secret expression. "What the devil do you mean?" the President said. He knew what the Secretary meant, just as the other three knew. A day or two after his guest had arrived without warning, and after the original shock had somewhat abated, the President had decreed the new clothing for them. He commanded, out of his own pocket, merchants and hatters as he would have commanded gunsmiths and bulletmakers in war emergency; incidentally he was thus able to estimate the number of them, the men at least, and within forty-eight hours he had transformed his guest's grave and motley train into the outward aspect of decorum at least. Then, two mornings after that, the guest—the half Chickasaw, half Frenchman, the squat, obese man with the face of a Gascon brigand and the mannerisms of a spoiled eunuch and dingy lace at throat and wrist, who for three weeks now had dogged his waking hours and his sleeping dreams with bland inescapability—called formally upon him while he and his wife were still in bed at five o'clock in the morning, with two of his retainers carrying a bundle and what seemed to the President at least a hundred others, men, women and children, thronging quietly into the bedroom, apparently to watch him array himself in it. For it was a costume—even in the shocked horror of the moment, the President found time to wonder wildly where in the capital Weddel (or Vidal) had found it—a mass, a network, of gold braid—frogs, epaulets, sash and sword—held loosely together by bright green cloth and presented to him in return. This is what the Secretary meant, while the President glared at him and while behind them both the three other men stood looking at the fire with immobile gravity. "Have your joke," the President said. "Have it quickly. Are you done laughing now?"

"I laugh?" the Secretary said. "At what?"

"Good," the President said. He thrust the dishes from him. "Then we can get down to business. Have you any documents you will need to refer to?"

The Secretary's secretary approached. "Shall I get the other papers, sir?"

"Papers?" the Secretary said; once more his crest began to rise. "What the devil do I need with papers? What else have I thought about night and day for three weeks?"

"Good; good," the President said. "Suppose you review the matter briefly, in case I have forgot anything else."

"Your Excellency is indeed a fortunate man, if you

have been able to forget," the Secretary said. From the pocket of his dressing gown he took a pair of steel-bowed spectacles. But he used them merely to glare again at the President in cockatoo-crested outrage. "This man, Weddel, Vidal—whatever his name is—he and his family or clan or whatever they are—claim to own the entire part of Mississippi which lies on the west side of this river in question. Oh, the grant is in order: that French father of his from New Orleans saw to that.— Well, it so happens that facing his home or plantation is the only ford in about three hundred miles."

"I know all this," the President said impatiently. "Naturally I regret now that there was any way of crossing the river at all. But otherwise I don't see . . ."

"Neither did they," the Secretary said. "Until the white man came."

"Ah," the President said. "The man who was mur . . ."

The Secretary raised his hand. "Wait. He stayed about a month with them, ostensibly hunting, since he would be absent all day long, though obviously what he was doing was assuring himself that there was no other ford close by. He never brought any game in; I imagine they laughed at that a good deal, in their pleasant way."

"Yes," the President said. "Weddel must have found that very amusing."

". . . or Vidal—whatever his name is," the Secretary said fretfully. "He don't even seem to know or even to care what his own name is."

"Get on," the President said. "About the ford."

"Yes. Then one day, after a month, the white man offered to buy some of Weddel's land—Weddel, Vidal— Damn, da . . ."

"Call him Weddel," the President said.

". . . from Weddel. Not much; a piece about the size of this room, for which Weddel or V— charged him about ten prices. Not out of any desire for usufruct, you understand; doubtless Weddel would have given the man the land or anyway wagered it on a game of mumble peg, it not having yet occurred to any of them apparently that the small plot which the man wanted contained the only available entrance to or exit from the ford. Doubtless the trading protracted itself over several days or perhaps weeks, as a kind of game to while away otherwise idle afternoons or evenings, with the bystanders laughing heartily and pleasantly at the happy scene. They must have laughed a great deal, especially when the man paid Weddel's price; they must have laughed hugely indeed later when they watched the white man out in the sun, building a fence around his property, it doubtless not even then occurring to them that what the white man had done was to fence off the only entrance to the ford."

"Yes," the President said impatiently. "But I still don't see . . ."

Again the Secretary lifted his hand, pontifical, admonitory. "Neither did they; not until the first traveler came along and crossed at the ford. The white man had built himself a tollgate."

"Oh," the President said.

"Yes. And now it must have been, indeed, amusing for them to watch the white man sitting now in the shade— he had a deerskin pouch fastened to a post for the travelers to drop their coins in, and the gate itself arranged so he could operate it by a rope from the veranda of his one-room domicile without having to even leave his seat; and to begin to acquire property—among which was the horse."

"Ah," the President said. "Now we are getting at it."

"Yes. They got at it swiftly from then on. It seems that the match was between the white man's horse and this nephew's horse, the wager the ford and tollgate against a thousand or so acres of land. The nephew's horse lost. And that night . . ."

"Ah," the President said. "I see. And that night the white man was mur . . ."

"Let us say, died," the Secretary said primly, "since it is so phrased in the agent's report. Though he did add in a private communication that the white man's disease seemed to be a split skull. But that is neither here nor there."

"No," the President said. "It's up yonder at the House." Where they had been for three weeks now, men, women, children and Negro slaves, coming for fifteen hundred miles in slow wagons since that day in late autumn when the Chickasaw agent had appeared to inquire into the white man's death. For fifteen hundred miles, across winter swamps and rivers, across the trackless eastern backbone of the continent, led by the bland, obese mongrel despot and patriarch in a carriage, dozing, his nephew beside him and one fat, ringed hand beneath its fall of soiled lace lying upon the nephew's knee to hold him in charge. "Why didn't the agent stop him?" the President said.

"Stop him?" the Secretary cried. "He finally compromised to the extent of offering to allow the nephew to be tried on the spot, by the Indians themselves, he reserving only the intention of abolishing the tollgate, since no one knew the white man anyway. But no. The nephew must come to you, to be absolved or convicted in person."

"But couldn't the agent stop the rest of them? Keep the rest of them from . . ."

"Stop them?" the Secretary cried again. "Listen. He moved in there and lived—Weddel, Vi—Damn! damn! ! Where was—Yes. Weddel told him that the house was his; soon it was. Because how could he tell there were fewer faces present each morning than the night before? Could you have? Could you now?"

"I wouldn't try," the President said. "I would just declare a national thanksgiving. So they slipped away at night."

"Yes. Weddel and the carriage and a few forage wagons went first; they had been gone about a month before the agent realized that each morning the number which remained had diminished somewhat. They would load the wagons and go at night, by families—grandparents, parents, children; slaves, chattels and dogs—everything. And why not? Why should they deny themselves this holiday at the expense of the Government? Why should they miss, at the mere price of a fifteen-hundred-mile journey through unknown country in the dead of winter, the privilege and pleasure of spending a few weeks or months in new beavers and broadcloth coats and underdrawers, in the home of the beneficent White Father?"

"Yes," the President said. He said: "And you have told him that there is no charge here against this nephew?"

"Yes. And that if they will go back home, the agent himself will declare the nephew innocent publicly, in whatever ceremony they think fit. And he said—how was it he put it?" The Secretary now spoke in a pleasant, almost lilting tone, in almost exact imitation of the man whom he repeated: "All we desire is justice. If this foolish boy has murdered a white man, I think that we should know it."

"Damn, damn, damn," the President said. "All right. We'll hold the investigation. Get them down here and let's have it over with."

"Here?" The Secretary started back. "In my house?"

"Why not? I've had them for three weeks; at least you can have them for an hour." He turned to the companion. "Hurry. Tell them we are waiting here to hold his nephew's trial."

And now the President and the Secretary sat behind the cleared table and looked at the man who stood as though framed by the opened doors through which he had entered, holding his nephew by the hand like an uncle conducting for the first time a youthful provincial kinsman into a metropolitan museum of wax figures. Immobile, they contemplated the soft, paunchy man facing them with his soft, bland, inscrutable face—the long, monk-like nose, the slumberous lids, the flabby, *café-au-lait*-colored jowls above a froth of soiled lace of an elegance fifty years outmoded and vanished; the mouth was full, small, and very red. Yet somewhere behind the face's expression of flaccid and weary disillusion, as behind the bland voice and the almost feminine mannerisms, there lurked something else: something willful, shrewd, unpredictable and despotic. Behind him clotted, quiet and gravely decorous, his dark retinue in beavers and broadcloth and woolen drawers, each with his neatly rolled pantaloons beneath his arm.

For a moment longer he stood, looking from face to face until he found the President. He said, in a voice of soft reproach: "This is not your house."

"No," the President said. "This is the house of this chief whom I have appointed myself to be the holder of justice between me and my Indian people. He will deal justice to you."

The uncle bowed slightly. "That is all that we desire."

"Good," the President said. On the table before him sat inkstand, quill, and sandbox, and many papers with ribbons and golden seals much in evidence, though none could have said if the heavy gaze had remarked them or not. The President looked at the nephew. Young, lean, the nephew stood, his right wrist clasped by his uncle's fat, lace-foamed hand, and contemplated the President quietly, with grave and alert repose. The President dipped the quill into the ink. "Is this the man who . . ."

"Who performed this murder?" the uncle said pleasantly. "That is what we made this long winter's journey to discover. If he did, if this white man really did not fall from that swift horse of his perhaps and strike his head upon a sharp stone, then this nephew of mine should be punished. We do not think that it is right to slay white men like a confounded Cherokee or Creek." Perfectly inscrutable, perfectly decorous, he looked at the two exalted personages playing behind the table their clumsy deception with dummy papers; for an instant the President himself met the slumbrous eyes and looked down. The Secretary though, upthrust, his crest roached violently upward, glared at the uncle.

"You should have held this horse-race across the ford itself," he said. "Water wouldn't have left that gash in the white man's skull."

The President, glancing quickly up, saw the heavy, secret face musing upon the Secretary with dark speculation. But almost immediately the uncle spoke. "So it would. But this white man would have doubtless required a coin of money from my nephew for passing through his gate." Then he laughed, mirthful, pleasant, decorous. "Perhaps it would have been better for that white man if he had allowed my nephew to pass through free. But that is neither here nor there now."

"No," the President said, almost sharply, so that they looked at him again. He held the quill above the paper. "What is the correct name? Weddel or Vidal?"

Again the pleasant, inflectionless voice came: "Weddel or Vidal. What does it matter by what name the White Chief calls us? We are but Indians: remembered yesterday and forgotten tomorrow."

The President wrote upon the paper. The quill scratched steadily in the silence in which there was but one other sound: a faint, steady, minor sound which seemed to emerge from the dark and motionless group behind the uncle and nephew. He sanded what he had written and folded it and rose and stood for a moment so while they watched him quietly—the soldier who had commanded men well on more occasions than this. "Your nephew is not guilty of this murder. My chief whom I have appointed to hold justice between us says for him to return home and never do this again, because next time he will be displeased."

His voice died into a shocked silence; even for that

instant the heavy lids fluttered, while from the dark throng behind him that faint, unceasing sound of quiet scratching by heat and wool engendered, like a faint, constant motion of the sea, also ceased for an instant. The uncle spoke in a tone of shocked unbelief: "My nephew is free?"

"He is free," the President said. The uncle's shocked gaze traveled about the room.

"This quick? And in here? In this house? I had thought. . . . But no matter." They watched him; again the face was smooth, enigmatic, blank. "We are only Indians; doubtless these busy white men have but little time for our small affairs. Perhaps we have already incommoded them too much."

"No, no," the President said quickly. "To me, my Indian and my white people are the same." But again the uncle's gaze was traveling quietly about the room; standing side by side, the President and the Secretary could feel from one to another the same dawning alarm. After a while the President said: "Where had you expected this council to be held?"

The uncle looked at him. "You will be amused. In my ignorance I had thought that even our little affair would have been concluded in . . . But no matter."

"In what?" the President said.

The bland, heavy face mused again upon him for a moment. "You will laugh; nevertheless, I will obey you. In the big white council house beneath the golden eagle."

"What?" the Secretary cried, starting again. "In the . . ."

The uncle looked away. "I said that you would be amused. But no matter. We will have to wait, anyway."

"Have to wait?" the President said. "For what?"

"This is really amusing," the uncle said. He laughed again, in his tone of mirthful detachment. "More of my people are about to arrive. We can wait for them, since they will wish to see and hear also." No one exclaimed at all now, not even the Secretary. They merely stared at him while the bland voice went on: "It seems that some of them mistook the town. They had heard the name of the White Chief's capital spoken, but it so happens that there is also a town in our country with the same name, so that when some of the People inquired on the road, they became misdirected and went there instead, poor ignorant Indians." He laughed, with fond and mirthful tolerance behind his enigmatic and sleepy face. "But a messenger has arrived; they will arrive themselves within the week. Then we will see about punishing this headstrong boy." He shook the nephew's arm lightly. Except for this the nephew did not move, watching the President with his grave and unwinking regard.

For a long moment there was no sound save the faint, steady scratching of the Indians. Then the Secretary began to speak, patiently, as though addressing a child: "Look. Your nephew is free. This paper says that he did not slay the white man and that no man shall so accuse him again, else both I and the great chief beside me will be angered. He can return home now, at once. Let all of you return home at once. For is it not well said that the graves of a man's fathers are never quiet in his absence?"

Again there was silence. Then the President said, "Besides, the white council house beneath the golden eagle is being used now by a council of chiefs who are more powerful there than I am."

The uncle's hand lifted; foamed with soiled lace, his forefinger waggled in reproachful deprecation. "Do not ask even an ignorant Indian to believe that," he said. Then he said, with no change of inflection whatever; the Secretary did not know until the President told him later, that the uncle was now addressing him: "And these chiefs will doubtless be occupying the white council hut for some time yet, I suppose."

"Yes," the Secretary said. "Until the last snow of winter has melted among the flowers and the green grass."

"Good," the uncle said. "We will wait, then. Then the rest of the People will have time to arrive."

And so it was that up that Avenue with a high destiny the cavalcade moved in the still falling snow, led by the carriage containing the President and the uncle and nephew, the fat, ringed hand lying again upon the nephew's knee, and followed by a second carriage containing the Secretary and his secretary, and this followed in turn by two files of soldiers between which walked the dark and decorous cloud of men, women and children on foot and in arms; so it was that behind the Speaker's desk of that chamber which was to womb and contemplate the high dream of a destiny superior to the injustice of events and the folly of mankind, the President and the Secretary stood, while below them, ringed about by the living manipulators of, and interspersed by the august and watching ghosts of the dreamers of, the destiny, the uncle and nephew stood, with behind them the dark throng of kin and friends and acquaintances from among which came steadily and unabated that faint sound of wool and flesh in friction. The President leaned to the Secretary.

"Are they ready with the cannon?" he whispered. "Are

you sure they can see my arm from the door? And suppose those damned guns explode: they have not been fired since Washington shot them last at Cornwallis: will they impeach me?"

"Yes," the Secretary hissed.

"Then God help us. Give me the book." The Secretary passed it to him: it was Petrarch's Sonnets, which the Secretary had snatched from his table in passing. "Let us hope that I remember enough law Latin to keep it from sounding like either English or Chickasaw," the President said. He opened the book, and then again the President, the conqueror of men, the winner of battles diplomatic, legal and martial, drew himself erect and looked down upon the dark, still, intent, waiting faces; when he spoke his voice was the voice which before this had caused men to pause and attend and then obey: "Francis Weddel, chief in the Chickasaw Nation, and you, nephew of Francis Weddel and some day to be a chief, hear my words." Then he began to read. His voice was full, sonorous, above the dark faces, echoing about the august dome in profound and solemn syllables. He read ten sonnets. Then, with his arm lifted, he perorated; his voice died profoundly away and he dropped his arm. A moment later, from outside the building, came a ragged crash of artillery. And now for the first time the dark throng stirred; from among them came a sound, a murmur, of pleased astonishment. The President spoke again: "Nephew of Francis Weddel, you are free. Return to your home."

And now the uncle spoke; again his finger waggled from out its froth of lace. "Heedless boy," he said. "Consider the trouble which you have caused these busy men." He turned to the Secretary, almost briskly; again his voice was bland, pleasant, almost mirthful: "And now, about the little matter of this cursed ford. . . ."

With the autumn sun falling warmly and pleasantly across his shoulders, the President said, "That is all," quietly and turned to his desk as the secretary departed. While he took up the letter and opened it the sun fell upon his hands and upon the page, with its inference of the splendid dying of the year, of approaching harvests and of columns of quiet wood smoke—serene pennons of peace—above peaceful chimneys about the land.

Suddenly the President started; he sprang up, the letter in his hand, glaring at it in shocked and alarmed consternation while the bland words seemed to explode one by one in his comprehension like musketry:

Dear sir and friend:

This is really amusing. Again this hot-headed nephew—he must have taken his character from his father's people, since it is none of mine—has come to trouble you and me. It is this cursed ford again. Another white man came among us, to hunt in peace we thought, since God's forest and the deer which He put in it belong to all. But he too became obsessed with the idea of owning this ford, having heard tales of his own kind who, after the curious and restless fashion of white men, find one side of a stream of water superior enough to the other to pay coins of money for the privilege of reaching it. So the affair was arranged as this white man desired it. Perhaps I did wrong, you will say. But—do I need to tell you?—I am a simple man and some day I shall be old, I trust, and the continuous interruption of these

*white men who wish to cross and the collecting and
care of the coins of money is only a nuisance. For
what can money be to me, whose destiny it apparently
is to spend my declining years beneath the shade of
familiar trees from whose peaceful shade my great
white friend and chief has removed the face of every
enemy save death? That was my thought, but when
you read further you will see that it was not to be.*

*Once more it is this rash and heedless boy. It
seems that he challenged this new white man of ours
(or the white man challenged him: the truth I will
leave to your unerring wisdom to unravel) to a swimming race in the river, the stakes to be this cursed
ford against a few miles of land, which (this will
amuse you) this wild nephew of mine did not even
own. The race took place, but unfortunately our
white man failed to emerge from the river until after
he was dead. And now your agent has arrived, and
he seems to feel that perhaps this swimming race
should not have taken place at all. And so now there
is nothing for me to do save to bestir old bones and
bring this rash boy to you for you to reprimand him.
We will arrive in about . . .*

The President sprang to the bell and pulled it violently. When his secretary entered, he grasped the man by
the shoulders and whirled him toward the door again.
"Get me the Secretary of War, and maps of all the country between here and New Orleans!" he cried. "Hurry."

And so again we see him; the President is absent now
and it is the Soldier alone who sits with the Secretary of
War behind the map-strewn table, while there face them
the officers of a regiment of cavalry. At the table his secretary is writing furiously while the President looks over

his shoulder. "Write it big," he says, "so that even an Indian cannot mistake it. *Know all men by these presents,*" he quotes. *"Francis Weddel his heirs, descendants and assigns from now on in perpetuity . . . provided*—Have you got provided? Good—*provided that neither he nor his do ever again cross to the eastern side of the above described River. . . .* And now to that damned agent," he said. "The sign must be in duplicate, at both ends of the ford: *The United States accepts no responsibility for any man, woman or child, black, white, yellow or red, who crosses this ford, and no white man shall buy, lease or accept it as a gift save under the severest penalty of the law.* Can I do that?"

"I'm afraid not, Your Excellency," the Secretary said.

The President mused swiftly. "Damn," he said. "Strike out *The United States,* then." The secretary did so. The President folded the two papers and handed them to the cavalry colonel. "Ride," he said. "Your orders are, Stop them."

"Suppose they refuse to stop," the colonel said. "Shall I fire then?"

"Yes," the President said. "Shoot every horse, mule, and ox. I know they won't walk. Off with you, now." The officers withdrew. The President turned back to the maps—the Soldier still: eager, happy, as though he rode himself with the regiment, or as if in spirit already he deployed it with that shrewd cunning which could discern and choose the place most disadvantageous to the enemy, and get there first. "It will be here," he said. He put his finger on the map. "A horse, General, that I may meet him here and turn his flank and drive him."

"Done, General," the Secretary said.

Turnabout

The American—the older one—wore no pink Bedfords. His breeches were of plain whipcord, like the tunic. And the tunic had no long London-cut skirts, so that below the Sam Browne the tail of it stuck straight out like the tunic of a military policeman beneath his holster belt. And he wore simple puttees and the easy shoes of a man of middle age, instead of Savile Row boots, and the shoes and the puttees did not match in shade, and the ordnance belt did not match either of them, and the pilot's wings on his breast were just wings. But the ribbon beneath them was a good ribbon, and the insigne on his shoulders were the twin bars of a captain. He was not tall. His face was thin, a little aquiline; the eyes intelligent and a little tired. He was past twenty-five; looking at him, one thought, not Phi Beta Kappa exactly, but Skull and Bones perhaps, or possibly a Rhodes scholarship.

One of the men who faced him probably could not see him at all. He was being held on his feet by an American military policeman. He was quite drunk, and in contrast with the heavy-jawed policeman who held him erect on his long, slim, boneless legs, he looked like a masquerading girl. He was possibly eighteen, tall, with a pink-and-white face and blue eyes, and a mouth like a girl's mouth. He wore a pea-coat, buttoned awry and stained with recent mud, and upon his blond head, at that unmistakable and rakish swagger which no other people can ever approach or imitate, the cap of a Royal Naval Officer.

"What's this, corporal?" the American captain said. "What's the trouble? He's an Englishman. You'd better let their M.P.'s take care of him."

"I know he is," the policeman said. He spoke heavily, breathing heavily, in the voice of a man under physical strain; for all his girlish delicacy of limb, the English boy was heavier—or more helpless—than he looked. "Stand up!" the policeman said. "They're officers!"

The English boy made an effort then. He pulled himself together, focusing his eyes. He swayed, throwing his arms about the policeman's neck, and with the other hand he saluted, his hand flicking, fingers curled a little, to his right ear, already swaying again and catching himself again. "Cheer-o, sir," he said. "Name's not Beatty, I hope."

"No," the captain said.

"Ah," the English boy said. "Hoped not. My mistake. No offense, what?"

"No offense," the captain said quietly. But he was looking at the policeman. The second American spoke. He was a lieutenant, also a pilot. But he was not twenty-five and he wore the pink breeches, the London boots, and his tunic might have been a British tunic save for the collar.

"It's one of those navy eggs," he said. "They pick them out of the gutters here all night long. You don't come to town often enough."

"Oh," the captain said. "I've heard about them. I remember now." He also remarked now that, though the street was a busy one—it was just outside a popular café—and there were many passers, soldier, civilian, women, yet none of them so much as paused, as though it were a familiar sight. He was looking at the policeman. "Can't you take him to his ship?"

"I thought of that before the captain did," the policeman said. "He says he can't go aboard his ship after dark because he puts the ship away at sundown."

"Puts it away?"

"Stand up, sailor!" the policeman said savagely, jerking at his lax burden. "Maybe the captain can make sense out of it. Damned if I can. He says they keep the boat under the wharf. Run it under the wharf at night, and that they can't get it out again until the tide goes out tomorrow."

"Under the wharf? A boat? What is this?" He was now speaking to the lieutenant. "Do they operate some kind of aquatic motorcycles?"

"Something like that," the lieutenant said. "You've seen them—the boats. Launches, camouflaged and all. Dashing up and down the harbor. You've seen them. They do that all day and sleep in the gutters here all night."

"Oh," the captain said. "I thought those boats were ship commanders' launches. You mean to tell me they use officers just to—"

"I don't know," the lieutenant said. "Maybe they use them to fetch hot water from one ship to another. Or buns. Or maybe to go back and forth fast when they forget napkins or something."

"Nonsense," the captain said. He looked at the English boy again.

"That's what they do," the lieutenant said. "Town's lousy with them all night long. Gutters full, and their M.P's carting them away in batches, like nursemaids in a park. Maybe the French give them the launches to get them out of the gutters during the day."

"Oh," the captain said, "I see." But it was clear that he didn't see, wasn't listening, didn't believe what he did hear. He looked at the English boy. "Well, you can't leave him here in that shape," he said.

Again the English boy tried to pull himself together. "Quite all right, 'sure you," he said glassily, his voice pleasant, cheerful almost, quite courteous. "Used to it. Confounded rough *pave*, though. Should force French do something about it. Visiting lads jolly well deserve decent field to play on, what?"

"And he was jolly well using all of it too," the policeman said savagely. "He must think he's a one-man team, maybe."

At that moment a fifth man came up. He was a British military policeman. "Nah then," he said. "What's this? What's this?" Then he saw the Americans' shoulder bars. He saluted. At the sound of his voice the English boy turned, swaying, peering.

"Oh, hullo, Albert," he said.

"Nah then, Mr. Hope," the British policeman said. He said to the American policeman, over his shoulder: "What is it this time?"

"Likely nothing," the American said. "The way you guys run a war. But I'm a stranger here. Here. Take him."

"What is this, corporal?" the captain said. "What was he doing?"

"He won't call it nothing," the American policeman

said, jerking his head at the British policeman. "He'll just call it a thrush or a robin or something. I turn into this street about three blocks back a while ago, and I find it blocked with a line of trucks going up from the docks, and the drivers all hollering ahead what the hell the trouble is. So I come on, and I find it is about three blocks of them, blocking the cross streets too; and I come on to the head of it where the trouble is, and I find about a dozen of the drivers out in front, holding a caucus or something in the middle of the street, and I come up and I say, 'What's going on here?' and they leave me through and I find this egg here laying—"

"Yer talking about one of His Majesty's officers, my man," the British policeman said.

"Watch yourself, corporal," the captain said. "And you found this officer—"

"He had done gone to bed in the middle of the street, with an empty basket for a pillow. Laying there with his hands under his head and his knees crossed, arguing with them about whether he ought to get up and move or not. He said that the trucks could turn back and go around by another street, but that he couldn't use any other street, because this street was his."

"His street?"

The English boy had listened, interested, pleasant. "Billet, you see," he said. "Must have order, even in war emergency. Billet by lot. This street mine; no poaching, eh? Next street Jamie Wutherspoon's. But trucks can go by that street because Jamie not using it yet. Not in bed yet. Insomnia. Knew so. Told them. Trucks go that way. See now?"

"Was that it, corporal?" the captain said.

"He told you. He wouldn't get up. He just laid there, arguing with them. He was telling one of them to go somewhere and bring back a copy of their articles of war—"

"King's Regulations; yes," the captain said.

"—and see if the book said whether he had the right of way, or the trucks. And then I got him up, and then the captain come along. And that's all. And with the captain's permission I'll now hand him over to His Majesty's wet nur—"

"That'll do, corporal," the captain said. "You can go. I'll see to this." The policeman saluted and went on. The British policeman was now supporting the English boy. "Can't you take him?" the captain said. "Where are their quarters?"

"I don't rightly know, sir, if they have quarters or not. We—I usually see them about the pubs until daylight. They don't seem to use quarters."

"You mean, they really aren't off of ships?"

"Well, sir, they might be ships, in a manner of speaking. But a man would have to be a bit sleepier than him to sleep in one of them."

"I see," the captain said. He looked at the policeman. "What kind of boats are they?"

This time the policeman's voice was immediate, final and completely inflectionless. It was like a closed door. "I don't rightly know, sir."

"Oh," the captain said. "Quite. Well, he's in no shape to stay about pubs until daylight this time."

"Perhaps I can find him a bit of a pub with a back table, where he can sleep," the policeman said. But the captain was not listening. He was looking across the street, where the lights of another café fell across the pavement. The English boy yawned terrifically, like a child does, his mouth pink and frankly gaped as a child's.

The captain turned to the policeman:

"Would you mind stepping across there and asking for Captain Bogard's driver? I'll take care of Mr. Hope."

The policeman departed. The captain now supported the English boy, his hand beneath the other's arm. Again the boy yawned like a weary child. "Steady," the captain said. "The car will be here in a minute."

"Right," the English boy said through the yawn.

II

Once in the car, he went to sleep immediately with the peaceful suddenness of babies, sitting between the two Americans. But though the aerodrome was only thirty minutes away, he was awake when they arrived, apparently quite fresh, and asking for whisky. When they entered the mess he appeared quite sober, only blinking a little in the lighted room, in his raked cap and his awry-buttoned pea-jacket and a soiled silk muffler, embroidered with a club insignia which Bogard recognized to have come from a famous preparatory school, twisted about his throat.

"Ah," he said, his voice fresh, clear now, not blurred, quite cheerful, quite loud, so that the others in the room turned and looked at him. "Jolly. Whisky, what?" He went straight as a bird dog to the bar in the corner, the lieutenant following. Bogard had turned and gone on to the other end of the room, where five men sat about a card table.

"What's he admiral of?" one said.

"Of the whole Scotch navy, when I found him," Bogard said.

Another looked up. "Oh, I thought I'd seen him in town." He looked at the guest. "Maybe it's because he was on his feet that I didn't recognize him when he came in. You usually see them lying down in the gutter."

"Oh," the first said. He, too, looked around. "Is he one of those guys?"

"Sure. You've seen them. Sitting on the curb, you know, with a couple of limey M.P.'s hauling at their arms."

"Yes. I've seen them," the other said. They all looked at the English boy. He stood at the bar, talking, his voice loud, cheerful. "They all look like him too," the speaker said. "About seventeen or eighteen. They run those little boats that are always dashing in and out."

"Is that what they do?" a third said. "You mean, there's a male marine auxiliary to the Waacs? Good Lord, I sure made a mistake when I enlisted. But this war never was advertised right."

"I don't know," Bogard said. "I guess they do more than just ride around."

But they were not listening to him. They were looking at the guest. "They run by clock," the first said. "You can see the condition of one of them after sunset and almost tell what time it is. But what I don't see is, how a man that's in that shape at one o'clock every morning can even see a battleship the next day."

"Maybe when they have a message to send out to a ship," another said, "they just make duplicates and line the launches up and point them toward the ship and give each one a duplicate of the message and let them go. And the ones that miss the ship just cruise around the harbor until they hit a dock somewhere."

"It must be more than that," Bogard said.

He was about to say something else, but at that moment the guest turned from the bar and approached, carrying a glass. He walked steadily enough, but his color was high and his eyes were bright, and he was talking, loud, cheerful, as he came up.

"I say. Won't you chaps join—" He ceased. He seemed to remark something; he was looking at their breasts. "Oh, I say. You fly. All of you. Oh, good gad! Find it jolly, eh?"

"Yes," somebody said. "Jolly."

"But dangerous, what?"

"A little faster than tennis," another said. The guest looked at him, bright, affable, intent.

Another said quickly, "Bogard says you command a vessel."

"Hardly a vessel. Thanks, though. And not command. Ronnie does that. Ranks me a bit. Age."

"Ronnie?"

"Yes. Nice. Good egg. Old, though. Stickler."

"Stickler?"

"Frightful. You'd not believe it. Whenever we sight smoke and I have the glass, he sheers away. Keeps the ship hull down all the while. No beaver then. Had me two down a fortnight yesterday."

The Americans glanced at one another. "No beaver?"

"We play it. With basket masts, you see. See a basket mast. Beaver! One up. The Ergenstrasse doesn't count any more, though."

The men about the table looked at one another. Bogard spoke. "I see. When you or Ronnie see a ship with basket masts, you get a beaver on the other. I see. What is the Ergenstrasse?"

"She's German. Interned. Tramp steamer. Foremast rigged so it looks something like a basket mast. Booms, cables, I dare say. I didn't think it looked very much like a basket mast, myself. But Ronnie said yes. Called it one day. Then one day they shifted her across the basin and I called her on Ronnie. So we decided to not count her any more. See now, eh?"

"Oh," the one who had made the tennis remark said, "I see. You and Ronnie run about in the launch, playing beaver. H'm'm. That's nice. Did you ever pl—"

"Jerry," Bogard said. The guest had not moved. He looked down at the speaker, still smiling, his eyes quite wide.

The speaker still looked at the guest. "Has yours and Ronnie's boat got a yellow stern?"

"A yellow stern?" the English boy said. He had quit smiling, but his face was still pleasant.

"I thought that maybe when the boats had two captains, they might paint the sterns yellow or something."

"Oh," the guest said. "Burt and Reeves aren't officers."

"Burt and Reeves," the other said, in a musing tone. "So they go, too. Do they play beaver too?"

"Jerry," Bogard said. The other looked at him. Bogard jerked his head a little. "Come over here." The other rose. They went aside. "Lay off of him," Bogard said. "I mean it, now. He's just a kid. When you were that age, how much sense did you have? Just about enough to get to chapel on time."

"My country hadn't been at war going on four years, though," Jerry said. "Here we are, spending our money and getting shot at by the clock, and it's not even our fight, and these limeys that would have been goosestepping twelve months now if it hadn't been—"

"Shut it," Bogard said. "You sound like a Liberty Loan."

"—taking it like it was a fair or something. 'Jolly.' " His voice was now falsetto, lilting. " 'But dangerous, what?' "

"Sh-h-h-h," Bogard said.

"I'd like to catch him and his Ronnie out in the harbor, just once. Any harbor. London's. I wouldn't want anything but a Jenny, either. Jenny? Hell, I'd take a bicycle and a pair of water wings! I'll show him some war."

"Well, you lay off him now. He'll be gone soon."

"What are you going to do with him?"

"I'm going to take him along this morning. Let him have Harper's place out front. He says he can handle a Lewis. Says they have one on the boat. Something he was telling me—about how he once shot out a channel-marker light at seven hundred yards."

"Well, that's your business. Maybe he can beat you."

"Beat me?"

"Playing beaver. And then you can take on Ronnie."

"I'll show him some war, anyway," Bogard said. He looked at the guest. "His people have been in it three years now, and he seems to take it like a sophomore in town for the big game." He looked at Jerry again. "But you lay off him now."

As they approached the table, the guest's voice was loud and cheerful: ". . . if he got the glasses first, he would go in close and look, but when I got them first, he'd sheer off where I couldn't see anything but the smoke. Frightful stickler. Frightful. But Ergenstrasse not counting any more. And if you make a mistake and call her, you lose two beaver from your score. If Ronnie were only to forget and call her we'd be even."

III

At two o'clock the English boy was still talking, his voice bright, innocent and cheerful. He was telling them how Switzerland had been spoiled by 1914, and instead of the vacation which his father had promised him for his sixteenth birthday, when that birthday came he and his tutor had had to do with Wales. But that he and the tutor had got pretty high and that he dared to say—with all due respect to any present who might have had the advantage of Switzerland, of course—that one could see probably as far from Wales as from Switzerland. "Perspire as much and breathe as hard, anyway," he added. And about him the Americans sat, a little hard-bitten, a little sober, somewhat older, listening to him with a kind of cold astonishment. They had been getting up for some time now and going out and returning in flying clothes, carrying helmets and goggles. An orderly entered with a tray of coffee cups, and the guest realized that for some time now he had been hearing engines in the darkness outside.

At last Bogard rose. "Come along," he said. "We'll get your togs." When they emerged from the mess, the sound of the engines was quite loud—an idling thunder. In alignment along the invisible tarmac was a vague rank of short banks of flickering blue-green fire suspended apparently in mid-air. They crossed the aerodrome to Bogard's quarters, where the lieutenant, McGinnis, sat on a cot fastening his flying boots. Bogard reached down a Sidcott suit and threw it across the cot. "Put this on," he said.

"Will I need all this?" the guest said. "Shall we be gone that long?"

"Probably," Bogard said. "Better use it. Cold upstairs."

The guest picked up the suit. "I say," he said. "I say, Ronnie and I have a do ourselves, tomor—today. Do you think Ronnie won't mind if I am a bit late? Might not wait for me."

"We'll be back before teatime," McGinnis said. He seemed quite busy with his boot. "Promise you." The English boy looked at him.

"What time should you be back?" Bogard said.

"Oh, well," the English boy said, "I dare say it will be all right. They let Ronnie say when to go, anyway. He'll wait for me if I should be a bit late."

"He'll wait," Bogard said. "Get your suit on."

"Right," the other said. They helped him into the suit. "Never been up before," he said, chattily, pleasantly. "Dare say you can see farther than from mountains, eh?"

"See more, anyway," McGinnis said. "You'll like it."

"Oh, rather. If Ronnie only waits for me. Lark. But dangerous, isn't it?"

"Go on," McGinnis said. "You're kidding me."

"Shut your trap, Mac," Bogard said. "Come along. Want some more coffee?" He looked at the guest, but McGinnis answered:

"No. Got something better than coffee. Coffee makes such a confounded stain on the wings."

"On the wings?" the English boy said. "Why coffee on the wings?"

"Stow it, I said, Mac," Bogard said. "Come along."

They recrossed the aerodrome, approaching the muttering banks of flame. When they drew near, the guest began to discern the shape, the outlines, of the Handley-Page. It looked like a Pullman coach run up-slanted aground into the skeleton of the first floor of an incomplete skyscraper. The guest looked at it quietly.

"It's larger than a cruiser," he said in his bright, interested voice. "I say, you know. This doesn't fly in one lump. You can't pull my leg. Seen them before. It comes in two parts: Captain Bogard and men in one; Mac and 'nother chap in other. What?"

"No," McGinnis said. Bogard had vanished. "It all goes up in one lump. Big lark, eh? Buzzard, what?"

"Buzzard?" the guest murmured. "Oh, I say. A cruiser. Flying. I say, now."

"And listen," McGinnis said. His hand came forth; something cold fumbled against the hand of the English boy—a bottle. "When you feel yourself getting sick, see? Take a pull at it."

"Oh, shall I get sick?"

"Sure. We all do. Part of flying. This will stop it. But if it doesn't. See?"

"What? Quite. What?"

"Not overside. Don't spew it overside."

"Not overside?"

"It'll blow back in Bogy's and my face. Can't see. Bingo. Finished. See?"

"Oh, quite. What shall I do with it?" Their voices were quiet, brief, grave as conspirators.

"Just duck your head and let her go."

"Oh, quite."

Bogard returned. "Show him how to get into the front pit, will you?" he said. McGinnis led the way through the trap. Forward, rising to the slant of the fuselage, the passage narrowed; a man would need to crawl.

"Crawl in there and keep going," McGinnis said.

"It looks like a dog kennel," the guest said.

"Doesn't it, though?" McGinnis agreed cheerfully. "Cut along with you." Stooping, he could hear the other scuttling forward. "You'll find a Lewis gun up there, like as not," he said into the tunnel.

The voice of the guest came back: "Found it."

"The gunnery sergeant will be along in a minute and show you if it is loaded."

"It's loaded," the guest said; almost on the heels of his words the gun fired, a brief staccato burst. There were shouts, the loudest from the ground beneath the nose of the aeroplane. "It's quite all right," the English boy's voice said. "I pointed it west before I let it off. Nothing back there but Marine office and your brigade headquarters. Ronnie and I always do this before we go anywhere. Sorry if I was too soon. Oh, by the way," he added, "my name's Claude. Don't think I mentioned it."

On the ground, Bogard and two other officers stood. They had come up running. "Fired it west," one said. "How in hell does he know which way is west?"

"He's a sailor," the other said. "You forgot that."

"He seems to be a machine gunner too," Bogard said.

"Let's hope he doesn't forget that," the first said.

IV

Nevertheless, Bogard kept an eye on the silhouetted head rising from the round gunpit in the nose ten feet ahead of him. "He even put the drum on himself, didn't he?"

"Yes," McGinnis said. "If he just doesn't forget and think that that gun is him and his tutor looking around from a Welsh alp."

"Maybe I should not have brought him," Bogard said. McGinnis didn't answer. Bogard jockeyed the wheel a little. Ahead, in the gunner's pit, the guest's head moved this way and that continuously, looking. "We'll get there and unload and haul air for home," Bogard said. "Maybe in the dark—Confound it, it would be a shame for his country to be in this mess for four years and him not even to see a gun pointed in his direction."

"He'll see one tonight if he don't keep his head in," McGinnis said.

But the boy did not do that. Not even when they had reached the objective and McGinnis had crawled down to the bomb toggles. And even when the searchlights found them and Bogard signaled to the other machines and dived, the two engines snarling full speed into and through the bursting shells, he could see the boy's face in the searchlight's glare, leaned far overside, coming sharply out as a spotlighted face on a stage, with an expression upon it of child-like interest and delight. "But he's firing that Lewis," Bogard thought. "Straight too"; nosing the machine farther down, watching the pinpoint swing into the sights, his right hand lifted, waiting to drop into McGinnis' sight. He dropped his hand; above the noise of the engines he seemed to hear the click and whistle of the released bombs as the machine, freed of the weight, shot zooming in a long upward bounce that carried it for an instant out of the light. Then he was pretty busy for a time, coming into and through the shells again, shooting athwart another beam that caught and held long enough for him to see the English boy leaning far over the side, looking back and down past the right wing, the undercarriage. "Maybe he's read about it somewhere," Bogard thought, turning, looking back to pick up the rest of the flight.

Then it was all over, the darkness cool and empty and peaceful and almost quiet, with only the steady sound of the engines. McGinnis climbed back into the office, and standing up in his seat, he fired the colored pistol this time and stood for a moment longer, looking backward toward where the searchlights still probed and sabered. He sat down again.

"O.K.," he said. "I counted all four of them. Let's haul air." Then he looked forward. "What's become of the King's Own? You didn't hang him onto a bomb release, did you?" Bogard looked. The forward pit was empty. It was in dim silhouette again now, against the stars, but there was nothing there now save the gun. "No," McGinnis said: "there he is. See? Leaning overside. Dammit, I told him not to spew it! There he comes back." The guest's head came into view again. But again it sank out of sight.

"He's coming back," Bogard said. "Stop him. Tell him we're going to have every squadron in the Hun Channel group on top of us in thirty minutes."

McGinnis swung himself down and stooped at the entrance to the passage. "Get back!" he shouted. The other was almost out; they squatted so, face to face like two dogs, shouting at one another above the noise of the still-unthrottled engines on either side of the fabric walls. The English boy's voice was thin and high.

"Bomb!" he shrieked.

"Yes," McGinnis shouted, "they were bombs! We gave them hell! Get back, I tell you! Have every Hun in France on us in ten minutes! Get back to your gun!"

Again the boy's voice came, high, faint above the noise: "Bomb! All right?"

"Yes! Yes! All right. Back to your gun, damn you!"

McGinnis climbed back into the office. "He went back. Want me to take her awhile?"

"All right," Bogard said. He passed McGinnis the wheel. "Ease her back some. I'd just as soon it was daylight when they come down on us."

"Right," McGinnis said. He moved the wheel suddenly. "What's the matter with that right wing?" he said. "Watch it. . . . See? I'm flying on the right aileron and a little rudder. Feel it."

Bogard took the wheel a moment. "I didn't notice that. Wire somewhere, I guess. I didn't think any of those shells were that close. Watch her, though."

"Right," McGinnis said. "And so you are going with him on his boat tomorrow—today."

"Yes. I promised him. Confound it, you can't hurt a kid, you know."

"Why don't you take Collier along, with his mandolin? Then you could sail around and sing."

"I promised him," Bogard said. "Get that wing up a little."

"Right," McGinnis said.

Thirty minutes later it was beginning to be dawn; the sky was gray. Presently McGinnis said: "Well, here they come. Look at them! They look like mosquitoes in September. I hope he don't get worked up now and think he's playing beaver. If he does he'll just be one down to Ronnie, provided the devil has a beard. . . . Want the wheel?"

V

At eight o'clock the beach, the Channel, was beneath them. Throttled back, the machine drifted down as Bogard ruddered it gently into the Channel wind. His face was strained, a little tired.

McGinnis looked tired, too, and he needed a shave.

"What do you guess he is looking at now?" he said. For again the English boy was leaning over the right side of the cockpit, looking backward and downward past the right wing.

"I don't know," Bogard said. "Maybe bullet holes." He blasted the port engine. "Must have the riggers—"

"He could see some closer than that," McGinnis said. "I'll swear I saw tracer going into his back at one time. Or maybe it's the ocean he's looking at. But he must have seen that when he came over from England." Then Bogard leveled off; the nose rose sharply, the sand, the curling tide edge fled alongside. Yet still the English boy hung far overside, looking backward and downward at something beneath the right wing, his face rapt, with utter and childlike interest. Until the machine was completely stopped he continued to do so. Then he ducked down, and in the abrupt silence of the engines they could hear him crawling in the passage. He emerged just as the two pilots climbed stiffly down from the office, his face bright, eager; his voice high, excited:

"Oh, I say! Oh, good gad! What a chap. What a judge of distance! If Ronnie could only have seen! Oh, good gad! Or maybe they aren't like ours—don't load themselves as soon as the air strikes them."

The Americans looked at him. "What don't what?" McGinnis said.

"The bomb. It was magnificent; I say, I shan't forget it. Oh, I say, you know! It was splendid!"

After a while McGinnis said, "The bomb?" in a fainting voice. Then the two pilots glared at each other; they said in unison: "That right wing!" Then as one they clawed down through the trap and, with the guest at their heels, they ran around the machine and looked beneath the right wing. The bomb, suspended by its tail, hung straight down like a plumb bob beside the right wheel, its tip just touching the sand. And parallel with the wheel track was the long delicate line in the sand where its ultimate tip had dragged. Behind them the English boy's voice was high, clear, childlike:

"Frightened, myself. Tried to tell you. But realized you knew your business better than I. Skill. Marvelous. Oh, I say, I shan't forget it."

VI

A marine with a bayoneted rifle passed Bogard onto the wharf and directed him to the boat. The wharf was empty, and he didn't even see the boat until he approached the edge of the wharf and looked directly down into it and upon the backs of two stooping men in greasy dungarees, who rose and glanced briefly at him and stooped again.

It was about thirty feet long and about three feet wide. It was painted with gray-green camouflage. It was quarterdecked forward, with two blunt, raked exhaust stacks. "Good Lord," Bogard thought, "if all that deck is engine—" Just aft the deck was the control seat; he saw a big wheel, an instrument panel. Rising to a height of about a foot above the free-board, and running from the stern forward to where the deck began, and continuing on across the after edge of the deck and thence back down the other gunwale to the stern, was a solid screen, also camouflaged, which inclosed the boat save for the width of the stern, which was open. Facing the steersman's seat like an eye was a hole in the screen about eight inches in diameter. And looking down into the long, narrow, still, vicious shape, he saw a machine gun swiveled at the stern, and he looked at the low screen—including which the whole vessel did not sit much more than a yard above water level—with its single empty forward-staring eye, and he thought quietly: "It's steel. It's made of steel." And his face was quite sober, quite thoughtful, and he drew his trench coat about him and buttoned it, as though he were getting cold.

He heard steps behind him and turned. But it was only an orderly from the aerodrome, accompanied by the marine with the rifle. The orderly was carrying a largish bundle wrapped in paper.

"From Lieutenant McGinnis to the captain," the orderly said.

Bogard took the bundle. The orderly and the marine

retreated. He opened the bundle. It contained some objects and a scrawled note. The objects were a new yellow silk sofa cushion and a Japanese parasol, obviously borrowed, and a comb and a roll of toilet paper. The note said:

> Couldn't find a camera anywhere and Collier wouldn't let me have his mandolin. But maybe Ronnie can play on the comb.
>
> MAC.

Bogard looked at the objects. But his face was still quite thoughtful, quite grave. He rewrapped the things and carried the bundle on up the wharf and dropped it quietly into the water.

As he returned toward the invisible boat he saw two men approaching. He recognized the boy at once—tall, slender, already talking, voluble, his head bent a little toward his shorter companion, who plodded along beside him, hands in pockets, smoking a pipe. The boy still wore the pea-coat beneath a flapping oilskin, but in place of the rakish and casual cap he now wore an infantryman's soiled Balaclava helmet, with, floating behind him as though upon the sound of his voice, a curtainlike piece of cloth almost as long as a burnous.

"Hullo, there!" he cried, still a hundred yards away.

But it was the second man that Bogard was watching, thinking to himself that he had never in his life seen a more curious figure. There was something stolid about the very shape of his hunched shoulders, his slightly down-looking face. He was a head shorter than the other. His face was ruddy, too, but its mold was of a profound gravity that was almost dour. It was the face of a man of twenty who has been for a year trying, even while asleep, to look twenty-one. He wore a high-necked sweater and dungaree slacks; above this a leather jacket; and above this a soiled naval officer's warmer that reached almost to his heels and which had one shoulder strap missing and not one remaining button at all. On his head was a plaid fore-and-aft deer stalker's cap tied on by a narrow scarf brought across and down, hiding his ears, and then wrapped once about his throat and knotted with a hang-man's noose beneath his left ear. It was unbelievably soiled, and with his hands elbow-deep in his pockets and his hunched shoulders and his bent head, he looked like someone's grandmother hung, say, for a witch. Clamped upside down between his teeth was a short brier pipe.

"Here he is!" the boy cried. "This is Ronnie. Captain Bogard."

"How are you?" Bogard said. He extended his hand. The other said no word, but his hand came forth, limp. It was quite cold, but it was hard, calloused. But he said no word; he just glanced briefly at Bogard and then away. But in that instant Bogard caught something in the look, something strange—a flicker; a kind of covert and curi-ous respect, something like a boy of fifteen looking at a circus trapezist.

But he said no word. He ducked on; Bogard watched him drop from sight over the wharf edge as though he had jumped feet first into the sea. He remarked now that the engines in the invisible boat were running.

"We might get aboard too," the boy said. He started toward the boat, then he stopped. He touched Bogard's arm. "Yonder!" he hissed. "See?" His voice was thin with excitement.

"What?" Bogard also whispered; automatically he looked backward and upward, after old habit. The other was gripping his arm and pointing across the harbor.

"There! Over there. The Ergenstrasse. They have shifted her again." Across the harbor lay an ancient, rusting, swaybacked hulk. It was small and nondescript, and, remembering, Bogard saw that the foremast was a strange mess of cables and booms, resembling—allowing for a great deal of license or looseness of imagery—a basket mast. Beside him the boy was almost chortling. "Do you think that Ronnie noticed?" he hissed. "Do you?"

"I don't know," Bogard said.

"Oh, good gad! If he should glance up and call her before he notices, we'll be even. Oh, good gad! But come along." He went on; he was still chortling. "Careful," he said. "Frightful ladder."

He descended first, the two men in the boat rising and saluting. Ronnie had disappeared, save for his backside, which now filled a small hatch leading forward beneath the deck. Bogard descended gingerly.

"Good Lord," he said. "Do you have to climb up and down this every day?"

"Frightful, isn't it?" the other said, in his happy voice. "But you know yourself. Try to run a war with makeshifts, then wonder why it takes so long." The narrow hull slid and surged, even with Bogard's added weight. "Sits right on top, you see," the boy said. "Would float on a lawn, in a heavy dew. Goes right over them like a bit of paper."

"It does?" Bogard said.

"Oh, absolutely. That's why, you see." Bogard didn't see, but he was too busy letting himself gingerly down to a sitting posture. There were no thwarts; no seats save a long, thick, cylindrical ridge which ran along the bottom of the boat from the driver's seat to the stern. Ronnie had backed into sight. He now sat behind the wheel, bent over the instrument panel. But when he glanced back over his shoulder he did not speak. His face was merely interrogatory. Across his face there was now a long smudge of grease. The boy's face was empty, too, now.

"Right," he said. He looked forward, where one of the seamen had gone. "Ready forward?" he said.

"Aye, sir," the seaman said.

The other seaman was at the stern line. "Ready aft?"

"Aye, sir."

"Cast off." The boat sheered away, purring, a boiling of water under the stern. The boy looked down at Bogard. "Silly business. Do it shipshape, though. Can't tell when silly fourstriper—" His face changed again, immediate, solicitous. "I say. Will you be warm? I never thought to fetch—"

"I'll be all right," Bogard said. But the other was already taking off his oilskin. "No, no," Bogard said. "I won't take it."

"You'll tell me if you get cold?"

"Yes. Sure." He was looking down at the cylinder on which he sat. It was a half cylinder—that is, like the hot-water tank to some Gargantuan stove, sliced down the middle and bolted, open side down, to the floor plates. It was twenty feet long and more than two feet thick. Its top rose as high as the gunwales and between it and the hull on either side was just room enough for a man to place his feet to walk.

"That's Muriel," the boy said.

"Muriel?"

"Yes. The one before that was Agatha. After my aunt. The first one Ronnie and I had was Alice in Wonderland. Ronnie and I were the White Rabbit. Jolly, eh?"

"Oh, you and Ronnie have had three, have you?"

"Oh, yes," the boy said. He leaned down. "He didn't notice," he whispered. His face was again bright, gleeful. "When we come back," he said. "You watch."

"Oh," Bogard said. "The Ergenstrasse." He looked astern, and then he thought: "Good Lord! We must be going—traveling." He looked out now, broadside, and saw the harbor line fleeing past, and he thought to himself that the boat was well-nigh moving at the speed at which the Handley-Page flew, left the ground. They were beginning to bound now, even in the sheltered water, from one wave crest to the next with a distinct shock. His hand still rested on the cylinder on which he sat. He looked down at it again, following it from where it seemed to emerge beneath Ronnie's seat, to where it beveled into the stern. "It's the air in her, I suppose," he said.

"The what?" the boy said.

"The air. Stored up in her. That makes the boat ride high."

"Oh, yes. I dare say. Very likely. I hadn't thought about it." He came forward, his burnous whipping in the wind, and sat down beside Bogard. Their heads were below the top of the screen.

Astern the harbor fled, diminishing, sinking into the sea. The boat had begun to lift now, swooping forward and down, shocking almost stationary for a moment, then lifting and swooping again; a gout of spray came aboard over the bows like a flung shovelful of shot. "I wish you'd take this coat," the boy said.

Bogard didn't answer. He looked around at the bright face. "We're outside, aren't we?" he said quietly.

"Yes. . . . Do take it, won't you?"

"Thanks, no. I'll be all right. We won't be long, anyway, I guess."

"No. We'll turn soon. It won't be so bad then."

"Yes. I'll be all right when we turn." Then they did turn. The motion became easier. That is, the boat didn't bang head-on, shuddering, into the swells. They came up beneath now, and the boat fled with increased speed, with a long, sickening, yawing motion, first to one side and then the other. But it fled on, and Bogard looked astern with that same soberness with which he had first looked down into the boat. "We're going east now," he said.

"With just a spot of north," the boy said. "Makes her ride a bit better, what?"

"Yes," Bogard said. Astern there was nothing now save empty sea and the delicate needlelike cant of the machine gun against the boiling and slewing wake, and the two seamen crouching quietly in the stern. "Yes. It's easier." Then he said: "How far do we go?"

The boy leaned closer. He moved closer. His voice was happy, confidential, proud, though lowered a little: "It's Ronnie's show. He thought of it. Not that I wouldn't have, in time. Gratitude and all that. But he's the older, you see. Thinks fast. Courtesy, *noblesse oblige*—all that. Thought of it soon as I told him this morning. I said, 'Oh, I say. I've been there. I've seen it'; and he said, 'Not flying'; and I said, 'Strewth'; and he said, 'How far? No lying now'; and I said, 'Oh, far. Tremendous. Gone all night'; and he said, 'Flying all night. That must have been to Berlin'; and I said, 'I don't know. I dare say'; and he thought. I could see him thinking. Because he is the older, you see. More experience in courtesy, right thing. And he said, 'Berlin. No fun to that chap, dashing out and back with us.' And he thought and I waited, and I said, 'But we can't take him to Berlin. Too far. Don't know the way, either'; and he said—fast, like a shot—said, 'But there's Kiel'; and I knew—"

"What?" Bogard said. Without moving, his whole body sprang. "Kiel? In this?"

"Absolutely. Ronnie thought of it. Smart, even if he is a stickler. Said at once, 'Zeebrugge no show at all for that chap. Must do best we can for him. Berlin,' Ronnie said. 'My Gad! Berlin.' "

"Listen," Bogard said. He had turned now, facing the other, his face quite grave. "What is this boat for?"

"For?"

"What does it do?" Then, knowing beforehand the answer to his own question, he said, putting his hand on the cylinder: "What is this in here? A torpedo, isn't it?"

"I thought you knew," the boy said.

"No," Bogard said. "I didn't know." His voice seemed to reach him from a distance, dry, cricketlike: "How do you fire it?"

"Fire it?"

"How do you get it out of the boat? When that hatch was open a while ago I could see the engines. They were right in front of the end of this tube."

"Oh," the boy said. "You pull a gadget there and the torpedo drops out astern. As soon as the screw touches the water it begins to turn, and then the torpedo is ready, loaded. Then all you have to do is turn the boat quickly and the torpedo goes on."

"You mean—" Bogard said. After a moment his voice obeyed him again. "You mean you aim the torpedo with the boat and release it and it starts moving, and you turn the boat out of the way and the torpedo passes through the same water that the boat just vacated?"

"Knew you'd catch on," the boy said. "Told Ronnie so. Airman. Tamer than yours, tough. But can't be helped. Best we can do, just on water. But knew you'd catch on."

"Listen," Bogard said. His voice sounded to him quite calm. The boat fled on, yawing over the swells. He sat quite motionless. It seemed to him that he could hear himself talking to himself: "Go on. Ask him. Ask him what? Ask him how close to the ship do you have to be before you fire. . . . Listen," he said, in that calm voice. "Now, you tell Ronnie, you see. You just tell him—just say—" He could feel his voice ratting off on him again, so he stopped it. He sat quite motionless, waiting for it to come back; the boy leaning now, looking at his face. Again the boy's voice was solicitous:

"I say. You're not feeling well. These confounded shallow boats."

"It's not that," Bogard said. "I just—Do your orders say Kiel?"

"Oh, no. They let Ronnie say. Just so we bring the boat back. This is for you. Gratitude. Ronnie's idea. Tame, after flying. But if you'd rather, eh?"

"Yes, some place closer. You see, I—"

"Quite. I see. No vacations in wartime. I'll tell Ronnie." He went forward. Bogard did not move. The boat fled in long, slewing swoops. Bogard looked quietly astern, at the scudding sea, the sky.

"My God!" he thought. "Can you beat it? Can you beat it?"

The boy came back; Bogard turned to him a face the color of dirty paper. "All right now," the boy said. "Not Kiel. Nearer place, hunting probably just as good. Ronnie says he knows you will understand." He was tugging at his pocket. He brought out a bottle. "Here. Haven't forgot last night. Do the same for you. Good for the stomach, eh?"

Bogard drank, gulping—a big one. He extended the bottle, but the boy refused. "Never touch it on duty," he said. "Not like you chaps. Tame here."

The boat fled on. The sun was already down the west. But Bogard had lost all count of time, of distance. Ahead he could see white seas through the round eye opposite Ronnie's face, and Ronnie's hand on the wheel and the granitelike jut of his profiled jaw and the dead upside-down pipe. The boat fled on.

Then the boy leaned and touched his shoulder. He half rose. The boy was pointing. The sun was reddish; against it, outside them and about two miles away, a vessel—a traveler, it looked like—at anchor swung a tall mast.

"Lightship!" the boy shouted. "Theirs." Ahead Bogard could see a low, flat mole—the entrance to a harbor. "Channel!" the boy shouted. He swept his arm in both directions. "Mines!" His voice swept back on the wind. "Place filthy with them. All sides. Beneath us too. Lark, eh?"

VII

Against the mole a fair surf was beating. Running before the seas now, the boat seemed to leap from one roller to the next; in the intervals while the screw was in the air the engine seemed to be trying to tear itself out by the roots. But it did not slow; when it passed the end of the mole the boat seemed to be standing almost erect on its rudder, like a sailfish. The mole was a mile away. From the end of it little faint lights began to flicker like fireflies. The boy leaned. "Down," he said. "Machine guns. Might stop a stray."

"What do I do?" Bogard shouted. "What can I do?"

"Stout fellow! Give them hell, what? Knew you'd like it!"

Crouching, Bogard looked up at the boy, his face wild. "I can handle the machine gun!"

"No need," the boy shouted back. "Give them first innings. Sporting. Visitors, eh?" He was looking forward. "There she is. See?" They were in the harbor now, the basin opening before them. Anchored in the channel was a big freighter. Painted midships of the hull was a huge Argentine flag. "Must get back to stations!" the boy shouted down to him. Then at that moment Ronnie spoke for the first time. The boat was hurtling along now in smoother water. Its speed did not slacken and Ronnie did not turn his head when he spoke. He just swung his jutting jaw and the clamped cold pipe a little, and said from the side of his mouth a single word:

"Beaver."

The boy, stooped over what he had called his gadget, jerked up, his expression astonished and outraged. Bogard also looked forward and saw Ronnie's arm pointing to starboard. It was a light cruiser at anchor a mile away. She had basket masts, and as he looked a gun flashed from her after turret. "Oh, damn!" the boy cried. "Oh, you putt! Oh, confound you, Ronnie! Now I'm three down!" But he had already stooped again over his gadget, his face bright and empty and alert again; not sober; just calm, waiting. Again Bogard looked forward and felt the boat pivot on its rudder and head directly for the freighter at terrific speed, Ronnie now with one hand on the wheel and the other lifted and extended at the height of his head.

But it seemed to Bogard that the hand would never drop. He crouched, not sitting, watching with a kind of quiet horror the painted flag increase like a moving picture of a locomotive taken from between the rails. Again the gun crashed from the cruiser behind them, and the freighter fired point-blank at them from its poop. Bogard heard neither shot.

"Man, man!" he shouted. "For God's sake!"

Ronnie's hand dropped. Again the boat spun on its rudder. Bogard saw the bow rise, pivoting; he expected the hull to slam broadside on into the ship. But it didn't. It shot off on a long tangent. He was waiting for it to make a wide sweep, heading seaward, putting the freighter astern, and he thought of the cruiser again. "Get a broadside, this time, once we clear the freighter," he thought. Then he remembered the freighter, the torpedo, and he looked back toward the freighter to watch the torpedo strike, and saw to his horror that the boat was now bearing down on the freighter again, in a skidding turn. Like a man in a dream, he watched himself rush down upon the ship and shoot past under her counter, still skidding, close enough to see the faces on her decks. "They missed and they are going to run down the torpedo and catch it and shoot it again," he thought idiotically.

So the boy had to touch his shoulder before he knew he was behind him. The boy's voice was quite calm: "Under Ronnie's seat there. A bit of a crank handle. If you'll just hand it to me—"

He found the crank. He passed it back; he was thinking dreamily: "Mac would say they had a telephone on board." But he didn't look at once to see what the boy was doing with it, for in that still and peaceful horror he was watching Ronnie, the cold pipe rigid in his jaw, hurling the boat at top speed round and round the freighter, so near that he could see the rivets in the plates. Then he looked aft, his face wild, importunate, and he saw what the boy was doing with the crank. He had fitted it into what was obviously a small windlass low on one flank of the tube near the head. He glanced up and saw Bogard's face. "Didn't go that time!" he shouted cheerfully.

"Go?" Bogard shouted. "It didn't—The torpedo—"

The boy and one of the seamen were quite busy, stooping over the windlass and the tube. "No. Clumsy. Always happening. Should think clever chaps like engineers—Happens, though. Draw her in and try her again."

"But the nose, the cap!" Bogard shouted. "It's still in the tube, isn't it? It's all right, isn't it?"

"Absolutely. But it's working now. Loaded. Screw's started turning. Get it back and drop it clear. If we should stop or slow up it would overtake us. Drive back into the tube. Bingo! What?"

Bogard was on his feet now, turned, braced to the terrific merry-go-round of the boat. High above them the freighter seemed to be spinning on her heel like a trick picture in the movies. "Let me have that winch!" he cried.

"Steady!" the boy said. "Mustn't draw her back too fast. Jam her into the head of the tube ourselves. Same bingo! Best let us. Every cobbler to his last, what?"

"Oh, quite," Bogard said. "Oh, absolutely." It was like someone else was using his mouth. He leaned, braced, his hands on the cold tube, beside the others. He was hot inside, but his outside was cold. He could feel all his flesh jerking with cold as he watched the blunt, grained hand of the seaman turning the windlass in short, easy, inch-long arcs while at the head of the tube the boy bent, tapping the cylinder with a spanner, lightly, his head turned with listening delicate and deliberate as a watchmaker. The boat rushed on in those furious, slewing turns. Bogard saw a long, drooping thread loop down from somebody's mouth, between his hands, and he found that the thread came from his own mouth.

He didn't hear the boy speak, nor notice when he stood up. He just felt the boat straighten out, flinging him to his knees beside the tube. The seaman had gone back to the stern and the boy stooped again over his gadget. Bogard knelt now, quite sick. He did not feel the boat when it swung again, nor hear the gun from the cruiser which had not dared to fire and the freighter which had not been able to fire, firing again. He did not feel anything at all when he saw the huge painted flag directly ahead and increasing with locomotive speed, and Ronnie's lifted hand drop. But this time he knew that the torpedo was gone; in pivoting and spinning this time the whole boat seemed to leave the water; he saw the bow of the boat shoot skyward like the nose of a pursuit ship going into a wingover. Then his outraged stomach denied him. He neither saw the geyser nor heard the detonation as he sprawled over the tube. He felt only a hand grasp him by the slack of his coat and the voice of one of the seamen: "Steady all, sir. I've got you."

VIII

A voice roused him, a hand. He was half sitting in the narrow starboard runway, half lying across the tube. He had been there for quite a while; quite a while ago he had felt someone spread a garment over him. But he had not raised his head. "I'm all right," he had said. "You keep it."

"Don't need it," the boy said. "Going home now."

"I'm sorry I—" Bogard said.

"Quite. Confounded shallow boats. Turn any stomach until you get used to them. Ronnie and I both, at first. Each time. You wouldn't believe it. Believe human stomach hold so much. Here." It was the bottle. "Good drink. Take enormous one. Good for stomach."

Bogard drank. Soon he did feel better, warmer. When the hand touched him later, he found that he had been asleep.

It was the boy again. The pea-coat was too small for him; shrunken, perhaps. Below the cuffs his long, slender, girl's wrists were blue with cold. Then Bogard realized what the garment was that had been laid over him. But before Bogard could speak, the boy leaned down, whispering; his face was gleeful: "He didn't notice!"

"What?"

"Ergenstrasse! He didn't notice that they had shifted her. Gad, I'd be just one down, then." He watched Bogard's face with bright, eager eyes. "Beaver, you know. I say. Feeling better, eh?"

"Yes," Bogard said, "I am."

"He didn't notice at all. Oh, gad! Oh, Jove!"

Bogard rose and sat on the tube. The entrance to the harbor was just ahead; the boat had slowed a little. It was just dusk. He said quietly: "Does this often happen?" The boy looked at him. Bogard touched the tube. "This. Failing to go out."

"Oh, yes. Why they put the windlass on them. That was later. Made first boat; whole thing blew up one day. So put on windlass."

"But it happens sometimes, even now? I mean, sometimes they blow up, even with the windlass?"

"Well, can't say, of course. Boats go out. Not come back. Possible. Not ever know, of course. Not heard of one captured yet, though. Possible. Not to us, though. Not yet."

"Yes," Bogard said. "Yes." They entered the harbor, the boat moving still fast, but throttled now and smooth, across the dusk-filled basin. Again the boy leaned down, his voice gleeful.

"Not a word, now!" he hissed. "Steady all!" He stood up; he raised his voice: "I say, Ronnie." Ronnie did not turn his head, but Bogard could tell that he was listening. "That Argentine ship was amusing, eh? In there. How do you suppose it got past us here? Might have stopped here as well. French would buy the wheat." He paused, diabolical—Machiavelli with the face of a strayed angel. "I say. How long has it been since we had a strange ship in here? Been months, eh?" Again he leaned, hissing. "Watch, now!" But Bogard could not see Ronnie's head move at all. "He's looking, though!" the boy whispered, breathed. And Ronnie was looking, though his head had not moved at all. Then there came into view, in silhouette against the dusk-filled sky, the vague, basketlike shape of the interned vessel's foremast. At once Ronnie's arm rose, pointing; again he spoke without turning his head, out of the side of his mouth, past the cold, clamped pipe, a single word:

"Beaver."

The boy moved like a released spring, like a heeled dog freed. "Oh, damn you!" he cried. "Oh, you putt! It's the Ergenstrasse! Oh, confound you! I'm just one down now!" He had stepped in one stride completely over Bogard, and he now leaned down over Ronnie. "What?" The boat was slowing in toward the wharf, the engine idle. "Aren't I, Ronnie? Just one down now?"

The boat drifted in; the seaman had again crawled forward onto the deck. Ronnie spoke for the third and last time. "Right," he said.

IX

"I want," Bogard said, "a case of Scotch. The best we've got. And fix it up good. It's to go to town. And I want a responsible man to deliver it." The responsible man came. "This is for a child," Bogard said, indicating the package. "You'll find him in the Street of the Twelve Hours, somewhere near the Café Twelve Hours. He'll be in the gutter. You'll know him. A child about six feet long. Any English M.P. will show him to you. If he is asleep, don't wake him. Just sit there and wait until he wakes up. Then give him this. Tell him it is from Captain Bogard."

X

About a month later a copy of the English Gazette which had strayed onto an American aerodrome carried the following item in the casualty lists:

> MISSING: Torpedo Boat XOOI. Midshipmen R. Boyce Smith and L. C. W. Hope, R. N. R., Boatswain's Mate Burt and Able Seaman Reeves. Channel Fleet, Light Torpedo Division. Failed to return from coast patrol duty.

Shortly after that the American Air Service headquarters also issued a bulletin:

> For extraordinary valor over and beyond the routine of duty, Captain H. S. Bogard, with his crew, composed of Second Lieutenant Darrel McGinnis and Aviation Gunners Watts and Harper, on a daylight raid and without scout protection, destroyed with bombs an ammunition depot several miles behind the enemy's lines. From here, beset by enemy aircraft in superior numbers, these men proceeded with what bombs remained to the enemy's corps headquarters at Blank and partially demolished this château, and then returned safely without loss of a man.

And regarding which exploit, it might have added, had it failed and had Captain Bogard come out of it alive, he would have been immediately and thoroughly court-martialed.

Carrying his remaining two bombs, he had dived that Handley-Page at the château where the generals sat at lunch, until McGinnis, at the toggles below him, began to shout at him, before he ever signaled. He didn't signal until he could discern separately the slate tiles of the roof. Then his hand dropped and he zoomed, and he held the aeroplane so, in its wild snarl, his lips parted, his breath hissing, thinking: "God! God! If they were all there—all the generals, the admirals, the presidents and the kings—theirs, ours—all of them."

Honor

I walked right through the anteroom without stopping. Miss West says, "He's in conference now," but I didn't stop. I didn't knock, either. They were talking and he quit and looked up across the desk at me.

"How much notice do you want to write me off?" I said.

"Write you off?" he said.

"I'm quitting," I said. "Will one day be notice enough?"

He looked at me, frog-eyed. "Isn't our car good enough for you to demonstrate?" he said. His hand lay on the desk, holding the cigar. He's got a ruby ring the size of a tail-light. "You've been with us three weeks," he says. "Not long enough to learn what that word on the door means."

He don't know it, but three weeks is pretty good; it's within two days of the record. And if three weeks is a record with him, he could have shaken hands with the new champion without moving.

The trouble is, I had never learned to do anything. You know how it was in those days, with even the college campuses full of British and French uniforms, and us all scared to death it would be over before we could get in and swank a pair of pilot's wings ourselves. And then to get in and find something that suited you right down to the ground, you see.

So after the Armistice I stayed in for a couple of years as a test pilot. That was when I took up wing-walking, to relieve the monotony. A fellow named Waldrip and I used to hide out at about three thousand on a Nine while I muscled around on top of it. Because Army life is pretty dull in peacetime: nothing to do but lay around and lie your head off all day and play poker all night. And isolation is bad for poker. You lose on tick, and on tick you always plunge.

There was a fellow named White lost a thousand one night. He kept on losing and I wanted to quit but I was winner and he wanted to play on, plunging and losing every pot. He gave me a check and I told him it wasn't any rush, to forget it, because he had a wife out in California. Then the next night he wanted to play again. I tried to talk him out of it, but he got mad. Called me yellow. So he lost fifteen hundred more that night.

Then I said I'd cut him, double or quit, one time. He cut a queen. So I said, "Well, that beats me. I won't even cut." And I flipped his cut over and riffled them and we saw a gob of face cards and three of the aces. But he insisted, and I said, "What's the use? The percentage would be against me, even with a full deck." But he insisted. I cut the case ace. I would have paid to lose. I offered again to tear up the checks, but he sat there and cursed me. I left him sitting at the table in his shirt sleeves and his collar open, looking at the ace.

The next day we had the job, the speed ship. I had done everything I could. I couldn't offer him the checks again. I will let a man who is worked up curse me once. But I won't let him twice. So we had the job, the speed ship. I wouldn't touch it. He took it up five thousand feet and dived the wings off at two thousand with a full gun.

So I was out again after four years, a civ again. And while I was still drifting around—that was when I first tried selling automobiles—I met Jack, and he told me about a bird that wanted a wing-walker for his barnstorming circus. And that was how I met her.

II

Jack—he gave me a note to Rogers—told me about what a good pilot Rogers was, and about her, how they said she was unhappy with him.

"So is your old man," I said.

"That's what they say," Jack said. So when I saw Rogers and handed him the note—he was one of these lean, quiet-looking birds—I said to myself he was just the kind that would marry one of these flighty, passionate, good-looking women they used to catch during the war with a set of wings, and have her run out on him the first chance. So I felt safe. I knew she'd not have had to wait any three years for one like me.

So I expected to find one of these long, dark, snakelike women surrounded by ostrich plumes and Woolworth incense, smoking cigarettes on the divan while Rogers ran out to the corner delicatessen for sliced ham and potato salad on paper plates. But I was wrong. She came in with an apron on over one of these little pale squashy dresses, with flour or something on her arms, without apologizing or flurrying around or anything. She said Howard—that was Rogers—had told her about me and I said, "What did he tell you?" But she just said:

"I expect you'll find this pretty dull for spending the evening, having to help cook your own dinner. I imagine you'd rather go out to dance with a couple of bottles of gin."

"Why do you think that?" I said. "Don't I look like I could do anything else?"

"Oh, don't you?" she said.

We had washed the dishes then and we were sitting in the firelight, with the lights off, with her on a cushion on the floor, her back against Rogers' knees, smoking and talking, and she said, "I know you had a dull time. Howard suggested that we go out for dinner and to dance somewhere. But I told him you'd just have to take us as we are, first as well as later. Are you sorry?"

She could look about sixteen, especially in the apron. By that time she had bought one for me to wear, and the three of us would all go back to the kitchen and cook dinner. "We don't expect you to enjoy doing this any more than we do," she said. "It's because we are so poor. We're just an aviator."

"Well, Howard can fly well enough for two people," I said. "So that's all right, too."

"When he told me you were just a flyer too, I said, 'My Lord, a wing-walker? When you were choosing a family friend,' I said, 'why didn't you choose a man we could invite to dinner a week ahead and not only count on his being there, but on his taking us out and spending his money on us?' But he had to choose one that is as poor as we are." And once she said to Rogers: "We'll have to find Buck a girl, too. He's going to get tired of just us some day." You know how they say things like that: things that sound like they meant something until you look at them and find their eyes perfectly blank, until you wonder if they were even thinking about you, let alone talking about you.

Or maybe I'd have them out to dinner and a show. "Only I didn't mean that like it sounded," she said. "That wasn't a hint to take us out."

"Did you mean that about getting me a girl too?" I said.

Then she looked at me with that wide, blank, innocent look. That was when I would take them by my place for a cocktail—Rogers didn't drink, himself—and when I would come in that night I'd find traces of powder on my dresser or maybe her handkerchief or something, and I'd go to bed with the room smelling like she was still there. She said: "Do you want us to find you one?" But nothing more was ever said about it, and after a while, when there was a high step or any of those little things which men do for women that means touching them, she'd turn to me like it was me was her husband and not him; and one night a storm caught us downtown and we went to my place and she and Rogers slept in my bed and I slept in a chair in the sitting-room.

One evening I was dressing to go out there when the 'phone rang. It was Rogers. "I am—" he said, then something cut him off. It was like somebody had put a hand on his mouth, and I could hear them talking, murmuring: her, rather. "Well, what—" Roger says. Then I could hear her breathing into the mouth-piece, and she said my name.

"Don't forget you're to come out tonight," she said.

"I hadn't," I said. "Or did I get the date wrong? If this is not the night—"

"You come on out," she said. "Goodbye."

When I got there he met me. His face looked like it always did, but I didn't go in. "Come on in," he said.

"Maybe I got the date wrong," I said. "So if you'll just—"

He swung the door back. "Come on in," he said.

She was lying on the divan, crying. I don't know what; something about money. "I just can't stick it," she said. "I've tried and I've tried, but I just can't stand it."

"You know what my insurance rates are," he said. "If something happened, where would you be?"

"Where am I, anyway? What tenement woman hasn't got more than I have?" She hadn't looked up, lying there on her face, with the apron twisted under her. "Why don't you quit and do something that you can get a decent insurance rate, like other men?"

"I must be getting along," I said. I didn't belong there. I just got out. He came down to the door with me, and then we were both looking back up the stairs toward the door where she was lying on her face on the couch.

"I've got a little stake," I said. "I guess because I've eaten so much of your grub I haven't had time to spend it. So if it's anything urgent. . . ." We stood there, he holding the door open. "Of course, I wouldn't try to muscle in where I don't . . ."

"I wouldn't, if I were you," he said. He opened the door. "See you at the field tomorrow."

"Sure," I said. "See you at the field."

I didn't see her for almost a week, didn't hear from

her. I saw him every day, and at last I said, "How's Mildred these days?"

"She's on a visit," he said. "At her mother's."

For the next two weeks I was with him every day. When I was out on top I'd look back at his face behind the goggles. But we never mentioned her name, until one day he told me she was home again and that I was invited out to dinner that night.

It was in the afternoon. He was busy all that day hopping passengers, so I was doing nothing, just killing time waiting for evening and thinking about her, wondering some, but mostly just thinking about her being home again, breathing the same smoke and soot I was breathing, when all of a sudden I decided to go out there. It was plain as a voice saying, "Go out there. Now, at once." So I went. I didn't even wait to change. She was alone, reading before the fire. It was like gasoline from a broken line blazing up around you.

III

It was funny. When I'd be out on top I'd look back at his face behind the windscreen, wondering what he knew. He must have known almost at once. Why, say, she didn't have any discretion at all. She'd say and do things, you know: insist on sitting close to me; touching me in that different way from when you hold an umbrella or a raincoat over them, and such that any man can tell at one look, when she thought he might not see: not when she knew he couldn't, but when she thought *maybe* he wouldn't. And when I'd unfasten my belt and crawl out

I'd look back at his face and wonder what he was thinking, how much he knew or suspected.

I'd go out there in the afternoon when he was busy. I'd stall around until I saw that he would be lined up for the rest of the day, then I'd give some excuse and beat it. One afternoon I was all ready to go, waiting for him to take off, when he cut the gun and leaned out and beckoned me. "Don't go off," he said. "I want to see you."

So I knew he knew then, and I waited until he made the last hop and was taking off his monkey suit in the office. He looked at me and I looked at him. "Come out to dinner," he said.

When I came in they were waiting. She had on one of those little squashy dresses and she came and put her arms around me and kissed me with him watching.

"I'm going with you," she said. "We've talked it over and have both agreed that we couldn't love one another any more after this and that this is the only sensible thing to do. Then he can find a woman he can love, a woman that's not bad like I am."

He was looking at me, and she running her hands over my face and making a little moaning sound against my neck, and me like a stone or something. Do you know what I was thinking? I wasn't thinking about her at all. I was thinking that he and I were upstairs and me out on top and I had just found that he had thrown the stick away and was flying her on the rudder alone and that he knew that I knew the stick was gone and so it was all right now, whatever happened. So it was like a piece of wood with another piece of wood leaning against it, and she held back and looked at my face.

"Don't you love me any more?" she said, watching my face. "If you love me, say so. I have told him everything."

I wanted to be out of there. I wanted to run. I wasn't scared. It was because it was all kind of hot and dirty. I wanted to be away from her a little while, for Rogers and me to be out where it was cold and hard and quiet, to settle things.

"What do you want to do?" I said. "Will you give her a divorce?"

She was watching my face very closely. Then she let me go and she ran to the mantel and put her face into the bend of her arm, crying.

"You were lying to me," she said. "You didn't mean what you said. Oh God, what have I done?"

You know how it is. Like there is a right time for everything. Like nobody is anything in himself: like a woman, even when you love her, is a woman to you just a part of the time and the rest of the time she is just a person that don't look at things the same way a man has learned to. Don't have the same ideas about what is decent and what is not. So I went over and stood with my arms about her, thinking, "God damn it, if you'll just keep out of this for a little while! We're both trying our best to take care of you, so it won't hurt you."

Because I loved her, you see. Nothing can marry two people closer than a mutual sin in the world's eyes. And he had had his chance. If it had been me that knew her first and married her and he had been me, I would have had my chance. But it was him that had had it, so when she said, "Then say what you tell me when we are alone. I tell you I have told him everything," I said:

"Everything? Have you told him everything?" He was watching us. "Has she told you everything?" I said.

"It doesn't matter," he said. "Do you want her?" Then before I could speak, he said: "Do you love her? Will you be good to her?"

His face was gray-looking, like when you see a man again after a long time and you say, "Good God, is that Rogers?" When I finally got away the divorce was all settled.

IV

So the next morning when I reached the field, Harris, the man who owned the flying circus, told me about the special job; I had forgotten it, I suppose. Anyway, he said he had told me about it. Finally I said I wouldn't fly with Rogers.

"Why not?" Harris said.

"Ask him," I said.

"If he agrees to fly you, will you go up?"

So I said yes. And then Rogers came out; he said that he would fly me. And so I believed that he had known about the job all the time and had laid for me, sucked me in. We waited until Harris went out. "So this is why you were so mealy-mouthed last night," I said. I cursed him. "You've got me now, haven't you?"

"Take the stick yourself," he said. "I'll do your trick."

"Have you ever done any work like this before?"

"No. But I can, as long as you fly her properly."

I cursed him. "You feel good," I said. "You've got me. Come on; grin on the outside of your face. Come on!"

He turned and went to the crate and began to get into

the front seat. I went and caught his shoulder and jerked him back. We looked at one another.

"I won't hit you now," he said, "if that's what you want. Wait till we get down again."

"No," I said. "Because I want to hit back once."

We looked at one another; Harris was watching us from the office.

"All right," Rogers said. "Let me have your shoes, will you? I haven't got any rubber soles out here."

"Take your seat," I said. "What the hell does it matter? I guess I'd do the same thing in your place."

The job was over an amusement park, a carnival. There must have been twenty-five thousand of them down there, like colored ants. I took chances that day that I had never taken, chances you can't see from the ground. But every time the ship was right under me, balancing me against side pressure and all, like he and I were using the same mind. I thought he was playing with me, you see. I'd look back at his face, yelling at him: "Come on; now you've got me. Where are your guts?"

I was a little crazy, I guess. Anyway, when I think of the two of us up there, yelling back and forth at one another, and all the little bugs watching and waiting for the big show, the loop. He could hear me, but I couldn't hear him; I could just see his lips moving. "Come on," I'd yell; "shake the wing a little; I'll go off easy, see?"

I was a little crazy. You know how it is, how you want to rush into something you know is going to happen, no matter what it is. I guess lovers and suicides both know that feeling. I'd yell back at him: "You want it to look all right, eh? And to lose me off the level ship wouldn't look so good, would it? All right," I yelled, "let's go." I went back to the center section and cast the rope loose where it loops around the forward jury struts and I got set against it and looked back at him and gave him the signal. I was a little crazy. I was still yelling at him; I don't know what I was yelling. I thought maybe I had already fallen off and was dead and didn't know it. The wires began to whine and I was looking straight down at the ground and the little colored dots. Then the wires were whistling proper and he gunned her and the ground began to slide back under the nose. I waited until it was gone and the horizon had slid back under too and I couldn't see anything but sky. Then I let go one end of the rope and jerked it out and threw it back at his head and held my arms out as she zoomed into the loop.

I wasn't trying to kill myself. I wasn't thinking about myself. I was thinking about him. Trying to show him up like he had shown me up. Give him something he must fail at like he had given me something I failed at. I was trying to break him.

We were over the loop before he lost me. The ground had come back, with the little colored dots, and then the pressure went off my soles and I was falling. I made a half somersault and was just going into the first turn of a flat spin, with my face to the sky, when something banged me in the back. It knocked the wind out of me, and for a second I must have been completely out. Then I opened my eyes and I was lying on my back on the top wing, with my head hanging over the back edge.

I was too far down the slope of the camber to bend my knees over the leading edge, and I could feel the wing creeping under me. I didn't dare move. I knew that if I tried to sit up against the slip stream, I would go off backward. I could see by the tail and the horizon that we were upside down now, in a shallow dive, and I could see Rogers standing up in his cockpit, unfastening his belt, and I could turn my head a little more and see that when I went off I would miss the fuselage altogether, or maybe hit it with my shoulder.

So I lay there with the wing creeping under me, feeling my shoulders beginning to hang over space, counting my backbones as they crept over the edge, watching Rogers crawl forward along the fuselage toward the front seat. I watched him for a long time, inching himself along against the pressure, his trouser-legs whipping. After a while I saw his legs slide into the front cockpit and then I felt his hands on me.

There was a fellow in my squadron. I didn't like him and he hated my guts. All right. One day he got me out of a tight jam when I was caught ten miles over the lines with a blowing valve. When we were down he said, "Don't think I was just digging you out. I was getting a Hun, and I got him." He cursed me, with his goggles cocked up and his hands on his hips, cursing me like he was smiling. But that's all right. You're each on a Camel; if you go out, that's too bad; if he goes out, it's just too bad. Not like when you're on the center section and he's at the stick, and just by stalling her for a second or ruddering her a little at the top of the loop.

But I was young, then. Good Lord, I used to be young! I remember Armistice night in '18, and me chasing all over Amiens with a lousy prisoner we had brought down that morning on an Albatross, trying to keep the frog M.P.'s from getting him. He was a good guy, and those damned infantrymen wanting to stick him in a pen full of S.O.S. and ginned-up cooks and such. I felt sorry for the bastard being so far from home and licked and all. I was sure young.

We were all young. I remember an Indian, a prince, an Oxford man, with his turban and his trick major's pips, that said we were all dead that fought in the war. "You will not know it," he said, "but you are all dead. With this difference: those out there"—jerking his arm toward where the front was—"do not care, and you do not know it." And something else he said, about breathing for a long time yet, some kind of walking funerals; catafalques and tombs and epitaphs of men that died on the fourth of August, 1914, without knowing that they had died, he said. He was a card, queer. A good little guy, too.

But I wasn't quite dead while I was lying on the top wing of that Standard and counting my backbones as they crawled over the edge like a string of ants, until Rogers grabbed me. And when he came to the station that night to say goodbye, he brought me a letter from her, the first I ever had. The handwriting looked exactly like her; I could almost smell the scent she used and feel her hands touching me. I tore it in two without opening it and threw the pieces down. But he picked them up and gave them back to me. "Don't be a fool," he said.

And that's all. They've got a kid now, a boy of six. Rogers wrote me; about six months afterward the letter caught up with me. I'm his godfather. Funny to have a godfather that's never seen you and that you'll never see, isn't it?

V

So I said to Reinhardt: "Will one day be enough notice?"

"One minute will be enough," he said. He pressed the buzzer. Miss West came in. She is a good kid. Now and then, when I'd just have to blow off some steam, she and I would have lunch at the dairy place across the street, and I could tell her about them, about the women. They are the worst. You know; you get a call for a demonstration, and there'll be a whole car full of them waiting on the porch and we'd pile in and all go shopping. Me dodging around in the traffic, hunting a place to park, and her saying, "John insisted that I try this car. But what I tell him, it's foolish to buy a car that is as difficult to find parking space for as this one appears to be."

And them watching the back of my head with that bright, hard, suspicious way. God knows what they thought we had; maybe one that would fold up like a deck chair and lean against a fire plug. But hell, I couldn't sell hair straightener to the widow of a nigger railroad accident.

So Miss West comes in; she is a good kid, only somebody told her I had had three or four other jobs in a year without sticking, and that I used to be a war pilot, and she'd keep on after me about why I quit flying and why I didn't go back to it, now that crates were more general, since I wasn't much good at selling automobiles or at anything else, like women will. You know: urgent and sympathetic, and you can't shut them up like you could a man; she came in and Reinhardt says, "We are letting Mr. Monaghan go. Send him to the cashier."

"Don't bother," I said. "Keep it to buy yourself a hoop with."

There Was a Queen

Elnora entered the back yard, coming up from her cabin. In the long afternoon the huge, square house, the premises, lay somnolent, peaceful, as they had lain for almost a hundred years, since John Sartoris had come from Carolina and built it. And he had died in it and his son Bayard had died in it, and Bayard's son John and John's son Bayard in turn had been buried from it even though the last Bayard didn't die there.

So the quiet was now the quiet of womenfolks. As Elnora crossed the back yard toward the kitchen door she remembered how ten years ago at this hour old Bayard, who was her half-brother (though possibly but not probably neither of them knew it, including Bayard's father), would be tramping up and down the back porch, shouting stableward for the Negro men and for his saddle mare. But he was dead now, and his grandson Bayard was also dead at twenty-six years old, and the Negro men were gone: Simon, Elnora's mother's husband, in the graveyard too, and Caspey, Elnora's husband, in the penitentiary for stealing, and Joby, her son, gone to Memphis to wear fine clothes on Beale Street. So there were left in the house only the first John Sartoris' sister, Virginia, who was ninety years old and who lived in a wheel chair beside a window above the flower garden, and Narcissa, young Bayard's widow, and her son. Virginia Du Pre had come out to Mississippi in '69, the last of the Carolina family, bringing with her the clothes in which she stood and a basket containing a few panes of colored glass from a Carolina window and a few flower cuttings and two bottles of port. She had seen her brother die and then her nephew and then her great-nephew and then her two great-great-nephews, and now she lived in the unmanned house with her great-great-nephew's wife and his son, Benbow, whom she persisted in calling Johnny after his uncle, who was killed in France. And for Negroes there were Elnora who cooked, and her son Isom who tended the grounds, and her daughter Saddie who slept on a cot beside Virginia Du Pre's bed and tended her as though she were a baby.

But that was all right. "I can take care of her," Elnora thought, crossing the back yard. "I don't need no help," she said aloud, to no one—a tall, coffee-colored woman with a small, high, fine head. "Because it's a Sartoris job. Cunnel knowed that when he died and tole me to take care of her. Tole me. Not no outsiders from town." She was thinking of what had caused her to come up to the house an hour before it was necessary. This was that, while busy in her cabin, she had seen Narcissa, young Bayard's wife, and the ten-year-old boy going down across the pasture in the middle of the afternoon. She had come to her door and watched them—the boy and the big young woman in white going through the hot afternoon, down across the pasture toward the creek. She had not wondered where they were going, nor why, as a white woman would have wondered. But she was half black, and she just watched the white woman with that expression of quiet and grave contempt with which she contemplated or listened to the orders of the wife of the house's heir even while he was alive. Just as she had listened two days ago when Narcissa had informed her that she was going to Memphis for a day or so and that Elnora would have to take care of the old aunt alone. "Like I ain't always done it," Elnora thought. "It's little you done for anybody since you come out here. We never needed you. Don't you never think it." But she didn't say this. She just thought it, and she helped Narcissa prepare for the trip and watched the carriage roll away toward town and the station without comment. "And you needn't to come back," she thought, watching the carriage disappear. But this morning Narcissa had returned, without offering to explain the sudden journey or the sudden return, and in the early afternoon Elnora from her cabin door had watched the woman and the boy go down across the pasture in the hot June sunlight.

"Well, it's her business where she going," Elnora said aloud, mounting the kitchen steps. "Same as it her business how come she went off to Memphis, leaving Miss Jenny setting yonder in her chair without nobody but niggers to look after her," she added, aloud still, with brooding inconsistency. "I ain't surprised she went. I just surprised she come back. No. I ain't even that. She ain't going to leave this place, now she done got in here." Then she said quietly, aloud, without rancor, without heat: "Trash. Town trash."

She entered the kitchen. Her daughter Saddie sat at the table, eating from a dish of cold turnip greens and looking at a thumbed and soiled fashion magazine. "What you doing back here?" she said. "Why ain't you up yonder where you can hear Miss Jenny if she call you?"

"Miss Jenny ain't need nothing," Saddie said. "She setting there by the window."

"Where did Miss Narcissa go?"

"I don't know'm," Saddie said. "Her and Bory went off somewhere. Ain't come back yet."

Elnora grunted. Her shoes were not laced, and she stepped out of them in two motions and left the kitchen and went up the quiet, high-ceiled hall filled with scent from the garden and with the drowsing and myriad sounds of the June afternoon, to the open library door. Beside the window (the sash was raised now, with its narrow border of colored Carolina glass which in the winter framed her head and bust like a hung portrait) an old woman sat in a wheel chair. She sat erect; a thin, upright woman with a delicate nose and hair the color of a whitewashed wall. About her shoulders lay a shawl of white wool, no whiter than her hair against her black dress. She was looking out the window; in profile her face was high-arched, motionless. When Elnora entered she turned her head and looked at the Negress with an expression immediate and interrogative.

"They ain't come in the back way, have they?" she said.

"Nome," Elnora said. She approached the chair.

The old woman looked out the window again. "I must say I don't understand this at all. Miss Narcissa's doing a mighty lot of traipsing around all of a sudden. Picking up and—"

Elnora came to the chair. "A right smart," she said in her cold, quiet voice, "for a woman lazy as her."

"Picking up—" the old woman said. She ceased. "You stop talking that way about her."

"I ain't said nothing but the truth," Elnora said.

"Then you keep it to yourself. She's Bayard's wife. A Sartoris woman, now."

"She won't never be a Sartoris woman," Elnora said.

The other was looking out the window. "Picking up all of a sudden two days ago and going to Memphis to spend two nights, that hadn't spent a night away from that boy since he was born. Leaving him for two whole nights, mind you, without giving any reason, and then coming home and taking him off to walk in the woods in the middle of the day. Not that he missed her. Do you think he missed her at all while she was gone?"

"Nome," Elnora said. "Ain't no Sartoris man never missed nobody."

"Of course he didn't." The old woman looked out the window. Elnora stood a little behind the chair. "Did they go on across the pasture?"

"I don't know. They went out of sight, still going. Toward the creek."

"Toward the creek? What in the world for?"

Elnora didn't answer. She stood a little behind the chair, erect, still as an Indian. The afternoon was drawing on. The sun was now falling level across the garden below the window, and soon the jasmine in the garden began to smell with evening, coming into the room in slow waves almost palpable; thick, sweet, oversweet. The two women were motionless in the window: the one leaning a little forward in the wheel chair, the Negress a little behind the chair, motionless too and erect as a caryatid.

The light in the garden was beginning to turn copper-colored when the woman and the boy entered the garden and approached the house. The old woman in the chair leaned suddenly forward. To Elnora it seemed as if the old woman in the wheel chair had in that motion escaped her helpless body like a bird and crossed the garden to meet the child; moving forward a little herself Elnora could see on the other's face an expression fond, immediate, and oblivious. So the two people had crossed the garden and were almost to the house when the old woman sat suddenly and sharply back. "Why, they're wet!" she said. "Look at their clothes. They have been in the creek with their clothes on!"

"I reckon I better go and get supper started," Elnora said.

II

In the kitchen Elnora prepared the lettuce and the tomatoes, and sliced the bread (not honest cornbread, not even biscuit) which the woman whose very name she did not speak unless it was absolutely necessary, had taught her to bake. Isom and Saddie sat in two chairs against the wall. "I got nothing against her," Elnora said. "I nigger and she white. But my black children got more blood than she got. More behavior."

"You and Miss Jenny both think ain't nobody been born since Miss Jenny," Isom said.

"Who is been?" Elnora said.

"Miss Jenny get along all right with Miss Narcissa," Isom said. "Seem to me like she the one to say. I ain't heard her say nothing about it."

"Because Miss Jenny quality," Elnora said. "That's why. And that's something you don't know nothing about, because you born too late to see any of it except her."

"Look to me like Miss Narcissa good quality as anybody else," Isom said. "I don't see no difference."

Elnora moved suddenly from the table. Isom as suddenly sprang up and moved his chair out of his mother's path. But she only went to the cupboard and took a platter from it and returned to the table, to the tomatoes. "Born Sartoris or born quality of any kind ain't *is,* it's *does.*" She talked in a level, inflectionless voice above her limber, brown, deft hands. When she spoke of the two women she used "she" indiscriminately, putting the least inflection on the one which referred to Miss Jenny. "Come all the way here by Herself, and the country still full of Yankees. All the way from Cal-lina, with Her folks all killed and dead except old Marse John, and him two hundred miles away in Missippi—"

"It's moren two hundred miles from here to Cal-lina," Isom said. "Learnt that in school. It's nigher two thousand."

Elnora's hands did not cease. She did not seem to have heard him. "With the Yankees done killed Her paw and Her husband and burned the Cal-lina house over Her and Her mammy's head, and She come all the way to Missippi by Herself, to the only kin She had left. Getting here in the dead of winter without nothing in this world of God's but a basket with some flower seeds and two bottles of wine and them colored window panes old Marse John put in the library window so She could look through it like it was Cal-lina. She got here at dusk-dark on

Christmas Day and old Marse John and the chillen and my mammy waiting on the porch, and Her setting high-headed in the wagon for old Marse John to lift Her down. They never even kissed then, out where folks could see them. Old Marse John just said, 'Well, Jenny,' and she just said, 'Well, Johnny,' and they walked into the house, him leading Her by the hand, until they was inside the house where the commonalty couldn't spy on them. Then She begun to cry, and old Marse John holding Her, after all them four thousand miles—"

"It ain't four thousand miles from here to Cal-lina," Isom said. "Ain't but two thousand. What the book say in school."

Elnora paid no attention to him at all; her hands did not cease. "It took Her hard, the crying did. 'It's because I ain't used to crying,' she said. 'I got out of the habit of it. I never had the time. Them goddamn Yankees,' she said. 'Them goddamn Yankees.'" Elnora moved again, to the cupboard. It was as though she walked out of the sound of her voice on her silent, naked feet, leaving it to fill the quiet kitchen though the voice itself had ceased. She took another platter down and returned to the table, her hands busy again among the tomatoes and lettuce, the food which she herself could not eat. "And that's how it is that she" (she was now speaking of Narcissa; the two Negroes knew it) "thinks she can pick up and go to Memphis and frolic, and leave Her alone in this house for two nights without nobody but niggers to look after Her. Move out here under a Sartoris roof and eat Sartoris food for ten years, and then pick up and go to Memphis same as a nigger on a excursion, without even telling why she was going."

"I thought you said Miss Jenny never needed nobody but you to take care of her," Isom said. "I thought you said yesterday you never cared if she come back or not."

Elnora made a sound, harsh, disparaging, not loud. "Her not come back? When she worked for five years to get herself married to Bayard? Working on Miss Jenny all the time Bayard was off to that war? I watched her. Coming out here two or three times a week, with Miss Jenny thinking she was just coming out to visit like quality. But I knowed. I knowed what she was up to all the time. Because I knows trash. I knows the way trash goes about working in with quality. Quality can't see that, because it quality. But I can."

"Then Bory must be trash, too," Isom said.

Elnora turned now. But Isom was already out of his chair before she spoke. "You shut your mouth and get yourself ready to serve supper." She watched him go to the sink and prepare to wash his hands. Then she turned back to the table, her long hands brown and deft among the red tomatoes and the pale absinth-green of the lettuce. "Needings," she said. "It ain't Bory's needings and it ain't Her needings. It's dead folks' needings. Old Marse John's and Cunnel's and Mister John's and Bayard's that's dead and can't do nothing about it. That's where the needings is. That's what I'm talking about. And not nobody to see to it except Her yonder in that chair, and me, a nigger, back here in this kitchen. I ain't got nothing against her. I just say to let quality consort with quality, and unquality do the same thing. You get that coat on, now. This here is all ready."

III

It was the boy who told her. She leaned forward in the wheel chair and watched through the window as the woman and the child crossed the garden and passed out of sight beyond the angle of the house. Still leaning forward and looking down into the garden, she heard them enter the house and pass the library door and mount the stairs. She did not move, nor look toward the door. She continued to look down into the garden, at the now stout shrubs which she had fetched from Carolina as shoots not much bigger than matches. It was in the garden that she and the younger woman who was to marry her nephew and bear a son, had become acquainted. That was back in 1918, and young Bayard and his brother John were still in France. It was before John was killed, and two or three times a week Narcissa would come out from town to visit her while she worked among the flowers. "And she engaged to Bayard all the time and not telling me," the old woman thought. "But it was little she ever told me about anything," she thought, looking down into the garden which was beginning to fill with twilight and which she had not entered in five years. "Little enough about anything. Sometimes I wonder how she ever got herself engaged to Bayard, talking so little. Maybe she did it by just being, filling some space, like she got that letter." That was one day shortly before Bayard returned home. Narcissa came out and stayed for two hours, then just before she left she showed the letter. It was anonymous and obscene; it sounded mad, and at the time she had tried to get Narcissa to let her show the letter to Bayard's grandfather and have him make some effort to find the man and punish him, but Narcissa refused. "I'll just burn it and forget about it," Narcissa said. "Well, that's your business," the older woman said. "But that should not be permitted. A lady should not be at the mercy of a man like that, even by mail. Any gentleman will believe that, act upon it. Besides, if you don't do something about it, he'll write you again." "Then I'll show it to Colonel Sartoris," Narcissa said. She was an orphan, her brother also in France. "But can't you see I just can't have any man know that anybody thought such things about me." "Well, I'd rather have the whole world know that somebody thought that way about me once and got horsewhipped for it, than to have him keep on thinking that way about me, unpunished. But it's your affair." "I'll just burn it and forget about it," Narcissa said. Then Bayard returned, and shortly afterward he and Narcissa were married and Narcissa came out to the house to live. Then she was pregnant, and before the child was born Bayard was killed in an airplane, and his grandfather, old Bayard, was dead and the child came, and it was two years before she thought to ask her niece if any more letters had come; and Narcissa told her no.

So they had lived quietly then, their women's life in the big house without men. Now and then she had urged Narcissa to marry again. But the other had refused, quietly, and they had gone on so for years, the two of them and the child whom she persisted in calling after his dead uncle. Then one evening a week ago, Narcissa had a guest for supper; when she learned that the guest was to be a man, she sat quite still in her chair for a time. "Ah," she thought, quietly. "It's come. Well. But it had to; she is young. And to live out here alone with a bedridden old woman. Well. But I wouldn't have her do as I did. Would not expect it of her. After all, she is not a Sartoris. She is no kin to them, to a lot of fool proud ghosts." The guest came. She did not see him until she was wheeled in to the supper table. Then she saw a bald, youngish man with a clever face and a Phi Beta Kappa key on his watch chain. The key she did not recognize, but she knew at once that he was a Jew, and when he spoke to her her outrage became fury and she jerked back in the chair like a striking snake, the motion strong enough to thrust the chair back from the table. "Narcissa," she said, "what is this Yankee doing here?"

There they were, about the candle-lit table, the three rigid people. Then the man spoke: "Madam," he said, "there'd be no Yankees left if your sex had ever taken the field against us."

"You don't have to tell me that, young man," she said. "You can thank your stars it was just men your grandfather fought." Then she had called Isom and had herself wheeled from the table, taking no supper. And even in her bedroom she would not let them turn on the light, and she refused the tray which Narcissa sent up. She sat beside her dark window until the stranger was gone.

Then three days later Narcissa made her sudden and mysterious trip to Memphis and stayed two nights, who had never before been separated overnight from her son since he was born. She had gone without explanation and returned without explanation, and now the old woman had just watched her and the boy cross the garden, their garments still damp upon them, as though they had been in the creek.

It was the boy who told her. He came into the room in fresh clothes, his hair still damp, though neatly combed now. She said no word as he entered and came to her chair. "We been in the creek," he said. "Not swimming, though. Just sitting in the water. She wanted me to show her the swimming hole. But we didn't swim. I don't reckon she can. We just sat in the water with our clothes on. All evening. She wanted to do it."

"Ah," the old woman said. "Oh. Well. That must have been fun. Is she coming down soon?"

"Yessum. When she gets dressed."

"Well. . . . You'll have time to go outdoors a while before supper, if you want to."

"I just as soon stay in here with you, if you want me to."

"No. You go outdoors. I'll be all right until Saddie comes."

"All right." He left the room.

The window faded slowly as the sunset died. The old woman's silver head faded too, like something motionless on a sideboard. The sparse colored panes which framed the window dreamed, rich and hushed. She sat there and presently she heard her nephew's wife descending the stairs. She sat quietly, watching the door, until the young woman entered.

She wore white: a large woman in her thirties, within the twilight something about her of that heroic quality of statuary. "Do you want the light?" she said.

"No," the old woman said. "No. Not yet." She sat erect in the wheel chair, motionless, watching the young woman cross the room, her white dress flowing slowly,

heroic, like a caryatid from a temple façade come to life.
She sat down.

"It was those let—" she said.

"Wait," the old woman said. "Before you begin. The
jasmine. Do you smell it?"

"Yes. It was those—"

"Wait. Always about this time of day it begins. It has
begun about this time of day in June for fifty-seven years
this summer. I brought them from Carolina, in a basket.
I remember how that first March I sat up all one night,
burning newspapers about the roots. Do you smell it?"

"Yes."

"If it's marriage, I told you. I told you five years ago
that I wouldn't blame you. A young woman, a widow.
Even though you have a child, I told you that a child
would not be enough. I told you I would not blame you
for not doing as I had done. Didn't I?"

"Yes. But it's not that bad."

"Not? Not how bad?" The old woman sat erect, her
head back a little, her thin face fading into the twilight
with a profound quality. "I won't blame you. I told you
that. You are not to consider me. My life is done; I need
little; nothing the Negroes can't do. Don't you mind me,
do you hear?" The other said nothing, motionless too,
serene; their voices seemed to materialize in the dusk
between them, unsourced of either mouth, either still and
fading face. "You'll have to tell me, then," the old woman
said.

"It was those letters. Thirteen years ago: don't you
remember? Before Bayard came back from France, before
you even knew that we were engaged. I showed you one

of them and you wanted to give it to Colonel Sartoris and let him find out who sent it and I wouldn't do it and you said that no lady would permit herself to receive anonymous love letters, no matter how badly she wanted to."

"Yes. I said it was better for the world to know that a lady had received a letter like that, than to have one man in secret thinking such things about her, unpunished. You told me you burned it."

"I lied. I kept it. And I got ten more of them. I didn't tell you because of what you said about a lady."

"Ah," the old woman said.

"Yes. I kept them all. I thought I had them hidden where nobody could ever find them."

"And you read them again. You would take them out now and then and read them again."

"I thought I had them hidden. Then you remember that night after Bayard and I were married when somebody broke into our house in town; the same night that bookkeeper in Colonel Sartoris' bank stole that money and ran away? The next morning the letters were gone, and then I knew who had sent them."

"Yes," the old woman said. She had not moved, her fading head like something inanimate in silver.

"So they were out in the world. They were somewhere. I was crazy for a while. I thought of people, men, reading them, seeing not only my name on them, but the marks of my eyes where I had read them again and again. I was wild. When Bayard and I were on our honeymoon, I was wild. I couldn't even think about him alone. It was like I was having to sleep with all the men in the world at the same time.

"Then it was almost twelve years ago, and I had Bory,

and I supposed I had got over it. Got used to having them out in the world. Maybe I had begun to think that they were gone, destroyed, and I was safe. Now and then I would remember them, but it was like somehow that Bory was protecting me, that they couldn't pass him to reach me. As though if I just stayed out here and was good to Bory and you—And then, one afternoon, after twelve years, that man came out to see me, that Jew. The one who stayed to supper that night."

"Ah," the old woman said. "Yes."

"He was a Federal agent. They were still trying to catch the man who had robbed the bank, and the agent had got hold of my letters. Found them where the book-keeper had lost them or thrown them away that night while he was running away, and the agent had had them twelve years, working on the case. At last he came out to see me, trying to find out where the man had gone, think-ing I must know, since the man had written me letters like that. You remember him: how you looked at him and you said, 'Narcissa, who is this Yankee?' "

"Yes. I remember."

"That man had my letters. He had had them for twelve years. He—"

"*Had* had?" the old woman said. "*Had* had?"

"Yes. I have them now. He hadn't sent them to Wash-ington yet, so nobody had read them except him. And now nobody will ever read them." She ceased; she breathed quietly, tranquil. "You don't understand yet, do you? He had all the information the letters could give him, but he would have to turn them in to the Depart-ment anyway and I asked him for them but he said he would have to turn them in and I asked him if he would make his final decision in Memphis and he said why Memphis and I told him why. I knew I couldn't buy them from him with money, you see. That's why I had to go to Memphis. I had that much regard for Bory and you, to go somewhere else. And that's all. Men are all about the same, with their ideas of good and bad. Fools." She breathed quietly. Then she yawned, deep, with utter relaxation. Then she stopped yawning. She looked again at the rigid, fading silver head opposite her. "Don't you understand yet?" she said. "I had to do it. They were mine; I had to get them back. That was the only way I could do it. But I would have done more than that. So I got them. And now they are burned up. Nobody will ever see them. Because he can't tell, you see. It would ruin him to ever tell that they even existed. They might even put him in the penitentiary. And now they are burned up."

"Yes," the old woman said. "And so you came back home and you took Johnny so you and he could sit together in the creek, the running water. In Jordan. Yes, Jordan at the back of a country pasture in Missippi."

"I had to get them back. Don't you see that?"

"Yes," the old woman said. "Yes." She sat bolt upright in the wheel chair. "Well, my Lord. Us poor, fool women—Johnny!" Her voice was sharp, peremptory.

"What?" the young woman said. "Do you want something?"

"No," the other said. "Call Johnny. I want my hat." The young woman rose. "I'll get it."

"No. I want Johnny to do it."

The young woman stood looking down at the other, the old woman erect in the wheel chair beneath the fading silver crown of her hair. Then she left the room. The old woman did not move. She sat there in the dusk until the boy entered, carrying a small black bonnet of an ancient shape. Now and then, when the old woman became upset, they would fetch her the hat and she would place it on the exact top of her head and sit there by the window. He brought the bonnet to her. His mother was with him. It was full dusk now; the old woman was invisible save for her hair. "Do you want the light now?" the young woman said.

"No," the old woman said. She set the bonnet on the top of her head. "You all go on to supper and let me rest a while. Go on, all of you." They obeyed, leaving her sitting there: a slender, erect figure indicated only by the single gleam of her hair, in the wheel chair beside the window framed by the sparse and defunctive Carolina glass.

IV

Since the boy's eighth birthday, he had had his dead grandfather's place at the end of the table. Tonight however his mother rearranged things. "With just the two of us," she said. "You come and sit by me." The boy hesitated. "Please. Won't you? I got so lonesome for you last night in Memphis. Weren't you lonesome for me?"

"I slept with Aunt Jenny," the boy said. "We had a good time."

"Please."

"All right," he said. He took the chair beside hers.

"Closer," she said. She drew the chair closer. "But we won't ever again, ever. Will we?" She leaned toward him, taking his hand.

"What? Sit in the creek?"

"Not ever leave one another again."

"I didn't get lonesome. We had a good time."

"Promise. Promise, Bory." His name was Benbow, her family name.

"All right."

Isom, in a duck jacket, served them and returned to the kitchen.

"She ain't coming to supper?" Elnora said.

"Nome," Isom said. "Setting yonder by the window, in the dark. She say she don't want no supper."

Elnora looked at Saddie. "What was they doing last time you went to the library?"

"Her and Miss Narcissa talking."

"They was still talking when I went to 'nounce supper," Isom said. "I tole you that."

"I know," Elnora said. Her voice was not sharp. Neither was it gentle. It was just peremptory, soft, cold. "What were they talking about?"

"I don't know'm," Isom said. "You the one taught me not to listen to white folks."

"What were they talking about, Isom?" Elnora said. She was looking at him, grave, intent, commanding.

" 'Bout somebody getting married. Miss Jenny say 'I tole you long time ago I ain't blame you. A young woman like you. I want you to marry. Not do like I done,' what she say."

"I bet she fixing to marry, too," Saddie said.

"Who marry?" Elnora said. "Her marry? What for? Give up what she got here? That ain't what it is. I wished I knowed what been going on here this last week. . . ." Her voice ceased; she turned her head toward the door as though she were listening for something. From the dining room came the sound of the young woman's voice. But Elnora appeared to listen to something beyond this. Then she left the room. She did not go hurriedly, yet her long silent stride carried her from sight with an abruptness like that of an inanimate figure drawn on wheels, off a stage.

She went quietly up the dark hall, passing the dining-room door unremarked by the two people at the table. They sat close. The woman was talking, leaning toward the boy. Elnora went on without a sound: a converging of shadows upon which her lighter face seemed to float without body, her eyeballs faintly white. Then she stopped suddenly. She had not reached the library door, yet she stopped, invisible, soundless, her eyes suddenly quite luminous in her almost-vanished face, and she began to chant in faint sing-song: "Oh, Lawd; oh, Lawd," not loud. Then she moved, went swiftly on to the library door and looked into the room where beside the dead window the old woman sat motionless, indicated only by that faint single gleam of white hair, as though for ninety years life had died slowly up her spare, erect frame, to linger for a twilit instant about her head before going out, though life itself had ceased. Elnora looked for only an instant into the room. Then she turned and retraced her swift and silent steps to the dining-room door. The woman still leaned toward the boy, talking. They did not remark Elnora at once. She stood in the doorway, tall, not touching the jamb on either side. Her face was blank; she did not appear to be looking at, speaking to, any one.

"You better come quick, I reckon," she said in that soft, cold, peremptory voice.

Mountain Victory

Through the cabin window the five people watched the cavalcade toil up the muddy trail and halt at the gate. First came a man on foot, leading a horse. He wore a broad hat low on his face, his body shapeless in a weathered gray cloak from which his left hand emerged, holding the reins. The bridle was silvermounted, the horse a gaunt, mudsplashed, thoroughbred bay, wearing in place of saddle a navy blue army blanket bound on it by a piece of rope. The second horse was a shortbodied, bigheaded, scrub sorrel, also mudsplashed. It wore a bridle contrived of rope and wire, and an army saddle in which, perched high above the dangling stirrups, crouched a shapeless something larger than a child, which at that distance appeared to wear no garment or garments known to man.

One of the three men at the cabin window left it quickly. The others, without turning, heard him cross the room swiftly and then return, carrying a long rifle.

"No, you don't," the older man said.

"Don't you see that cloak?" the younger said. "That rebel cloak?"

"I wont have it," the other said. "They have surrendered. They have said they are whipped."

Through the window they watched the horses stop at

the gate. The gate was of sagging hickory, in a rock fence which straggled down a gaunt slope sharp in relief against the valley and a still further range of mountains dissolving into the low, dissolving sky.

They watched the creature on the second horse descend and hand his reins also into the same left hand of the man in gray that held the reins of the Thoroughbred. They watched the creature enter the gate and mount the path and disappear beyond the angle of the window. Then they heard it cross the porch and knock at the door. They stood there and heard it knock again.

After a while the older man said, without turning his head, "Go and see."

One of the women, the older one, turned from the window, her feet making no sound on the floor, since they were bare. She went to the front door and opened it. The chill, wet light of the dying April afternoon fell upon her—upon a small woman with a gnarled expressionless face, in a gray shapeless garment. Facing her across the sill was a creature a little larger than a large monkey, dressed in a voluminous blue overcoat of a private in the Federal army, with, tied tentlike over his head and falling about his shoulders, a piece of oilcloth which might have been cut square from the hood of a sutler's wagon; within the orifice the woman could see nothing whatever save the whites of two eyes, momentary and phantomlike, as with a single glance the Negro examined the woman standing barefoot in her faded calico garment, and took in the bleak and barren interior of the cabin hall.

"Marster Major Soshay Weddel send he compliments en say he wishful fo sleeping room fo heself en boy en two hawses," he said in a pompous, parrot-like voice. The woman looked at him. Her face was like a spent mask. "We been up yonder a ways, fighting dem Yankees," the Negro said. "Done quit now. Gwine back home."

The woman seemed to speak from somewhere behind her face, as though behind an effigy or a painted screen: "I'll ask him."

"We ghy pay you," the Negro said.

"Pay?" Pausing, she seemed to muse upon him. "Hit aint near a ho-tel on the mou-tin."

The Negro made a large gesture. "Dont make no diffunce. We done stayed de night in worse places den whut dis is. You just tell um it Marse Soshay Weddel." Then he saw that the woman was looking past him. He turned and saw the man in the worn gray cloak already halfway up the path from the gate. He came on and mounted the porch, removing with his left hand the broad slouched hat bearing the tarnished wreath of a Confederate field officer. He had a dark face, with dark eyes and black hair, his face at once thick yet gaunt, and arrogant. He was not tall, yet he topped the Negro by five or six inches. The cloak was weathered, faded about the shoulders where the light fell strongest. The skirts were bedraggled, frayed, mudsplashed: the garment had been patched again and again, and brushed again and again; the nap was completely gone.

"Goodday, madam," he said. "Have you stableroom for my horses and shelter for myself and my boy for the night?"

The woman looked at him with a static, musing quality, as though she had seen without alarm an apparition.

"I'll have to see," she said.

"I shall pay," the man said. "I know the times."

"I'll have to ask him," the woman said. She turned, then stopped. The older man entered the hall behind her. He was big, in jean clothes, with a shock of iron-gray hair and pale eyes.

"I am Saucier Weddel," the man in gray said. "I am on my way home to Mississippi from Virginia. I am in Tennessee now?"

"You are in Tennessee," the other said. "Come in."

Weddel turned to the Negro. "Take the horses on to the stable," he said.

The Negro returned to the gate, shapeless in the oil-cloth cape and the big overcoat, with that swaggering arrogance which he had assumed as soon as he saw the woman's bare feet and the meagre, barren interior of the cabin. He took up the two bridle reins and began to shout at the horses with needless and officious vociferation, to which the two horses paid no heed, as though they were long accustomed to him. It was as if the Negro himself paid no attention to his cries, as though the shouting were merely concomitant to the action of leading the horses out of sight of the door, like an effluvium by both horses and Negro accepted and relegated in the same instant.

II

Through the kitchen wall the girl could hear the voices of the men in the room from which her father had driven her when the stranger approached the house. She was about twenty: a big girl with smooth, simple hair and big, smooth hands, standing barefoot in a single garment made out of flour-sacks. She stood close to the wall, motionless, her head bent a little, her eyes wide and still and empty like a sleep-walker's, listening to her father and the guest enter the room beyond it.

The kitchen was a plank leanto built against the log wall of the cabin proper. From between the logs beside her the clay chinking, dried to chalk by the heat of the stove, had fallen away in places. Stooping, the movement slow and lush and soundless as the whispering of her bare feet on the floor, she leaned her eye to one of these cracks. She could see a bare table on which sat an earthenware jug and a box of musket cartridges stenciled *U.S. Army*. At the table her two brothers sat in splint chairs, though it was only the younger one, the boy, who looked toward the door, though she knew, could hear now, that the stranger was in the room. The older brother was taking the cartridges one by one from the box and crimping them and setting them upright at his hand like a mimic parade of troops, his back to the door where she knew the stranger was now standing. She breathed quietly. "Vatch would have shot him," she said, breathed, to herself, stooping. "I reckon he will yet."

Then she heard feet again and her mother came toward the door to the kitchen, crossing and for a moment blotting the orifice. Yet she did not move, not even when her mother entered the kitchen. She stooped to the crack, her breathing regular and placid, hearing her mother clattering the stovelids behind her. Then she saw the stranger for the first time and then she was holding her breath quietly, not even aware that she had ceased to breathe. She saw him standing beside the table in his shabby cloak, with his hat in his left hand. Vatch did not look up.

"My name is Saucier Weddel," the stranger said.

"Soshay Weddel," the girl breathed into the dry chinking, the crumbled and powdery wall. She could see him at full length, in his stained and patched and brushed cloak, with his head lifted a little and his face worn, almost gaunt, stamped with a kind of indomitable weariness and yet arrogant too, like a creature from another world with other air to breathe and another kind of blood to warm the veins. "Soshay Weddel," she breathed.

"Take some whiskey," Vatch said without moving.

Then suddenly, as it had been with the suspended breathing, she was not listening to the words at all, as though it were no longer necessary for her to hear, as though curiosity too had no place in the atmosphere in which the stranger dwelled and in which she too dwelled for the moment as she watched the stranger standing beside the table, looking at Vatch, and Vatch now turned in his chair, a cartridge in his hand, looking up at the stranger. She breathed quietly into the crack through which the voices came now without heat or significance out of that dark and smoldering and violent and childlike vanity of men:

"I reckon you know these when you see them then?"

"Why not? We used them too. We never always had the time nor the powder to stop and make our own. So we had to use yours now and then. Especially during the last."

"Maybe you would know them better if one exploded in your face."

"Vatch." She now looked at her father, because he had spoken. Her younger brother was raised a little in his chair, leaning a little forward, his mouth open a little. He was seventeen. Yet still the stranger stood looking quietly down at Vatch, his hat clutched against his worn cloak, with on his face that expression arrogant and weary and a little quizzical.

"You can show your other hand too," Vatch said. "Don't be afraid to leave your pistol go."

"No," the stranger said. "I am not afraid to show it."

"Take some whiskey, then," Vatch said, pushing the jug forward with a motion slighting and contemptuous.

"I am obliged infinitely," the stranger said. "It's my stomach. For three years of war I have had to apologize to my stomach; now, with peace, I must apologize for it. But if I might have a glass for my boy? Even after four years, he cannot stand cold."

"Soshay Weddel," the girl breathed into the crumbled dust beyond which the voices came, not yet raised yet forever irreconcilable and already doomed, the one blind victim, the other blind executioner:

"Or maybe behind your back you would know it better."

"You, Vatch."

"Stop, sir. If he was in the army for as long as one year, he has run too, once. Perhaps oftener, if he faced the Army of Northern Virginia."

"Soshay Weddel," the girl breathed, stooping. Now she saw Weddel, walking apparently straight toward her, a thick tumbler in his left hand and his hat crumpled beneath the same arm.

"Not that way," Vatch said. The stranger paused and looked back at Vatch. "Where are you aiming to go?"

"To take this out to my boy," the stranger said. "Out to the stable. I thought perhaps this door—" His face was in profile now, worn, haughty, wasted, the eyebrows lifted with quizzical and arrogant interrogation. Without rising Vatch jerked his head back and aside. "Come away from that door." But the stranger did not stir. Only his head moved a little, as though he had merely changed the direction of his eyes.

"He's looking at paw," the girl breathed. "He's waiting for paw to tell him. He aint skeered of Vatch. I knowed it."

"Come away from that door," Vatch said. "You damn nigra."

"So it's my face and not my uniform," the stranger said. "And you fought four years to free us, I understand."

Then she heard her father speak again. "Go out the front way and around the house, stranger," he said.

"Soshay Weddel," the girl said. Behind her her mother clattered at the stove. "Soshay Weddel," she said. She did not say it aloud. She breathed again, deep and quiet and without haste. "It's like a music. It's like a singing."

III

The Negro was squatting in the hallway of the barn, the sagging and broken stalls of which were empty save for the two horses. Beside him was a worn rucksack, open. He was engaged in polishing a pair of thin dancing slippers with a cloth and a tin of paste, empty save for a thin rim of polish about the circumference of the tin. Beside him on a piece of plank sat one finished shoe. The upper was cracked; it had a crude sole nailed recently and crudely on by a clumsy hand.

"Thank de Lawd folks cant see de bottoms of yo feets," the Negro said. "Thank de Lawd it's just dese hyer mountain trash. I'd even hate fo Yankees to see yo feets in dese things." He rubbed the shoe, squinted at it, breathed upon it, rubbed it again upon his squatting flank.

"Here," Weddel said, extending the tumbler. It contained a liquid as colorless as water.

The Negro stopped, the shoe and the cloth suspended. "Which?" he said. He looked at the glass. "Whut's dat?"

"Drink it," Weddel said.

"Dat's water. Whut you bringing me water fer?"

"Take it," Weddel said. "It's not water."

The Negro took the glass gingerly. He held it as if it contained nitroglycerin. He looked at it, blinking, bringing the glass slowly under his nose. He blinked. "Where'd you git dis hyer?" Weddel didn't answer. He had taken up the finished slipper, looking at it. The Negro held the glass under his nose. "It smell kind of like it ought to," he said. "But I be dawg ef it look like anything. Dese folks fixing to pizen you." He tipped the glass and sipped gingerly and lowered the glass, blinking.

"I didn't drink any of it," Weddel said. He set the slipper down.

"You better hadn't," the Negro said. "When here I done been fo years trying to take care of you en git you back home like whut Mistis tole me to do, and here you sleeping in folks' barns at night like a tramp, like a pater-roller nigger—" He put the glass to his lips, tilting it and his head in a single jerk. He lowered the glass, empty; his eyes were closed; he said, "Whuf!" shaking his head with a violent, shuddering motion. "It smells right, and it act right. But I be dawg ef it look right. I reckon you better let it alone, like you started out. When dey try to make you drink it you send um to me. I done already stood so much I reckon I can stand a little mo fer Mistis' sake."

He took up the shoe and the cloth again. Weddel stooped above the rucksack. "I want my pistol," he said.

Again the Negro ceased, the shoe and the cloth poised. "Whut fer?" He leaned and looked up the muddy slope toward the cabin. "Is dese folks Yankees?" he said in a whisper.

"No," Weddel said, digging in the rucksack with his left hand. The Negro did not seem to hear him.

"In Tennessee? You tole me we was in Tennessee, where Memphis is, even if you never tole me it was all disyer up-and-down land in de Memphis country. I know I never seed none of um when I went to Memphis wid yo paw dat time. But you says so. And now you telling me dem Memphis folks is Yankees?"

"Where is the pistol?" Weddel said.

"I done tole you," the Negro said. "Acting like you does. Letting dese folks see you come walking up de road, leading Caesar caze you think he tired; making me ride whilst you walks when I can outwalk you any day you ever lived and you knows it, even if I is fawty en you twenty-eight. I ghy tell yo maw. I ghy tell um."

Weddel rose, in his hand a heavy cap-and-ball revolver. He chuckled it in his single hand, drawing the hammer back, letting it down again. The Negro watched him, crouched like an ape in the blue Union army overcoat. "You put dat thing back," he said. "De war done wid now. Dey tole us back dar at Ferginny it was done wid. You dont need no pistol now. You put it back, you hear me?"

"I'm going to bathe," Weddel said. "Is my shirt—"

"Bathe where? In whut? Dese folks aint never seed a bathtub."

"Bathe at the well. Is my shirt ready?"

"Whut dey is of it. . . . You put dat pistol back, Marse Soshay. I ghy tell yo maw on you. I ghy tell um. I just wish Marster was here."

"Go to the kitchen," Weddel said. "Tell them I wish to bathe in the well house. Ask them to draw the curtain on that window there." The pistol had vanished beneath the gray cloak. He went to the stall where the Thoroughbred was. The horse nuzzled at him, its eyes rolling soft and wild. He patted its nose with his left hand. It whickered, not loud, its breath sweet and warm.

IV

The Negro entered the kitchen from the rear. He had removed the oilcloth tent and he now wore a blue forage cap which, like the overcoat, was much too large for him, resting upon the top of his head in such a way that the unsupported brim oscillated faintly when he moved as though with a life of its own. He was completely invisible save for his face between cap and collar like a dried Dyak trophy and almost as small and dusted lightly over as with a thin pallor of wood ashes by the cold. The older woman was at the stove on which frying food now hissed and sputtered; she did not look up when the Negro entered. The girl was standing in the middle of the room, doing nothing at all. She looked at the Negro, watching him with a slow, grave, secret, unwinking gaze as he crossed the kitchen with that air of swaggering caricatured assurance, and upended a block of wood beside the stove and sat upon it.

"If disyer is de kind of weather yawl has up here all de time," he said, "I dont care ef de Yankees does has dis country." He opened the overcoat, revealing his legs and feet as being wrapped, shapeless and huge, in some muddy and anonymous substance resembling fur, giving them the appearance of two muddy beasts the size of half-grown dogs lying on the floor; moving a little nearer the girl, the girl thought quietly *Hit's fur. He taken and cut up a fur coat to wrap his feet in* "Yes, suh," the Negro said. "Just yawl let me git home again, en de Yankees kin have all de rest of it."

"Where do you-uns live?" the girl said.

The Negro looked at her. "In Miss'ippi. On de Domain. Aint you never hyeard tell of Countymaison?"

"Countymaison?"

"Dat's it. His grandpappy named it Countymaison caze it's bigger den a county to ride over. You cant ride across it on a mule betwixt sunup and sundown. Dat's how come." He rubbed his hands slowly on his thighs. His face was now turned toward the stove; he snuffed loudly. Already the ashy overlay on his skin had disappeared, leaving his face dead black, wizened, his mouth a little loose, as though the muscles had become slack with usage, like rubber bands—not the eating muscles, the talking ones. "I reckon we is gittin nigh home, after all. Leastways dat hawg meat smell like it do down whar folks lives."

"Countymaison," the girl said in a rapt, bemused tone, looking at the Negro with her grave, unwinking regard. Then she turned her head and looked at the wall, her face perfectly serene, perfectly inscrutable, without haste, with a profound and absorbed deliberation.

"Dat's it," the Negro said. "Even Yankees is heard tell of Weddel's Countymaison en erbout Marster Francis Weddel. Maybe yawl seed um pass in de carriage dat time he went to Washn'ton to, tell yawl's president how he aint like de way yawl's president wuz treating de people. He rid all de way to Washn'ton in de carriage, wid two niggers to drive en to heat de bricks to kept he foots warm, en de man done gone on ahead wid de wagon en de fresh hawses. He carried yawl's president two whole dressed bears en eight sides of smoked deer venison. He must a passed right out dar in front yawl's house. I reckon yo pappy or maybe his pappy seed um pass." He talked on, voluble, in soporific singsong, his face beginning to glisten, to shine a little with the rich warmth, while the mother bent over the stove and the girl, motionless, static, her bare feet cupped smooth and close to the rough puncheons, her big, smooth, young body cupped soft and richly mammalian to the rough garment, watching the Negro with her ineffable and unwinking gaze, her mouth open a little.

The Negro talked on, his eyes closed, his voice interminable, boastful, his air lazily intolerant, as if he were still at home and there had been no war and no harsh rumors of freedom and of change, and he (a stableman, in the domestic hierarchy a man of horses) were spending the evening in the quarters among field hands, until the older woman dished the food and left the room, closing the door behind her. He opened his eyes at the sound and looked toward the door and then back to the girl. She was looking at the wall, at the closed door through which her mother had vanished. "Dont dey lets you eat at de table wid um?" he said.

The girl looked at the Negro, unwinking. "County-maison," she said. "Vatch says he is a nigra too."

"Who? Him? A nigger? Marse Soshay Weddel? Which un is Vatch?" The girl looked at him. "It's caze yawl aint never been nowhere. Aint never seed nothing. Living up here on a nekkid hill whar you cant even see smoke. Him a nigger? I wish his maw could hear you say dat." He looked about the kitchen, wizened, his eyeballs rolling white, ceaseless, this way and that. The girl watched him.

"Do the girls there wear shoes all the time?" she said.

The Negro looked about the kitchen. "Where does yawl keep dat ere Tennessee spring water? Back here somewhere?"

"Spring water?"

The Negro blinked slowly. "Dat ere light-drinking kahysene."

"Kahysene?"

"Dat ere light-colored lamp oil whut yawl drinks. Aint you got a little of it hid back here somewhere?"

"Oh," the girl said. "You mean corn." She went to a corner and lifted a loose plank in the floor, the Negro watching her, and drew forth another earthen jug. She filled another thick tumbler and gave it to the Negro and watched him jerk it down his throat, his eyes closed. Again he said, "Whuf!" and drew his back hand across his mouth.

"Whut wuz dat you axed me?" he said.

"Do the girls down there at Countymaison wear shoes?"

"De ladies does. If dey didn't have none, Marse Soshay

could sell a hun'ed niggers en buy um some . . . Which un is it say Marse Soshay a nigger?"

The girl watched him. "Is he married?"

"Who married? Marse Soshay?" The girl watched him. "How he have time to git married, wid us fighting de Yankees for fo years? Aint been home in fo years now where no ladies to marry is." He looked at the girl, his eyewhites a little bloodshot, his skin shining in faint and steady highlights. Thawing, he seemed to have increased in size a little too. "Whut's it ter you, if he married or no?"

They looked at each other. The Negro could hear her breathing. Then she was not looking at him at all, though she had not yet even blinked nor turned her head. "I dont reckon he'd have any time for a girl that didn't have any shoes," she said. She went to the wall and stooped again to the crack. The Negro watched her. The older woman entered and took another dish from the stove and departed without having looked at either of them.

V

The four men, the three men and the boy, sat about the supper table. The broken meal lay on thick plates. The knives and forks were iron. On the table the jug still sat. Weddel was now cloakless. He was shaven, his still damp hair combed back. Upon his bosom the ruffles of the shirt frothed in the lamplight, the right sleeve, empty, pinned across his breast with a thin gold pin. Under the table the frail and mended dancing slippers rested among the brogans of the two men and the bare splayed feet of the boy.

"Vatch says you are a nigra," the father said.

Weddel was leaning a little back in his chair. "So that

explains it," he said. "I was thinking that he was just congenitally illtempered. And having to be a victor, too."

"Are you a nigra?" the father said.

"No," Weddel said. He was looking at the boy, his weathered and wasted face a little quizzical. Across the back of his neck his hair, long, had been cut roughly as though with a knife or perhaps a bayonet. The boy watched him in complete and rapt immobility. *As if I might be an apparition* he thought. *A hunt. Maybe I am.* "No," he said. "I am not a Negro."

"Who are you?" the father said.

Weddel sat a little sideways in his chair, his hand lying on the table. "Do you ask guests who they are in Tennessee?" he said. Vatch was filling a tumbler from the jug. His face was lowered, his hands big and hard. His face was hard. Weddel looked at him. "I think I know how you feel," he said. "I expect I felt that way once. But it's hard to keep on feeling any way for four years. Even feeling at all."

Vatch said something, sudden and harsh. He clapped the tumbler on to the table, splashing some of the liquor out. It looked like water, with a violent, dynamic odor. It seemed to possess an inherent volatility which carried a splash of it across the table and on to the foam of frayed yet immaculate linen on Weddel's breast, striking sudden and chill through the cloth against his flesh.

"Vatch!" the father said.

Weddel did not move; his expression arrogant, quizzical, and weary, did not change. "He did not mean to do that," he said.

"When I do," Vatch said, "it will not look like an accident."

Weddel was looking at Vatch. "I think I told you once," he said. "My name is Saucier Weddel. I am a Mississippian. I live at a place named Contalmaison. My father built it and named it. He was a Choctaw chief named Francis Weddel, of whom you have probably not heard. He was the son of a Choctaw woman and a French émigré of New Orleans, a general of Napoleon's and a knight of the Legion of Honor. His name was François Vidal. My father drove to Washington once in his carriage to remonstrate with President Jackson about the Government's treatment of his people, sending on ahead a wagon of provender and gifts and also fresh horses for the carriage, in charge of the man, the native overseer, who was a full-blood Choctaw and my father's cousin. In the old days The Man was the hereditary title of the head of our clan; but after we became Europeanised like the white people, we lost the title to the branch which refused to become polluted, though we kept the slaves and the land. The Man now lives in a house a little larger than the cabins of the Negroes—an upper servant. It was in Washington that my father met and married my mother. He was killed in the Mexican War. My mother died two years ago, in '63, of a complication of pneumonia acquired while superintending the burying of some silver on a wet night when Federal troops entered the county, and of unsuitable food; though my boy refuses to believe that she is dead. He refuses to believe that the country would have permitted the North to deprive her of the imported Martinique coffee and the beaten biscuit which she had each Sunday noon and Wednesday night. He believes that the country would have risen in arms first. But then, he is only a Negro, member of an oppressed race burdened with freedom. He has a daily list of my misdoings which he is going to tell her on me when we reach home. I went to school in France, but not very hard. Until two weeks ago I was a major of Mississippi infantry in the corps of a man named Longstreet, of whom you may have heard."

"So you were a major," Vatch said.

"That appears to be my indictment; yes."

"I have seen a rebel major before," Vatch said. "Do you want me to tell you where I saw him?"

"Tell me," Weddel said.

"He was lying by a tree. We had to stop there and lie down, and he was lying by the tree, asking for water. 'Have you any water, friend?' he said. 'Yes. I have water,' I said. 'I have plenty of water.' I had to crawl; I couldn't stand up. I crawled over to him and I lifted him so that his head would be propped against the tree. I fixed his face to the front."

"Didn't you have a bayonet?" Weddel said. "But I forgot; you couldn't stand up."

"Then I crawled back. I had to crawl back a hundred yards, where—"

"Back?"

"It was too close. Who can do decent shooting that close? I had to crawl back, and then the damned musket—"

"Damn musket?" Weddel sat a little sideways in his chair, his hand on the table, his face quizzical and sardonic, contained.

"I missed the first shot. I had his face propped up and turned, and his eyes open watching me, and then I missed. I hit him in the throat and I had to shoot again because of the damned musket."

"Vatch," the father said.

Vatch's hands were on the table. His head, his face, were like his father's, though without the father's deliberation. His face was furious, still, unpredictable. "It was that damn musket. I had to shoot three times. Then he had three eyes, in a row across his face propped against the tree, all three of them open, like he was watching me with three eyes. I gave him another eye, to see better with. But I had to shoot twice because of the damn musket."

"You, Vatch," the father said. He stood now, his hands on the table, propping his gaunt body. "Don't you mind Vatch, stranger. The war is over now."

"I dont mind him," Weddel said. His hand went to his bosom, disappearing into the foam of linen while he watched Vatch steadily with his alert, quizzical, sardonic gaze. "I have seen too many of him for too long a time to mind one of him any more."

"Take some whiskey," Vatch said.

"Are you just making a point?"

"Damn the pistol," Vatch said. "Take some whiskey."

Weddel laid his hand on the table. But instead of pouring, Vatch held the jug poised over the tumbler. He was looking past Weddel's shoulder. Weddel turned. The girl was in the room, standing in the doorway with her mother just behind her. The mother said as if she were speaking to the floor under her feet: "I tried to keep her back, like you said. I tried to. But she is strong as a man; hard-headed like a man."

"You go back," the father said.

"Me to go back?" the mother said to the floor.

The father spoke a name; Weddel did not catch it; he did not even know that he had missed it. "You go back."

The girl moved. She was not looking at any of them. She came to the chair on which lay Weddel's worn and mended cloak and opened it, revealing the four ragged slashes where the sable lining had been cut out as though with a knife. She was looking at the cloak when Vatch grasped her by the shoulder, but it was at Weddel that she looked. "You cut hit out and gave hit to that nigra to wrap his feet in," she said. Then the father grasped Vatch in turn. Weddel had not stirred, his face turned over his shoulder; beside him the boy was upraised out of his chair by his arms, his young, slacked face leaned forward into the lamp. But save for the breathing of Vatch and the father there was no sound in the room.

"I am stronger than you are, still," the father said. "I am a better man still, or as good."

"You wont be always," Vatch said.

The father looked back over his shoulder at the girl. "Go back," he said. She turned and went back toward the hall, her feet silent as rubber feet. Again the father called that name which Weddel had not caught; again he did not catch it and was not aware again that he had not. She went out the door. The father looked at Weddel. Weddel's attitude was unchanged, save that once more his hand was hidden inside his bosom. They looked at one another—the cold, Nordic face and the half Gallic half Mongol face thin and worn like a bronze casting, with eyes like those of the dead, in which only vision has ceased and not sight. "Take your horses, and go," the father said.

VI

It was dark in the hall, and cold, with the black chill of the mountain April coming up through the floor about her bare legs and her body in the single coarse garment. "He cut the lining outen his cloak to wrap that nigra's feet in," she said. "He done hit for a nigra." The door behind her opened. Against the lamplight a man loomed, then the door shut behind him. "Is it Vatch or paw?" she said. Then something struck her across the back—a leather strap. "I was afeared it would be Vatch," she said. The blow fell again.

"Go to bed," the father said.

"You can whip me, but you cant whip him," she said.

The blow fell again: a thick, flat, soft sound upon her immediate flesh beneath the coarse sacking.

VII

In the deserted kitchen the Negro sat for a moment longer on the upturned block beside the stove, looking at the door. Then he rose carefully, one hand on the wall.

"Whuf!" he said. "Wish us had a spring on de Domain whut run dat. Stock would git tromped to death, sho mon." He blinked at the door, listening, then he moved, letting himself carefully along the wall, stopping now and then to look toward the door and listen, his air cunning, unsteady, and alert. He reached the corner and lifted the loose plank, stooping carefully, bracing himself against the wall. He lifted the jug out, whereupon he lost his balance and sprawled on his face, his face ludicrous and earnest with astonishment. He got up and sat flat on the floor, carefully, the jug between his knees, and lifted the jug and drank. He drank a long time.

"Whuf!" he said. "On de Domain we'd give disyer stuff to de hawgs. But deseyer ign'unt mountain trash—" He drank again; then with the jug poised there came into his face an expression of concern and then consternation. He set the jug down and tried to get up, sprawling above the jug, gaining his feet at last, stooped, swaying, drooling, with that expression of outraged consternation on his face. Then he fell headlong to the floor, overturning the jug.

VIII

They stooped above the Negro, talking quietly to one another—Weddel in his frothed shirt, the father and the boy.

"We'll have to tote him," the father said.

They lifted the Negro. With his single hand Weddel jerked the Negro's head up, shaking him. "Jubal," he said.

The Negro struck out, clumsily, with one arm. "Le'm be," he muttered. "Le'm go."

"Jubal!" Weddel said.

The Negro thrashed, sudden and violent. "You le'm be," he said. "I ghy tell de Man. I ghy tell um." He ceased, muttering: "Field hands. Field niggers."

"We'll have to tote him," the father said.

"Yes," Weddel said. "I'm sorry for this. I should have warned you. But I didn't think there was another jug he could have gained access to." He stooped, getting his single hand under the Negro's shoulders.

"Get away," the father said. "Me and Hule can do it." He and the boy picked the Negro up. Weddel opened the door. They emerged into the high black cold. Below them the barn loomed. They carried the Negro down the slope. "Get them horses out, Hule," the father said.

"Horses?" Weddel said. "He cant ride now. He cant stay on a horse."

They looked at one another, each toward the other voice, in the cold, the icy silence.

"You wont go now?" the father said.

"I am sorry. You see I cannot depart now. I will have to stay until daylight, until he is sober. We will go then."

"Leave him here. Leave him one horse, and you ride on. He is nothing but a nigra."

"I am sorry. Not after four years." His voice was quizzical, whimsical almost, yet with that quality of indomitable weariness. "I've worried with him this far; I reckon I will get him on home."

"I have warned you," the father said.

"I am obliged. We will move at daylight. If Hule will be kind enough to help me get him into the loft."

The father had stepped back. "Put that nigra down, Hule," he said.

"He will freeze here," Weddel said. "I must get him into the loft." He hauled the Negro up and propped him against the wall and stooped to hunch the Negro's lax body onto his shoulder. The weight rose easily, though he did not understand why until the father spoke again:

"Hule. Come away from there."

"Yes; go," Weddel said quietly. "I can get him up the ladder." He could hear the boy's breathing, fast, young, swift with excitement perhaps. Weddel did not pause to speculate, nor at the faintly hysterical tone of the boy's voice:

"I'll help you."

Weddel didn't object again. He slapped the Negro awake and they set his feet on the ladder rungs, pushing him upward. Halfway up he stopped; again he thrashed out at them. "I ghy tell um. I ghy tell de Man. I ghy tell Mistis. Field hands. Field niggers."

IX

They lay side by side in the loft, beneath the cloak and the two saddle blankets. There was no hay. The Negro snored, his breath reeking and harsh, thick. Below, in its stall, the Thoroughbred stamped now and then. Weddel lay on his back, his arm across his chest, the hand clutching the stub of the other arm. Overhead, through the cracks in the roof the sky showed—the thick chill, black sky which would rain again tomorrow and on every tomorrow until they left the mountains. "If I leave the mountains," he said quietly, motionless on his back beside the snoring Negro, staring upward. "I was concerned. I had thought that it was exhausted; that I had lost the privilege of being afraid. But I have not. And so I am happy. Quite happy." He lay rigid on his back in the cold darkness, thinking of home. "Contalmaison. Our lives are summed up in sounds and made significant. Victory. Defeat. Peace. Home. That's why we must do so much to invent meanings for the sounds, so damned much. Especially if you are unfortunate enough to be victorious: so damned much. It's nice to be whipped; quiet to be whipped. To be whipped and to lie under a broken roof, thinking of home." The Negro snored. "So damned much"; seeming to watch the words shape quietly in the darkness above his mouth. "What would happen, say, a man in the lobby of the Gayoso, in Memphis, laughing suddenly aloud. But I am quite happy—" Then he heard the sound. He lay utterly still then, his hand clutching the butt of the pistol warm beneath the stub of his right arm, hearing the quiet, almost infinitesimal sound as it mounted the ladder. But he made no move until he saw the dim orifice of the trap door blotted out. "Stop where you are," he said.

"It's me," the voice said; the voice of the boy, again with that swift, breathless quality which even now Weddel did not pause to designate as excitement or even to remark at all. The boy came on his hands and knees across the dry, sibilant chaff which dusted the floor. "Go ahead and shoot," he said. On his hands and knees he loomed above Weddel with his panting breath. "I wish I was dead. I so wish hit. I wish we was both dead. I could wish like Vatch wishes. Why did you uns have to stop here?"

Weddel had not moved. "Why does Vatch wish I was dead?"

"Because he can still hear you uns yelling. I used to sleep with him and he wakes up at night and once paw had to keep him from choking me to death before he waked up and him sweating, hearing you uns yelling still. Without nothing but unloaded guns, yelling, Vatch said, like scarecrows across a cornpatch, running." He was crying now, not aloud. "Damn you! Damn you to hell!"

"Yes," Weddel said. "I have heard them, myself. But why do you wish you were dead?"

"Because she was trying to come, herself. Only she had to—"

"Who? She? Your sister?"

"—had to go through the room to get out. Paw was awake. He said, 'If you go out that door, dont you never come back.' And she said, 'I dont aim to.' And Vatch was awake too and he said, 'Make him marry you quick because you are going to be a widow at daylight.' And she come back and told me. But I was awake too. She told me to tell you."

"Tell me what?" Weddel said. The boy cried quietly, with a kind of patient and utter despair.

"I told her if you was a nigra, and if she done that — I told her that I—"

"What? If she did what? What does she want you to tell me?"

"About the window into the attic where her and me sleep. There is a foot ladder I made to come back from hunting at night for you to get in. But I told her if you was a nigra and if she done that I would—"

"Now then," Weddel said sharply; "pull yourself together now. Dont you remember? I never even saw her but that one time when she came in the room and your father sent her out."

"But you saw her then. And she saw you."

"No," Weddel said.

The boy ceased to cry. He was quite still above Weddel. "No what?"

"I wont do it. Climb up your ladder."

For a while the boy seemed to muse above him, motionless, breathing slow and quiet now; he spoke now in a musing, almost dreamy tone: "I could kill you easy.

You aint got but one arm, even if you are older. . . ."
Suddenly he moved, with almost unbelievable quickness;
Weddel's first intimation was when the boy's hard, over-
large hands took him by the throat. Weddel did not
move. "I could kill you easy. And wouldn't none mind."

"Shhhhhh," Weddel said. "Not so loud."

"Wouldn't none care." He held Weddel's throat with
hard, awkward restraint. Weddel could feel the choking
and the shaking expend itself somewhere about the boy's
forearms before it reached his hands, as though the connection between brain and hands was incomplete.
"Wouldn't none care. Except Vatch would be mad."

"I have a pistol," Weddel said.

"Then shoot me with it. Go on."

"No."

"No what?"

"I told you before."

"You swear you wont do it? Do you swear?"

"Listen a moment," Weddel said; he spoke now with
a sort of soothing patience, as though he spoke one-syl-
lable words to a child: "I just want to go home. That's all.
I have been away from home for four years. All I want
is to go home. Dont you see? I want to see what I have
left there, after four years."

"What do you do there?" The boy's hands were loose
and hard about Weddel's throat, his arms still, rigid. "Do
you hunt all day, and all night too if you want, with a
horse to ride and nigras to wait on you, to shine your
boots and saddle the horse, and you setting on the gallery,
eating, until time to go hunting again?"

"I hope so. I haven't been home in four years, you see.
So I dont know any more."

"Take me with you."

"I dont know what's there, you see. There may not be anything there: no horses to ride and nothing to hunt. The Yankees were there, and my mother died right afterward, and I dont know what we would find there, until I can go and see."

"I'll work. We'll both work. You can get married in Mayesfield. It's not far."

"Married? Oh. Your . . . I see. How do you know I am not already married?" Now the boy's hands shut on his throat, shaking him. "Stop it!" he said.

"If you say you have got a wife, I will kill you," the boy said.

"No," Weddel said. "I am not married."

"And you dont aim to climb up that foot ladder?"

"No. I never saw her but once. I might not even know her if I saw her again."

"She says different. I dont believe you. You are lying."

"No," Weddel said.

"Is it because you are afraid to?"

"Yes. That's it."

"Of Vatch?"

"Not Vatch. I'm just afraid. I think my luck has given out. I know that it has lasted too long; I am afraid that I shall find that I have forgot how to be afraid. So I cant risk it. I cant risk finding that I have lost touch with truth. Not like Jubal here. He believes that I still belong to him; he will not believe that I have been freed. He wont even let me tell him so. He does not need to bother about truth, you see."

"We would work. She might not look like the

Miss'ippi women that wear shoes all the time. But we would learn. We would not shame you before them."

"No," Weddel said. "I cannot."

"Then you go away. Now."

"How can I? You see that he cannot ride, cannot stay on a horse." The boy did not answer at once; an instant later Weddel could almost feel the tenseness, the utter immobility, though he himself had heard no sound; he knew that the boy, crouching, not breathing, was looking toward the ladder. "Which one is it?" Weddel whispered.

"It's paw."

"I'll go down. You stay here. You keep my pistol for me."

X

The dark air was high, chill, cold. In the vast invisible darkness the valley lay, the opposite cold and invisible range black on the black sky. Clutching the stub of his missing arm across his chest, he shivered slowly and steadily.

"Go," the father said.

"The war is over," Weddel said. "Vatch's victory is not my trouble."

"Take your horses and nigra, and ride on."

"If you mean your daughter, I never saw her but once and I never expect to see her again."

"Ride on," the father said. "Take what is yours, and ride on."

"I cannot." They faced one another in the darkness. "After four years I have bought immunity from running."

"You have till daylight."

"I have had less than that in Virginia for four years. And this is just Tennessee." But the other had turned; he dissolved into the black slope. Weddel entered the stable and mounted the ladder. Motionless above the snoring Negro the boy squatted.

"Leave him here," the boy said. "He aint nothing but a nigra. Leave him, and go."

"No," Weddel said.

The boy squatted above the snoring Negro. He was not looking at Weddel, yet there was between them, quiet and soundless, the copse, the sharp dry report, the abrupt wild thunder of upreared horse, the wisping smoke. "I can show you a short cut down to the valley. You will be out of the mountains in two hours. By daybreak you will be ten miles away."

"I cant. He wants to go home too. I must get him home too." He stooped; with his single hand he spread the cloak awkwardly, covering the Negro closer with it. He heard the boy creep away, but he did not look. After a while he shook the Negro. "Jubal," he said. The Negro groaned; he turned heavily, sleeping again. Weddel squatted above him as the boy had done. "I thought that I had lost it for good," he said.—"The peace and the quiet; the power to be afraid again."

XI

The cabin was gaunt and bleak in the thick cold dawn when the two horses passed out the sagging gate and into the churned road, the Negro on the Thoroughbred, Weddel on the sorrel. The Negro was shivering. He sat hunched and high, with updrawn knees, his face almost invisible in the oilcloth hood.

"I tole you dey wuz fixing to pizen us wid dat stuff," he said. "I tole you. Hillbilly rednecks. En you not only let um pizen me, you fotch me de pizen wid yo own hand. O Lawd, O Lawd! If we ever does git home."

Weddel looked back at the cabin, at the weathered, blank house where there was no sign of any life, not even smoke. "She has a young man, I suppose—a beau." He spoke aloud, musing, quizzical. "And that boy. Hule. He said to come within sight of a laurel copse where the road disappears, and take a path to the left. He said we must not pass that copse."

"Who says which?" the Negro said. "I aint going nowhere. I going back to dat loft en lay down."

"All right," Weddel said. "Get down."

"Git down?"

"I'll need both horses. You can walk on when you are through sleeping."

"I ghy tell yo maw," the Negro said. "I ghy tell um. Ghy tell how after four years you aint got no more sense than to not know a Yankee when you seed um. To stay de night wid Yankees en let um pizen one of Mistis' niggers. I ghy tell um."

"I thought you were going to stay here," Weddel said. He was shivering too. "Yet I am not cold," he said. "I am not cold."

"Stay here? Me? How in de world you ever git home widout me? Whut I tell Mistis when I come in widout you en she ax me whar you is?"

"Come," Weddel said. He lifted the sorrel into motion. He looked quietly back at the house, then rode on. Behind him on the Thoroughbred the Negro muttered and mumbled to himself in woebegone singsong. The road, the long hill which yesterday they had toiled up, descended now. It was muddy, rockchurned, scarred across the barren and rocky land beneath the dissolving sky, jolting downward to where the pines and laurel began. After a while the cabin had disappeared.

"And so I am running away," Weddel said. "When I get home I shall not be very proud of this. Yes, I will. It means that I am still alive. Still alive, since I still know fear and desire. Since life is an affirmation of the past and a promise to the future. So I am still alive—Ah." It was the laurel copse. About three hundred yards ahead it seemed to have sprung motionless and darkly secret in the air which of itself was mostly water. He drew rein sharply, the Negro, hunched, moaning, his face completely hidden, overiding him unawares until the Thoroughbred stopped of its own accord. "But I dont see any path—" Weddel said; then a figure emerged from the copse, running toward them. Weddel thrust the reins beneath his groin and withdrew his hand inside his cloak. Then he saw that it was the boy. He came up trotting. His face was white, strained, his eyes quite grave.

"It's right yonder," he said.

"Thank you," Weddel said. "It was kind of you to come and show us, though we could have found it, I imagine."

"Yes," the boy said as though he had not heard. He had already taken the sorrel's bridle. "Right tother of the brush. You can't see hit until you are in hit."

"In whut?" the Negro said. "I ghy tell um. After four years you aint got no more sense. . . ."

"Hush," Weddel said. He said to the boy, "I am obliged to you. You'll have to take that in lieu of anything better. And now you get on back home. We can find the path. We will be all right now."

"They know the path too," the boy said. He drew the sorrel forward. "Come on."

"Wait," Weddel said, drawing the sorrel up. The boy still tugged at the bridle, looking on ahead toward the copse. "So we have one guess and they have one guess. Is that it?"

"Damn you to hell, come on!" the boy said, in a kind of thin frenzy. "I am sick of hit. Sick of hit."

"Well," Weddel said. He looked about, quizzical, sardonic, with his gaunt, weary, wasted face. "But I must move. I cant stay here, not even if I had a house, a roof to live under. So I have to choose between three things. That's what throws a man off—that extra alternative. Just when he has come to realize that living consists in choosing wrongly between two alternatives, to have to choose among three. You go back home."

The boy turned and looked up at him. "We'd work. We could go back to the house now, since paw and Vatch are . . . We could ride down the mou-tin, two on one horse and two on tother. We could go back to the valley and get married at Mayesfield. We would not shame you."

"But she has a young man, hasn't she? Somebody that waits for her at church on Sunday and walks home and takes Sunday dinner, and maybe fights the other young men because of her?"

"You wont take us, then?"

"No. You go back home."

For a while the boy stood, holding the bridle, his face lowered. Then he turned; he said quietly: "Come on, then. We got to hurry."

"Wait," Weddel said; "what are you going to do?"

"I'm going a piece with you. Come on." He dragged the sorrel forward, toward the roadside.

"Here," Weddel said, "you go on back home. The war is over now. Vatch knows that."

The boy did not answer. He led the sorrel into the underbrush. The Thoroughbred hung back. "Whoa, you Caesar!" the Negro said. "Wait, Marse Soshay. I aint gwine ride down no . . ."

The boy looked over his shoulder without stopping. "You keep back there," he said. "You keep where you are."

The path was a faint scar, doubling and twisting among the brush. "I see it now," Weddel said. "You go back."

"I'll go a piece with you," the boy said; so quietly that Weddel discovered that he had been holding his breath, in a taut, strained alertness. He breathed again, while the sorrel jolted stiffly downward beneath him. "Nonsense," he thought. "He will have me playing Indian also in five minutes more. I had wanted to recover the power to be afraid, but I seem to have outdone myself." The path widened; the Thoroughbred came alongside, the boy walking between them; again he looked at the Negro.

"You keep back, I tell you," he said.

"Why back?" Weddel said. He looked at the boy's wan, strained face; he thought swiftly, "I dont know whether I am playing Indian or not." He said aloud: "Why must he keep back?"

The boy looked at Weddel; he stopped, pulling the sorrel up. "We'd work," he said. "We wouldn't shame you."

Weddel's face was now as sober as the boy's. They looked at one another. "Do you think we have guessed wrong? We had to guess. We had to guess one out of three."

Again it was as if the boy had not heard him. "You wont think hit is me? You swear hit?"

"Yes. I swear it." He spoke quietly, watching the boy; they spoke now as two men or two children. "What do you think we ought to do?"

"Turn back. They will be gone now. We could . . ." He drew back on the bridle; again the Thoroughbred came abreast and forged ahead.

"You mean, it could be along here?" Weddel said. Suddenly he spurred the sorrel, jerking the clinging boy forward. "Let go," he said. The boy held onto the bridle, swept forward until the two horses were again abreast. On the Thoroughbred the Negro perched, high-kneed, his mouth still talking, flobbed down with ready speech, easy and worn with talk like an old shoe with walking.

"I done told him en tole him," the Negro said.

"Let go!" Weddel said, spurring the sorrel, forcing its shoulder into the boy. "Let go!"

"You wont turn back?" the boy said. "You wont?"

"Let go!" Weddel said. His teeth showed a little beneath his mustache; he lifted the sorrel bodily with the spurs. The boy let go of the bridle and ducked beneath the Thoroughbred's neck; Weddel, glancing back as the sorrel leaped, saw the boy surge upward and on to the

Thoroughbred's back, shoving the Negro back along its spine until he vanished.

"They think you will be riding the good horse," the boy said in a thin, panting voice; "I told them you would be riding . . . Down the mou-tin!" he cried as the Thoroughbred swept past; "the horse can make hit! Git outen the path! Git outen the. . . ." Weddel spurred the sorrel; almost abreast the two horses reached the bend where the path doubled back upon itself and into a matted shoulder of laurel and rhododendron. The boy looked back over his shoulder. "Keep back!" he cried. "Git outen the path!" Weddel rowelled the sorrel. On his face was a thin grimace of exasperation and anger almost like smiling.

It was still on his dead face when he struck the earth, his foot still fast in the stirrup. The sorrel leaped at the sound and dragged Weddel to the path side and halted and whirled and snorted once, and began to graze. The Thoroughbred however rushed on past the curve and whirled and rushed back, the blanket twisted under its belly and its eyes rolling, springing over the boy's body where it lay in the path, the face wrenched sideways against a stone, the arms backsprawled, openpalmed, like a woman with lifted skirts springing across a puddle. Then it whirled and stood above Weddel's body, whinnying, with tossing head, watching the laurel copse and the fading gout of black powder smoke as it faded away.

The Negro was on his hands and knees when the two men emerged from the copse. One of them was running. The Negro watched him run forward, crying monotonously, "The durned fool! The durned fool! The durned fool!" and then stop suddenly and drop the gun; squatting, the Negro saw him become stone still above the fallen gun, looking down at the boy's body with an expression of shock and amazement like he was waking from a dream. Then the Negro saw the other man. In the act of stopping, the second man swung the rifle up and began to reload it. The Negro did not move. On his hands and knees he watched the two white men, his irises rushing and wild in the bloodshot whites. Then he too moved and, still on hands and knees, he turned and scuttled to where Weddel lay beneath the sorrel and crouched over Weddel and looked again and watched the second man backing slowly away up the path, loading the rifle. He watched the man stop; he did not close his eyes nor look away. He watched the rifle elongate and then rise and diminish slowly and become a round spot against the white shape of Vatch's face like a period on a page. Crouching, the Negro's eyes rushed wild and steady and red, like those of a cornered animal.

Beyond

The hard round ear of the stethoscope was cold and unpleasant upon his naked chest; the room, big and square, furnished with clumsy walnut—the bed where he had first slept alone, which had been his marriage bed, in which his son had been conceived and been born and lain dressed for the coffin—the room familiar for sixty-five years, by ordinary peaceful and lonely and so peculiarly his own as to have the same odor which he had, seemed to be cluttered with people, though there were but three of them and all of them he knew: Lucius Peabody who should have been down town attending to his medical practice, and the two Negroes, the one who should be in the kitchen and the other with the lawn mower on the lawn, making some pretence toward earning the money which on Saturday night they would expect.

But worst of all was the hard cold little ear of the stethoscope, worse even than the outrage of his bared chest with its fine delicate matting of gray hair. In fact, about the whole business there was just one alleviating circumstance. "At least," he thought with fretted and sardonic humor, "I am spared that uproar of female connections which might have been my lot, which is the ordinary concomitant of occasions of marriage or divorcement. And if he will just move his damned little toy telephone and let my niggers go back to work—"

And then, before he had finished the thought, Peabody did remove the stethoscope. And then, just as he was settling himself back into the pillow with a sigh of fretted relief, one of the Negroes, the woman, set up such a pandemonium of wailing as to fetch him bolt upright in the bed, his hands to his ears. The Negress stood at the foot of the bed, her long limber black hands motionless on the footboard, her eyes whitely backrolled into her skull and her mouth wide open, while from it rolled slow billows of soprano sound as mellow as high-register organ tones and wall-shattering as a steamer siren.

"Chlory!" he shouted. "Stop that!" She didn't stop. Apparently she could neither see nor hear. "You, Jake!" he shouted to the Negro man who stood beside her, his hands too on the footboard, his face brooding upon the bed with an expression darkly and profoundly enigmatic; "get her out of here! At once!" But Jake too did not move, and he then turned to Peabody in angry outrage. "Here! Loosh! Get these damn niggers out of here!" But Peabody also did not seem to hear him. The Judge watched him methodically folding the stethoscope into its case; glared at him for a moment longer while the woman's shattering noise billowed through the room. Then he flung the covers back and rose from the bed and hurried furiously from the room and from the house.

At once he realized that he was still in his pajamas, so he buttoned his overcoat. It was of broadcloth, black, brushed, of an outmoded elegance, with a sable collar. "At least they didn't have time to hide this from me," he thought in fretted rage. "Now, if I just had my. . . ." He looked down at his feet. "Ah. I seem to have. . . ." He looked at his shoes. "That's fortunate, too." Then the momentary surprise faded too, now that outrage had space in which to disseminate itself. He touched his hat, then he put his hand to his lapel. The jasmine was there. Say what he would, curse Jake as he often had to do, the Negro never forgot whatever flower in its season. Always it would be there, fresh and recent and unblemished, on the morning coffee tray. The flower and the. . . . He clasped his ebony stick beneath his arm and opened the briefcase. The two fresh handkerchiefs were there, beside the book. He thrust one of them into his breast pocket and went on. After a while the noise of Chlory's wailing died away.

Then for a little while it was definitely unpleasant. He detested crowds: the milling and aimless and patient stupidity; the concussion of life-quick flesh with his own. But presently, if not soon, he was free, and standing so, still a little ruffled, a little annoyed, he looked back with fading outrage and distaste at the throng as it clotted quietly through the entrance. With fading distaste until the distaste was gone, leaving his face quiet and quite intelligent, with a faint and long constant overtone of quizzical bemusement not yet tinctured with surprised speculation, not yet puzzled, not yet wary. That was to come later. Hence it did not show in his voice, which was now merely light, quizzical, contained, "There seems to be quite a crowd of them."

"Yes," the other said. The Judge looked at him and saw a young man in conventional morning dress with some subtle effluvium of weddings, watching the entrance with a strained, patient air.

"You are expecting someone?" the Judge said.

Now the other looked at him. "Yes. You didn't see— But you don't know her."

"Know whom?"

"My wife. That is, she is not my wife yet. But the wedding was to be at noon."

"Something happened, did it?"

"I had to do it." The young man looked at him, strained, anxious. "I was late. That's why I was driving fast. A child ran into the road. I was going too fast to stop. So I had to turn."

"But you missed the child?"

"Yes." The other looked at him. "You don't know her?"

"And are you waiting here to. . . ." The Judge stared at the other. His eyes were narrowed, his gaze was piercing, hard. He said suddenly, sharply, "Nonsense."

"What? What did you say?" the other asked with his vague, strained, almost beseeching air. The Judge looked away. His frowning concentration, his reflex of angry astonishment, was gone. He seemed to have wiped it from his face by a sudden deliberate action. He was like a man who, not a swordsman, has practiced with a blade a little against a certain improbable crisis, and who suddenly finds himself, blade in hand, face to face with the event. He looked at the entrance, his face alert, musing swiftly: he seemed to muse upon the entering faces with a still and furious concentration, and quietly; quietly he looked about, then at the other again. The young man still watched him.

"You're looking for your wife too, I suppose," he said. "I hope you find her. I hope you do." He spoke with a sort of quiet despair. "I suppose she is old, as you are. It must be hell on the one who has to watch and wait for the other one he or she has grown old in marriage with, because it is so terrible to wait and watch like me, for a girl who is a maiden to you. Of course I think mine is the most unbearable. You see if it had only been the next day—anything. But then if it had, I guess I could not have turned out for that kid. I guess I just think mine is so terrible. It can't be as bad as I think it is. It just can't be. I hope you find her."

The Judge's lip lifted. "I came here to escape someone; not to find anyone." He looked at the other. His face was still broken with that grimace which might have been smiling. But his eyes were not smiling. "If I were look-ing for anybody, it would probably be my son."

"Oh. A son. I see."

"Yes. He would be about your age. He was ten when he died."

"Look for him here."

Now the Judge laughed outright, save for his eyes. The other watched him with that grave anxiety leavened now with quiet interested curiosity. "You mean you don't believe?" The Judge laughed aloud. Still laughing, he pro-duced a cloth sack of tobacco and rolled a slender ciga-rette. When he looked up, the other was watching the entrance again. The Judge ceased to laugh.

"Have you a match?" he said. The other looked at him. The Judge raised the cigarette. "A match."

The other sought in his pockets. "No." He looked at the Judge. "Look for him here," he said.

"Thank you," the Judge answered. "I may avail myself of your advice later." He turned away. Then he paused and looked back. The young man was watching the entrance. The Judge watched him, bemused, his lip lifted. He turned on, then he stopped still. His face was now completely shocked, into complete immobility like a mask; the sensitive, worn mouth, the delicate nostrils, the eyes all pupil or pupilless. He could not seem to move at all. Then Mothershed turned and saw him. For an instant Mothershed's pale eyes flickered, his truncated jaw, collapsing steadily with a savage, toothless motion, ceased.

"Well?" Mothershed said.

"Yes," the Judge said; "it's me." Now it was that, as the mesmerism left him, the shadow bewildered and wary and complete, touched his face. Even to himself his words sounded idiotic. "I thought that you were dea. . . ." Then he made a supreme and gallant effort, his voice light, quizzical, contained again, "Well?"

Mothershed looked at him—a squat man in a soiled and mismatched suit stained with grease and dirt, his soiled collar innocent of tie—with a pale, lightly slumbering glare filled with savage outrage. "So they got you here, too, did they?"

"That depends on who you mean by 'they' and what you mean by 'here.' "

Mothershed made a savage, sweeping gesture with one arm. "Here, by God! The preachers. The Jesus shouters."

"Ah," the Judge said. "Well, if I am where I am beginning to think I am, I don't know whether I am here or not. But you are not here at all, are you?" Mothershed cursed violently. "Yes," the Judge said, "we never thought, sitting in my office on those afternoons, discussing Voltaire and Ingersoll, that we should ever be brought to this, did we? You, the atheist whom the mere sight of a church spire on the sky could enrage; and I who have never been able to divorce myself from reason enough to accept even your pleasant and labor-saving theory of nihilism."

"Labor-saving!" Mothershed cried. "By God, I. . . ." He cursed with impotent fury. The Judge might have been smiling save for his eyes. He sealed the cigarette again.

"Have you a match?"

"What?" Mothershed said. He glared at the Judge, his mouth open. He sought through his clothes. From out the savage movement, strapped beneath his armpit, there peeped fleetly the butt of a heavy pistol. "No," he said. "I ain't."

"Yes," the Judge said. He twisted the cigarette, his gaze light, quizzical. "But you still haven't told me what you are doing here. I heard that you had. . . ."

Again Mothershed cursed, prompt, outraged. "I ain't. I just committed suicide." He glared at the Judge. "God damn it, I remember raising the pistol; I remember the little cold ring it made against my ear; I remember when I told my finger on the trigger. . . ." He glared at the Judge. "I thought that that would be one way I could escape the preachers, since by the church's own token. . . ." He glared at the Judge, his pale gaze apoplectic and outraged. "Well, I know why you are here. You come here looking for that boy."

The Judge looked down, his lip lifted, the movement pouched upward about his eyes. He said quietly, "No."

Mothershed watched him, glared at him. "Looking for that boy. Agnosticism." He snarled it. "Won't say 'Yes' and won't say 'No' until you see which way the cat will jump. Ready to sell out to the highest bidder. By God, I'd rather have give up and died in sanctity, with every heaven-yelping fool in ten miles around. . . ."

"No," the Judge said quietly behind the still, dead gleam of his teeth. Then his teeth vanished quietly, though he did not look up. He sealed the cigarette carefully again. "There seem to be a lot of people here." Mothershed now began to watch him with speculation, tasting his savage gums, his pale furious glare arrested. "You have seen other familiar faces besides my own here, I suppose. Even those of men whom you know only by name, perhaps?"

"Oh," Mothershed said. "I see. I get you now." The Judge seemed to be engrossed in the cigarette. "You want to take a whirl at them too, do you? Go ahead. I hope you will get a little more out of them that will stick to your guts than I did. Maybe you will, since you don't seem to want to know as much as you want something new to be uncertain about. Well, you can get plenty of that from any of them."

"You mean you have. . . ."

Again Mothershed cursed, harsh, savage. "Sure. Ingersoll. Paine. Every bastard one of them that I used to waste my time reading when I had better been sitting on the sunny side of a log."

"Ah," the Judge said. "Ingersoll. Is he. . . ."

"Sure. On a bench just inside the park yonder. And maybe on the same bench you'll find the one that wrote the little women books. If he ain't there, he ought to be."

So the Judge sat forward, elbows on knees, the unlighted cigarette in his fingers. "So you too are reconciled," he said. The man who Mothershed said was Ingersoll looked at his profile quietly. "To this place."

"Ah," the other said. He made a brief, short gesture. "Reconciled."

The Judge did not look up. "You accept it? You acquiesce?" He seemed to be absorbed in the cigarette. "If I could just see Him, talk to Him." The cigarette turned slowly in his fingers. "Perhaps I was seeking Him. Perhaps I was seeking Him all the time I was reading your books, and Voltaire and Montesquieu. Perhaps I was." The cigarette turned slowly. "I have believed in you. In your sincerity. I said, if Truth is to be found by man, this man will be among those who find it. At one time—I was in the throes of that suffering from a still green hurt which causes even an intelligent man to cast about for anything, any straw—I had a foolish conceit: you will be the first to laugh at it as I myself did later. I thought, perhaps there is a hereafter, a way station into nothingness perhaps, where for an instant lesser men might speak face to face with men like you whom they could believe; could hear from such a man's own lips the words: 'There is hope,' or: 'There is nothing.' I said to myself, in such case it will not be Him whom I shall seek; it will be Ingersoll or Paine or Voltaire." He watched the cigarette. "Give me your word now. Say either of these to me. I will believe."

The other looked at the Judge for a time. Then he said, "Why? Believe why?"

The paper about the cigarette had come loose. The Judge twisted it carefully back, handling the cigarette carefully. "You see, I had a son. He was the last of my name and race. After my wife died we lived alone, two men in the house. It had been a good name, you see. I wanted him to be manly, worthy of it. He had a pony which he rode all the time. I have a photograph of them which I use as a bookmark. Often, looking at the picture or watching them unbeknownst as they passed the library window, I would think *What hopes ride yonder;* of the pony I would think *What burden do you blindly bear, dumb brute.* One day they telephoned me at my office. He had been found dragging from the stirrup. Whether the pony had kicked him or he had struck his head in falling, I never knew."

He laid the cigarette carefully on the bench beside him and opened the briefcase. He took out a book. "Voltaire's *Philosophical Dictionary,*" he said. "I always carry a book with me. I am a great reader. It happens that my life is a solitary one, owing to the fact that I am the last of my family, and perhaps to the fact that I am a Republican officeholder in a Democratic stronghold. I am a Federal judge, from a Mississippi district. My wife's father was a Republican." He added quickly, "I believe the tenets of the Republican Party to be best for the country. You will not believe it, but for the last fifteen years my one intellectual companion has been a rabid atheist, almost an illiterate, who not only scorns all logic and science, but who has a distinct body odor as well. Sometimes I have thought, sitting with him in my office on a summer afternoon—a damp one—that if a restoration of faith could remove his prejudice against bathing, I should be justified in going to that length myself even." He took a photograph from the book and extended it. "This was my son."

The other looked at the picture without moving, without offering to take it. From the brown and fading cardboard a boy of ten, erect upon the pony, looked back at them with a grave and tranquil hauteur. "He rode practically all the time. Even to church (I attended church regularly then. I still do, at times, even now). We had to take an extra groom along in the carriage to. . . ." He looked at the picture, musing. "After his mother died I never married again. My own mother was sickly, an invalid. I could cajole her. In the absence of my aunts I could browbeat her into letting me go barefoot in the garden, with two house servants on watch to signal the approach of my aunts. I would return to the house, my manhood triumphant, vindicated, until I entered the room where she waited for me. Then I would know that for every grain of dust which pleasured my feet, she would pay with a second of her life. And we would sit in the dusk like two children, she holding my hand and crying quietly, until my aunts entered with the lamp. 'Now, Sophia. Crying again. What have you let him bulldoze you into doing this time?' She died when I was fourteen; I was twenty-eight before I asserted myself and took the wife of my choice; I was thirty-seven when my son was born." He looked at the photograph, his eyes pouched, netted by two delicate hammocks of myriad lines as fine as etching. "He rode all the time. Hence the picture of the two of them, since they were inseparable. I have used this picture as a bookmark in the printed volumes where his and my ancestry can be followed for ten generations in our American annals, so that as the pages progressed it would be as though with my own eyes I watched him ride in the flesh down the long road which his blood and bone had traveled before it became his." He held the picture. With his other hand he took up the cigarette. The paper had come loose: he held it raised a little and then arrested so, as if he did not dare raise it farther. "And you can give me your word. I will believe."

"Go seek your son," the other said. "Go seek him."

Now the Judge did not move at all. Holding the picture and the dissolving cigarette, he sat in a complete immobility. He seemed to sit in a kind of terrible and unbreathing suspension. "And find him? And find him?" The other did not answer. Then the Judge turned and looked at him, and then the cigarette dropped quietly into dissolution as the tobacco rained down upon his neat, gleaming shoe. "Is that your word? I will believe, I tell you." The other sat, shapeless, gray, sedentary, almost nondescript, looking down. "Come. You cannot stop with that. You cannot."

Along the path before them people passed constantly. A woman passed, carrying a child and a basket, a young woman in a plain, worn, brushed cape. She turned upon the man who Mothershed had said was Ingersoll a plain, bright, pleasant face and spoke to him in a pleasant, tranquil voice. Then she looked at the Judge, pleasantly, a full look without boldness or diffidence, and went on. "Come. You cannot. You cannot." Then his face went completely blank. In the midst of speaking his face emptied; he repeated "cannot. *Cannot*" in a tone of musing consternation. "Cannot," he said. "You mean, you *can*not give me any word? That you do not know? That you, yourself, do not *know*? You, Robert Ingersoll? Robert *Ingersoll*?" The other did not move. "Is Robert Ingersoll telling me that for twenty years I have leaned upon a reed no stronger than myself?"

Still the other did not look up. "You saw that young

woman who just passed, carrying a child. Follow her. Look into her face."

"A young woman. With a. . . ." The Judge looked at the other. "Ah. I see. Yes. I will look at the child and I shall see scars. Then I am to look into the woman's face. Is that it?" The other didn't answer. "That is your answer? your final word?" The other did not move. The Judge's lip lifted. The movement pouched upward about his eyes as though despair, grief, had flared up for a final instant like a dying flame, leaving upon his face its ultimate and fading gleam in a faint grimace of dead teeth. He rose and put the photograph back into the briefcase. "And this is the man who says that he was once Robert Ingersoll." Above his teeth his face mused in that expression which could have been smiling save for the eyes. "It is not proof that I sought. I, of all men, know that proof is but a fallacy invented by man to justify to himself and his fellows his own crass lust and folly. It was not proof that I sought." With the stick and the briefcase clasped beneath his arm he rolled another slender cigarette. "I don't know who you are, but I don't believe you are Robert Ingersoll. Perhaps I could not know it even if you were. Anyway, there is a certain integral consistency which, whether it be right or wrong, a man must cherish because it alone will ever permit him to die. So what I have been, I am; what I am, I shall be until that instant comes when I am not. And then I shall have never been. How does it go? *Non fui. Sum. Fui. Non sum.*"

With the unlighted cigarette in his fingers he thought at first that he would pass on. But instead he paused and looked down at the child. It sat in the path at the woman's feet, surrounded by tiny leaden effigies of men, some erect and some prone. The overturned and now empty basket lay at one side. Then the Judge saw that the effigies were Roman soldiers in various stages of dismemberment—some headless, some armless and legless—scattered about, lying profoundly on their faces or staring up with martial and battered inscrutability from the mild and inscrutable dust. On the exact center of each of the child's insteps was a small scar. There was a third scar in the palm of its exposed hand, and as the Judge looked down with quiet and quizzical bemusement, the child swept flat the few remaining figures and he saw the fourth scar. The child began to cry.

"Shhhhhhhhh," the woman said. She glanced up at the Judge, then she knelt and set the soldiers up. The child cried steadily, with a streaked and dirty face, strong, unhurried, passionless, without tears. "Look!" the woman said, "see? Here! Here's Pilate too! Look!" The child ceased. Tearless, it sat in the dust, looking at the soldiers with an expression as inscrutable as theirs, suspended, aldermanic, and reserved. She swept the soldiers flat. "There!" she cried in a fond, bright voice, "see?" For a moment longer the child sat. Then it began to cry. She took it up and sat on the bench, rocking it back and forth, glancing up at the Judge. "Now, now," she said. "Now, now."

"Is he sick?" the Judge said.

"Oh, no. He's just tired of his toys, as children will get." She rocked the child with an air fond and unconcerned. "Now, now. The gentleman is watching you."

The child cried steadily. "Hasn't he other toys?" the Judge said.

"Oh, yes. So many that I don't dare walk about the

house in the dark. But he likes his soldiers the best. An old gentleman who has lived here a long time, they say, and is quite wealthy, gave them to him. An old gentleman with a white mustache and that kind of popping eyes that old people have who eat too much; I tell him so. He has a footman to carry his umbrella and overcoat and steamer rug, and he sits here with us for more than an hour, sometimes, talking and breathing hard. He always has candy or something." She looked down at the child, her face brooding and serene. It cried steadily. Quizzical, bemused, the Judge stood, looking quietly down at the child's scarred, dirty feet. The woman glanced up and followed his look. "You are looking at his scars and wondering how he got them, aren't you? The other children did it one day when they were playing. Of course they didn't know they were going to hurt him. I imagine they were as surprised as he was. You know how children are when they get too quiet."

"Yes," the Judge said. "I had a son too."

"You have? Why don't you bring him here? I'm sure we would be glad to have him play with our soldiers too."

The Judge's teeth glinted quietly. "I'm afraid he's a little too big for toys." He took the photograph from the briefcase. "This was my son."

The woman took the picture. The child cried steady and strong. "Why, it's Howard. Why, we see him every day. He rides past here every day. Sometimes he stops and lets us ride too. I walk beside to hold him on," she added, glancing up. She showed the picture to the child. "Look! See Howard on his pony? See?" Without ceasing to cry, the child contemplated the picture, its face streaked with tears and dirt, its expression detached, suspended, as though it were living two distinct and separate lives at one time. She returned the picture. "I suppose you are looking for him."

"Ah," the Judge said behind his momentary teeth. He replaced the picture carefully in the briefcase, the unlighted cigarette in his fingers.

The woman moved on the bench, gathering her skirts in with invitation. "Won't you sit down? You will be sure to see him pass here."

"Ah," the Judge said again. He looked at her, quizzical, with the blurred eyes of the old. "It's like this, you see. He always rides the same pony, you say?"

"Why, yes." She looked at him with grave and tranquil surprise.

"And how old would you say the pony is?"

"Why, I. . . . It looks just the right size for him."

"A young pony, you would say then?"

"Why . . . yes. Yes." She watched him, her eyes wide.

"Ah," the Judge said again behind his faint still teeth. He closed the briefcase carefully. From his pocket he took a half dollar. "Perhaps he is tired of the soldiers too. Perhaps with this. . . ."

"Thank you," she said. She did not look again at the coin. "Your face is so sad. There: when you think you are smiling it is sadder than ever. Aren't you well?" She glanced down at his extended hand. She did not offer to take the coin. "He'd just lose it, you see. And it's so pretty and bright. When he is older, and can take care of small playthings. . . . He's so little now, you see."

"I see," the Judge said. He put the coin back into his pocket. "Well, I think I shall—"

"You wait here with us. He always passes here. You'll find him quicker that way."

"Ah," the Judge said. "On the pony, the same pony. You see, by that token, the pony would have to be thirty years old. That pony died at eighteen, six years unridden, in my lot. That was twelve years ago. So I had better get on."

And again it was quite unpleasant. It should have been doubly so, what with the narrow entrance and the fact that, while the other time he was moving with the crowd, this time he must fight his way inch by inch against it. "But at least I know where I am going," he thought, beneath his crushed hat, his stick and briefcase dragging at his arms; "which I did not seem to know before." But he was free at last, and looking up at the clock on the courthouse, as he never failed to do on descending his office stairs, he saw that he had a full hour before supper would be ready, before the neighbors would be ready to mark his clocklike passing.

"I shall have time to go to the cemetery," he thought, and looking down at the raw and recent excavation, he swore with fretful annoyance, for some of the savage clods had fallen or been thrown upon the marble slab beside it. "Damn that Pettigrew," he said. "He should have seen to this. I told him I wanted the two of them as close as possible, but at least I thought that he. . . ." Kneeling, he tried to remove the earth which had fallen upon the slab. But it was beyond his strength to do more than clear away that which partially obscured the lettering: *Howard Allison II. April 3, 1903. August 22, 1913*, and the quietly cryptic Gothic lettering at the foot: *Auf Wiedersehen, Lit-*

tle Boy. He continued to smooth, to stroke the letters after the earth was gone, his face bemused, quiet, as he spoke to the man who Mothershed had said was Ingersoll, "You see, if I could believe that I shall see and touch him again, I shall not have lost him. And if I have not lost him, I shall never have had a son. Because I am I through bereavement and because of it. I do not know what I was nor what I shall be. But because of death, I know that I am. And that is all the immortality of which intellect is capable and flesh should desire. Anything else is for peasants, clods, who could never have loved a son well enough to have lost him." His face broke, myriad, quizzical, while his hand moved lightly upon the quiet lettering. "No. I do not require that. To lie beside him will be sufficient for me. There will be a wall of dust between us: that is true, and he is already dust these twenty years. But some day I shall be dust too. And—" he spoke now firmly, quietly, with a kind of triumph: "who is he who will affirm that there must be a web of flesh and bone to hold the shape of love?"

Now it was late. "Probably they are setting their clocks back at this very moment," he thought, pacing along the street toward his home. Already he should have been hearing the lawn mower, and then in the instant of exasperation at Jake, he remarked the line of motor cars before his gate and a sudden haste came upon him. But not so much but what, looking at the vehicle at the head of the line, he cursed again. "Damn that Pettigrew! I told him, in the presence of witnesses when I signed my will, that I would not be hauled feet first through Jefferson at forty miles an hour. That if he couldn't find me a decent pair of horses. . . . I am a good mind to come back and haunt him, as Jake would have me do."

But the haste, the urgency, was upon him. He hurried round to the back door (he remarked that the lawn was freshly and neatly trimmed, as though done that day) and entered. Then he could smell the flowers faintly and hear the voice; he had just time to slip out of his overcoat and pajamas and leave them hanging neatly in the closet, and cross the hall into the odor of cut flowers and the drone of the voice, and slip into his clothes. They had been recently pressed, and his face had been shaved too. Nevertheless they were his own, and he fitted himself to the olden and familiar embrace which no iron could change, with the same lascivious eagerness with which he shaped his limbs to the bedclothes on a winter night.

"Ah," he said to the man who Mothershed had said was Ingersoll, "this is best, after all. An old man is never at home save in his own garments: his own old thinking and beliefs; old hands and feet, elbow, knee, shoulder which he knows will fit."

Now the light vanished with a mute, faint, decorous hollow sound which drove for a fading instant down upon him the dreadful, macabre smell of slain flowers; at the same time he became aware that the droning voice had ceased. "In my own house too," he thought, waiting for the smell of the flowers to fade; "yet I did not once think to notice who was speaking, nor when he ceased." Then he heard or felt the decorous scuffing of feet about him, and he lay in the close dark, his hands folded upon his breast as he slept, as the old sleep, waiting for the moment. It came. He said quietly aloud, quizzical, humorous, peaceful, as he did each night in his bed in his lonely and peaceful room when a last full exhalation had emptied his body of waking and he seemed for less than an instant to look about him from the portal of sleep, "Gentlemen of the Jury, you may proceed."

Race at Morning

I was in the boat when I seen him. It was jest dust-dark; I had jest fed the horses and clumb back down the bank to the boat and shoved off to cross back to camp when I seen him, about half a quarter up the river, swimming; jest his head above the water, and it no more than a dot in that light. But I could see that rocking chair he toted on it and I knowed it was him, going right back to that canebrake in the fork of the bayou where he lived all year until the day before the season opened, like the game wardens had give him a calendar, when he would clear out and disappear, nobody knowed where, until the day after the season closed. But here he was, coming back a day ahead of time, like maybe he had got mixed up and was using last year's calendar by mistake. Which was jest too bad for him, because me and Mister Ernest would be setting on the horse right over him when the sun rose tomorrow morning.

So I told Mister Ernest and we et supper and fed the dogs, and then I holp Mister Ernest in the poker game, standing behind his chair until about ten o'clock, when Roth Edmonds said, "Why don't you go to bed, boy?"

"Or if you're going to set up," Willy Legate said, "why don't you take a spelling book to set up over? He

289

290 / WILLIAM FAULKNER

knows every cuss word in the dictionary, every poker
hand in the deck and every whisky label in the distillery,
but he can't even write his name. Can you?" he says
to me.

"I don't need to write my name down," I said. "I can
remember in my mind who I am."

"You're twelve years old," Walter Ewell said. "Man
to man now, how many days in your life did you ever
spend in school?"

"He ain't got time to go to school," Willy Legate said.
"What's the use in going to school from September to
middle of November, when he'll have to quit then to
come in here and do Ernest's hearing for him? And
what's the use in going back to school in January, when in
jest eleven months it will be November fifteenth again
and he'll have to start all over telling Ernest which way
the dogs went?"

"Well, stop looking into my hand, anyway," Roth
Edmonds said.

"What's that? What's that?" Mister Ernest said. He
wore his listening button in his ear all the time, but he
never brought the battery to camp with him because the
cord would bound to get snagged ever time we run
through a thicket.

"Willy says for me to go to bed!" I hollered.

"Don't you never call nobody 'mister'?" Willy said.

"I call Mister Ernest 'mister,' " I said.

"All right," Mister Ernest said. "Go to bed then. I
don't need you."

"That ain't no lie," Willy said. "Deaf or no deaf, he
can hear a fifty-dollar raise if you don't even move your
lips."

So I went to bed, and after a while Mister Ernest come in and I wanted to tell him again how big them horns looked even half a quarter away in the river. Only I would 'a' had to holler, and the only time Mister Ernest agreed he couldn't hear was when we would be setting on Dan, waiting for me to point which way the dogs was going. So we jest laid down, and it wasn't no time Simon was heating the bottom of the dishpan with the spoon, hollering, "Raise up and get your four-o'clock coffee!" and I crossed the river in the dark this time, with the lantern, and fed Dan and Roth Edmondziz horse. It was going to be a fine day, cold and bright; even in the dark I could see the white frost on the leaves and bushes—jest exactly the kind of day that big old son of a gun laying up there in that brake would like to run.

Then we et, and set the stand-holder across for Uncle Ike McCaslin to put them on the stands where he thought they ought to be, because he was the oldest one in camp. He had been hunting deer in these woods for about a hundred years, I reckon, and if anybody would know where a buck would pass, it would be him. Maybe with a big old buck like this one, that had been running the woods for what would amount to a hundred years in a deer's life, too, him and Uncle Ike would sholy manage to be at the same place at the same time this morning—provided, of course, he managed to git away from me and Mister Ernest on the jump. Because me and Mister Ernest was going to git him.

Then me and Mister Ernest and Roth Edmonds sent the dogs over, with Simon holding Eagle and the other old dogs on leash because the young ones, the puppies, wasn't going nowhere until Eagle let them, nohow. Then me and

Mister Ernest and Roth saddled up, and Mister Ernest got up and I handed him up his pump gun and let Dan's bridle go for him to git rid of the spell of bucking he had to git shut of ever morning until Mister Ernest hit him between the ears with the gun barrel. Then Mister Ernest loaded the gun and give me the stirrup, and I got up behind him and we taken the fire road up toward the bayou, the four big dogs dragging Simon along in front with his single-barrel britch-loader slung on a piece of plow line across his back, and the puppies moiling along in ever'body's way. It was light now and it was going to be jest fine; the east already yellow for the sun and our breaths smoking in the cold still bright air until the sun would come up and warm it, and a little skim of ice in the ruts, and ever leaf and twig and switch and even the frozen clods frosted over, waiting to sparkle like a rainbow when the sun finally come up and hit them. Until all my insides felt light and strong as a balloon, full of that light cold strong air, so that it seemed to me like I couldn't even feel the horse's back I was straddle of—jest the hot strong muscles moving under the hot strong skin, setting up there without no weight atall, so that when old Eagle struck and jumped, me and Dan and Mister Ernest would go jest like a bird, not even touching the ground. It was jest fine. When that big old buck got killed today, I knowed that even if he had put it off another ten years, he couldn't 'a' picked a better one.

And sho enough, as soon as we come to the bayou we seen his foot in the mud where he had come up out of the river last night, spread in the soft mud like a cow's foot, big as a cow's, big as a mule's, with Eagle and the other dogs laying into the leash rope now until Mister Ernest told me to jump down and help Simon hold them. Because me and Mister Ernest knowed exactly where he would be—a little canebrake island in the middle of the bayou, where he could lay up until whatever doe or little deer the dogs had happened to jump could go up or down the bayou in either direction and take the dogs on away, so he could steal out and creep back down the bayou to the river and swim it, and leave the country like he always done the day the season opened.

Which is jest what we never aimed for him to do this time. So we left Roth on his horse to cut him off and turn him over Uncle Ike's standers if he tried to slip back down the bayou, and me and Simon, with the leashed dogs, walked on up the bayou until Mister Ernest on the horse said it was fur enough; then turned up into the woods about half a quarter above the brake because the wind was going to be south this morning when it riz, and turned down toward the brake, and Mister Ernest give the word to cast them, and we slipped the leash and Mister Ernest give me the stirrup again and I got up.

Old Eagle had done already took off because he knowed where that old son of a gun would be laying as good as we did, not making no racket atall yet, but jest boring on through the buck vines with the other dogs trailing along behind him, and even Dan seemed to know about that buck, too, beginning to souple up and jump a little through the vines, so that I taken my holt on Mister Ernest's belt already before the time had come for Mister Ernest to touch him. Because when we got strung out, going fast behind a deer, I wasn't on Dan's back much of the time nohow, but mostly jest strung out from my holt on Mister Ernest's belt, so that Willy Legate said that when we was going through the woods fast, it looked like Mister Ernest had a boy-size pair of empty overalls blowing out of his hind pocket.

So it wasn't even a strike, it was a jump. Eagle must 'a' walked right up behind him or maybe even stepped on him while he was laying there still thinking it was day after tomorrow. Eagle jest throwed his head back and up and said, "There he goes," and we even heard the buck crashing through the first of the cane. Then all the other dogs was hollering behind him, and Dan give a squat to jump, but it was against the curb this time, not jest the snaffle, and Mister Ernest let him down into the bayou and swung him around the brake and up the other bank. Only he never had to say, "Which way?" because I was already pointing past his shoulder, freshening my holt on the belt jest as Mister Ernest touched Dan with that big old rusty spur on his nigh heel, because when Dan felt it he would go off jest like a stick of dynamite, straight through whatever he could bust and over or under what he couldn't, over it like a bird or under it crawling on his knees like a mole or a big coon, with Mister Ernest still on him because he had the saddle to hold on to, and me still there because I had Mister Ernest to hold on to; me and Mister Ernest not riding him, but jest going along with him, provided we held on. Because when the jump come, Dan never cared who else was there neither; I believe to my soul he could 'a' cast and run them dogs by hisself, without me or Mister Ernest or Simon or nobody.

That's what he done. He had to; the dogs was already almost out of hearing. Eagle must 'a' been looking right up that big son of a gun's tail until he finally decided he better git on out of there. And now they must 'a' been getting pretty close to Uncle Ike's standers, and Mister Ernest reined Dan back and held him, squatting and bouncing and trembling like a mule having his tail roached, while we listened for the shots. But never none come, and I hollered to Mister Ernest we better go on while I could still hear the dogs, and he let Dan off, but still there wasn't no shots, and now we knowed the race had done already passed the standers, like that old son of a gun actually was a hant, like Simon and the other field hands said he was, and we busted out of a thicket, and sho enough there was Uncle Ike and Willy standing beside his foot in a soft patch.

"He got through us all," Uncle Ike said. "I don't know how he done it. I just had a glimpse of him. He looked big as a elephant, with a rack on his head you could cradle a yellin' calf in. He went right on down the ridge. You better get on, too; that Hog Bayou camp might not miss him."

So I freshened my holt and Mister Ernest touched Dan again. The ridge run due south; it was clear of vines and bushes so we could go fast, into the wind, too, because it had riz now, and now the sun was up, too; though I hadn't had time to notice it, bright and strong and level through the woods, shining and sparking like a rainbow on the frosted leaves. So we would hear the dogs again any time now as the wind got up; we could make time now, but still holding Dan back to a canter, because it was either going to be quick, when he got down to the standers from that Hog Bayou camp eight miles below ourn, or a long time, in case he got by them, too. And sho enough, after a while we heard the dogs; we was walking

Dan now to let him blow a while, and we heard them, the sound coming faint up the wind, not running now, but trailing because the big son of a gun had decided a good piece back, probably, to put a end to this foolishness, and picked hisself up and souled out and put about a mile between hisself and the dogs—until he run up on them other standers from that camp below. I could almost see him stopped behind a bush, peeping out and saying, "What's this? What's this? Is this whole durn country full of folks this morning?" Then looking back over his shoulder at where old Eagle and the others was hollering along after him while he decided how much time he had to decide what to do next.

Except he almost shaved it too fine. We heard the shots; it sounded like a war. Old Eagle must 'a' been looking right up his tail again and he had to bust on through the best way he could. "Pow, pow, pow, pow" and then "Pow, pow, pow, pow," like it must 'a' been three or four ganged right up on him before he had time even to swerve, and me hollering, "No! No! No! No!" because he was ourn. It was our beans and oats he et and our brake he laid in; we had been watching him every year, and it was like we had raised him, to be killed at last on our jump, in front of our dogs, by some strangers that would probably try to beat the dogs off and drag him away before we could even git a piece of the meat.

"Shut up and listen," Mister Ernest said. So I done it and we could hear the dogs; not just the others, but Eagle, too, not trailing no scent now and not baying no downed meat neither, but running hot on sight long after the shooting was over. I jest had time to freshen my holt. Yes, sir, they was running on sight. Like Willy Legate would say, if Eagle jest had a drink of whisky he would ketch that deer; going on, done already gone when we broke out of the thicket and seen the fellers that had done the shooting, five or six of them, squatting and crawling around, looking at the ground and the bushes, like maybe if they looked hard enough, spots of blood would bloom out on the stalks and leaves like frogstools or hawberries, with old Eagle still in hearing and still telling them that what blood they found wasn't coming out of nothing in front of him.

"Have any luck, boys?" Mister Ernest said.

"I think I hit him," one of them said. "I know I did. We're hunting blood now."

"Well, when you find him, blow your horn and I'll come back and tote him in to camp for you," Mister Ernest said.

So we went on, going fast now because the race was almost out of hearing again, going fast, too, like not jest the buck, but the dogs, too, had took a new leash on life from all the excitement and shooting.

We was in strange country now because we never had to run this fur before, we had always killed before now; now we had come to Hog Bayou that runs into the river a good fifteen miles below our camp. It had water in it, not to mention a mess of down trees and logs and such, and Mister Ernest checked Dan again, saying, "Which way?" I could just barely hear them, off to the east a little, like the old son of a gun had give up the idea of Vicksburg or New Orleans, like he first seemed to have, and had decided to have a look at Alabama, maybe, since he was already up and moving; so I pointed and we turned up the bayou hunting for a crossing, and maybe we could 'a' found one, except that I reckon Mister Ernest decided we never had time to wait.

We come to a place where the bayou had narrowed down to about twelve or fifteen feet, and Mister Ernest said, "Look out, I'm going to touch him" and done it; I didn't even have time to freshen my holt when we was already in the air, and then I seen the vine—it was a loop of grapevine nigh as big as my wrist, looping down right across the middle of the bayou—and I thought he seen it, too, and was jest waiting to grab it and fling it up over our heads to go under it, and I know Dan seen it because he even ducked his head to jump under it. But Mister Ernest never seen it atall until it skun back along Dan's neck and hooked under the head of the saddle horn, us flying on through the air, the loop of the vine gitting tighter and tighter until something somewhere was going to have to give. It was the saddle girth. It broke, and Dan going on and scrabbling up the other bank bare nekkid except for the bridle, and me and Mister Ernest and the saddle, Mister Ernest still setting in the saddle holding the gun, and me still holding onto Mister Ernest's belt, hanging in the air over the bayou in the tightened loop of that vine like in the drawed-back loop of a big rubber-banded slingshot, until it snapped back and shot us back across the bayou and flang us clear, me still holding onto Mister Ernest's belt and on the bottom now, so that when we lit I would 'a' had Mister Ernest and the saddle both on top of me if I hadn't clumb fast around the saddle and up Mister Ernest's side, so that when we landed, it was the saddle first, then Mister Ernest, and me on top, until I jumped up, and Mister Ernest still laying there with jest the white rim of his eyes showing.

"Mister Ernest!" I hollered, and then clumb down to the bayou and scooped my cap full of water and clumb back and throwed it in his face, and he opened his eyes and laid there on the saddle cussing me.

"God dawg it," he said, "why didn't you stay behind where you started out?"

"You was the biggest!" I said. "You would 'a' mashed me flat!"

"What do you think you done to me?" Mister Ernest said. "Next time, if you can't stay where you start out, jump clear. Don't climb up on top of me no more. You hear?"

"Yes, sir," I said.

So he got up then, still cussing and holding his back, and clumb down to the water and dipped some in his hand onto his face and neck and dipped some more up and drunk it, and I drunk some, too, and clumb back and got the saddle and the gun, and we crossed the bayou on the down logs. If we could jest ketch Dan; not that he would have went them fifteen miles back to camp, because, if anything, he would have went on by hisself to try to help Eagle ketch that buck. But he was about fifty yards away, eating buck vines, so I brought him back, and we taken Mister Ernest's galluses and my belt and the whang leather loop off Mister Ernest's horn and tied the saddle back on Dan. It didn't look like much, but maybe it would hold.

"Provided you don't let me jump him through no more grapevines without hollering first," Mister Ernest said.

"Yes, sir," I said. "I'll holler first next time—provided you'll holler a little quicker when you touch him next time, too." But it was all right; we jest had to be a little easy getting up. "Now which-a-way?" I said. Because we couldn't hear nothing now, after wasting all this time. And this was new country, sho enough. It had been cut over and growed up in thickets we couldn't 'a' seen over even standing up on Dan.

But Mister Ernest never even answered. He jest turned Dan along the bank of the bayou where it was a little more open and we could move faster again, soon as Dan and us got used to that homemade cinch strop and got a little confidence in it. Which jest happened to be east, or so I thought then, because I never paid no particular attention to east then because the sun—I don't know where the morning had went, but it was gone, the morning and the frost, too—was up high now, even if my insides had told me it was past dinnertime.

And then we heard him. No, that's wrong; what we heard was shots. And that was when we realized how fur he had come, because the only camp we knowed about in that direction was the Hollyknowe camp, and Hollyknowe was exactly twenty-eight miles from Van Dorn, where me and Mister Ernest lived—jest the shots, no dogs nor nothing. If old Eagle was still behind him and the buck was still alive, he was too wore out now to even say, "Here he comes."

"Don't touch him!" I hollered. But Mister Ernest remembered that cinch strop, too, and he jest let Dan off the snaffle. And Dan heard them shots, too, picking his way through the thickets, hopping the vines and logs when he could and going under them when he couldn't. And sho enough, it was jest like before—two or three men squatting and creeping among the bushes, looking for blood that Eagle had done already told them wasn't there.

But we never stopped this time, jest trotting on by with Dan hopping and dodging among the brush and vines dainty as a dancer. Then Mister Ernest swung Dan until we was going due north.

"Wait!" I hollered. "Not this way."

But Mister Ernest jest turned his face back over his shoulder. It looked tired, too, and there was a smear of mud on it where that ere grapevine had snatched him off the horse.

"Don't you know where he's heading?" he said. "He's done done his part, give everybody a fair open shot at him, and now he's going home, back to that brake in our bayou. He ought to make it exactly at dark."

And that's what he was doing. We went on. It didn't matter to hurry now. There wasn't no sound nowhere; it was that time in the early afternoon in November when don't nothing move or cry, not even birds, the pecker-woods and yellowhammers and jays, and it seemed to me like I could see all three of us—me and Mister Ernest and Dan—and Eagle, and the other dogs, and that big old buck, moving through the quiet woods in the same direction, headed for the same place, not running now but walking, that had all run the fine race the best we knowed how, and all three of us now turned like on a agreement to walk back home, not together in a bunch because we didn't want to worry or tempt one another, because what we had all three spent this morning doing was no play-acting jest for fun, but was serious, and all three of us was still what we was—that old buck that had to run, not because he was skeered, but because running was what he done the best and was proudest at; and Eagle and the dogs that chased him, not because they hated or feared him, but because that was the thing they done the best and was proudest at; and me and Mister Ernest and Dan, that run him not because we wanted his meat, which would be too tough to eat anyhow, or his head to hang on a wall, but because now we could go back and work hard for eleven months making a crop, so we would have the right to come back here next November—all three of us going back home now, peaceful and separate, but still side by side, until next year, next time.

Then we seen him for the first time. We was out of the cut-over now; we could even 'a' cantered, except that all three of us was long past that, and now you could tell where west was because the sun was already halfway down it. So we was walking, too, when we come on the dogs—the puppies and one of the old ones—played out, laying in a little wet swag, panting, jest looking up at us when we passed, but not moving when we went on. Then we come to a long open glade, you could see about half a quarter, and we seen the three other old dogs and about a hundred yards ahead of them Eagle, all walking, not making no sound; and then suddenly, at the fur end of the glade, the buck hisself getting up from where he had been resting for the dogs to come up, getting up without no hurry, big, big as a mule, tall as a mule, and turned without no hurry still, and the white underside of his tail for a second or two more before the thicket taken him.

It might 'a' been a signal, a good-bye, a farewell. Still walking, we passed the other three old dogs in the middle of the glade, laying down, too, now jest where they was when the buck vanished, and not trying to get up neither when we passed; and still that hundred yards ahead of them, Eagle, too, not laying down, because he was still on his feet, but his legs was spraddled and his head was down; maybe jest waiting until we was out of sight of his shame, his eyes saying plain as talk when we passed, "I'm sorry, boys, but this here is all."

Mister Ernest stopped Dan. "Jump down and look at his feet," he said.

"Ain't nothing wrong with his feet," I said. "It's his wind has done give out."

"Jump down and look at his feet," Mister Ernest said.

So I done it, and while I was stooping over Eagle I could hear the pump gun go, "Snick-cluck. Snick-cluck. Snick-cluck" three times, except that I never thought nothing then. Maybe he was jest running the shells through to be sho it would work when we seen him again or maybe to make sho they was all buckshot. Then I got up again, and we went on, still walking; a little west of north now, because when we seen his white flag that second or two before the thicket hid it, it was on a beeline for that notch in the bayou. And it was evening, too, now. The wind had done dropped and there was a edge to the air and the sun jest touched the tops of the trees now, except jest now and then, when it found a hole to come almost level through onto the ground. And he was taking the easiest way, too, now, going straight as he could. When we seen his foot in the soft places he was running for a while at first after his rest. But soon he was walking, too, like he knowed, too, where Eagle and the dogs was.

And then we seen him again. It was the last time—a thicket, with the sun coming through a hole onto it like a searchlight. He crashed jest once; then he was standing there broadside to us, not twenty yards away, big as a statue and red as gold in the sun, and the sun sparking on the tips of his horns—they was twelve of them—so that he looked like he had twelve lighted candles branched around his head, standing there looking at us while Mister Ernest raised the gun and aimed at his neck, and the gun went, "Click. Snick-cluck. Click. Snick-cluck. Click. Snick-cluck" three times, and Mister Ernest still holding the gun aimed while the buck turned and give one long bound, the white underside of his tail like a blaze of fire, too, until the thicket and the shadows put it out; and Mister Ernest laid the gun slow and gentle back across the saddle in front of him, saying quiet and peaceful, and not much louder than jest breathing, "God dawg. God dawg."

Then he jogged me with his elbow and we got down, easy and careful because of that ere cinch strop and he reached into his vest and taken out one of the cigars. It was busted where I had fell on it, I reckon, when we hit the ground. He throwed it away and taken out the other one. It was busted, too, so he bit off a hunk of it to chew and throwed the rest away. And now the sun was gone even from the tops of the trees and there wasn't nothing left but a big red glare in the west.

"Don't worry," I said. "I ain't going to tell them you forgot to load your gun. For that matter, they don't need to know we ever seed him."

"Much oblige," Mister Ernest said. There wasn't going to be no moon tonight neither, so he taken the compass off the whang leather loop in his buttonhole and handed me the gun and set compass on a stump and stepped back and looked at it. "Just about the way we're headed now," he said, and taken the gun from me and opened it and put one shell in the britch and taken up the compass, and I taken Dan's reins and we started, with him in front with the compass in his hand.

And after a while it was full dark; Mister Ernest would have to strike a match ever now and then to read the compass, until the stars come out good and we could pick out one to follow, because I said, "How fur do you reckon it is?" and he said, "A little more than one box of matches." So we used a star when we could, only we couldn't see it all the time because the woods was too dense and we would git a little off until he would have to spend another match. And now it was good and late, and he stopped and said, "Get on the horse."

"I ain't tired," I said.

"Get on the horse," he said. "We don't want to spoil him."

Because he had been a good feller ever since I had knowed him, which was even before that day two years ago when maw went off with the Vicksburg roadhouse feller and the next day pap didn't come home neither, and on the third one Mister Ernest rid Dan up to the door of the cabin on the river he let us live in, so pap could work his piece of land and run his fish line, too, and said, "Put that gun down and come on here and climb up behind."

So I got in the saddle even if I couldn't reach the stirrups, and Mister Ernest taken the reins and I must 'a' went to sleep, because the next thing I knowed a buttonhole of my lumberjack was tied to the saddle horn with that ere whang cord off the compass, and it was good and late now and we wasn't fur, because Dan was already smelling water, the river. Or maybe it was the feed lot itself he smelled, because we struck the fire road not a quarter below it, and soon I could see the river, too, with the white mist laying on it soft and still as cotton. Then the lot, home; and up yonder in the dark, not no piece akchully, close enough to hear us unsaddling and shucking corn prob'ly, and sholy close enough to hear Mister Ernest blowing his horn at the dark camp for Simon to come in the boat and git us, that old buck in his brake in the bayou; home, too, resting, too, after the hard run, waking hisself now and then, dreaming of dogs behind him or maybe it was the racket we was making would wake him, but not neither of them for more than jest a little while before sleeping again.

Then Mister Ernest stood on the bank blowing until Simon's lantern went bobbing down into the mist; then we clumb down to the landing and Mister Ernest blowed again now and then to guide Simon, until we seen the lantern in the mist, and then Simon and the boat; only it looked like ever time I set down and got still, I went back to sleep, because Mister Ernest was shaking me again to git out and climb the bank into the dark camp, until I felt a bed against my knees and tumbled into it.

Then it was morning, tomorrow; it was all over now until next November, next year, and we could come back. Uncle Ike and Willy and Walter and Roth and the rest of them had come in yestiddy, soon as Eagle taken the buck out of hearing and they knowed that deer was gone, to pack up and be ready to leave this morning for Yoknapatawpha, where they lived, until it would be November again and they could come back again.

So, as soon as we et breakfast, Simon run them back up the river in the big boat to where they left their cars and pickups, and now it wasn't nobody but jest me and Mister Ernest setting on the bench against the kitchen wall in the sun; Mister Ernest smoking a cigar—a whole one this time that Dan hadn't had no chance to jump him through a grapevine and bust. He hadn't washed his face neither where that vine had throwed him into the mud. But that was all right, too; his face usually did have a smudge of mud or tractor grease or beard stubble on it, because he wasn't jest a planter; he was a farmer, he worked as hard as ara one of his hands and tenants—which is why I knowed from the very first that we would git along, that I wouldn't have no trouble with him and he wouldn't have no trouble with me, from that very first day when I woke up and maw had done gone off with that Vicksburg road-house feller without even waiting to cook breakfast, and the next morning pap was gone, too, and it was almost night the next day when I heard a horse coming up and I taken the gun that I had already throwed a shell into the britch when pap never came home last night, and stood in the door while Mister Ernest rid up and said, "Come on. Your paw ain't coming back neither."

"You mean he give me to you?" I said.

"Who cares?" he said. "Come on. I brought a lock for the door. We'll send the pickup back tomorrow for whatever you want."

So I come home with him and it was all right, it was jest fine—his wife had died about three years ago—without no women to worry us or take off in the middle of the night with a durn Vicksburg roadhouse jake without even waiting to cook breakfast. And we would go home this afternoon, too, but not jest yet; we always stayed one more day after the others left because Uncle Ike always left what grub they hadn't et, and the rest of the homemade corn whisky he drunk and that town whisky of Roth Edmondziz he called Scotch that smelled like it come out of a old bucket of roof paint; setting in the sun for one more day before we went back home to git ready to put in next year's crop of cotton and oats and beans and hay; and across the river yonder, behind the wall of trees where the big woods started, that old buck laying up today in the sun, too—resting today, too, without nobody to bother him until next November.

So at least one of us was glad it would be eleven months and two weeks before he would have to run that fur that fast again. So he was glad of the very same thing we was sorry of, and so all of a sudden I thought about how maybe planting and working and then harvesting oats and cotton and beans and hay wasn't jest something me and Mister Ernest done three hundred and fifty-one days to fill in the time until we could come back hunting again, but it was something we had to do, and do honest and good during the three hundred and fifty-one days, to have the right to come back into the big woods and hunt for the other fourteen; and the fourteen days that old buck run in front of dogs wasn't jest something to fill his time until the three hundred and fifty-one when he didn't have to, but the running and the risking in front of guns and dogs was something he had to do for fourteen days to have the right not to be bothered for the other three hundred and fifty-one. And so the hunting and the farming wasn't two different things atall—they was jest the other side of each other.

"Yes," I said. "All we got to do now is put in that next year's crop. Then November won't be no time away atall."

"You ain't going to put in the crop next year," Mister Ernest said. "You're going to school."

So at first I didn't even believe I had heard him. "What?" I said. "Me? Go to school?"

"Yes," Mister Ernest said. "You must make something out of yourself."

"I am," I said. "I'm doing it now. I'm going to be a hunter and a farmer like you."

"No," Mister Ernest said. "That ain't enough any more. Time was when all a man had to do was just farm eleven and a half months, and hunt the other half. But not now. Now just to belong to the farming business and the hunting business ain't enough. You got to belong to the business of mankind."

"Mankind?" I said.

"Yes," Mister Ernest said. "So you're going to school. Because you got to know why. You can belong to the farming and hunting business and you can learn the difference between what's right and what's wrong, and do right. And that used to be enough—just to do right. But not now. You got to know why it's right and why it's wrong, and be able to tell the folks that never had no chance to learn it; teach them how to do what's right, not just because they know it's right, but because they know now why it's right because you just showed them, told them, taught them why. So you're going to school."

"It's because you been listening to that durn Will Legate and Walter Ewell!" I said.

"No," Mister Ernest said.

"Yes!" I said. "No wonder you missed that buck yestiddy, taking ideas from the very fellers that let him git away, after me and you had run Dan and the dogs durn nigh clean to death! Because you never even missed him! You never forgot to load that gun! You had done already unloaded it a purpose! I heard you!"

"All right, all right," Mister Ernest said. "Which would you rather have? His bloody head and hide on the kitchen floor yonder and half his meat in a pickup truck on the way to Yoknapatawpha County, or him with his head and hide and meat still together over yonder in that brake, waiting for next November for us to run him again?"

"And git him, too," I said. "We won't even fool with no Willy Legate and Walter Ewell next time."

"Maybe," Mister Ernest said.

"Yes," I said.

"Maybe," Mister Ernest said. "The best word in our language, the best of all. That's what mankind keeps going on: Maybe. The best days of his life ain't the ones when he said 'Yes' beforehand: they're the ones when all he knew to say was 'Maybe.' He can't say 'Yes' until afterward because he not only don't know it until then, he don't want to know 'Yes' until then. . . . Step in the kitchen and make me a toddy. Then we'll see about dinner."

"All right," I said. I got up. "You want some of Uncle Ike's corn or that town whisky of Roth Edmondziz?"

"Can't you say Mister Roth or Mister Edmonds?" Mister Ernest said.

"Yes, sir," I said. "Well, which do you want? Uncle Ike's corn or that ere stuff of Roth Edmondziz?"

A NOTE ON THE TYPE

The principal text of this Modern Library edition
was composed in a digitized version of
Horley Old Style, a typeface issued by
the English type foundry Monotype in 1925.
It is an old-style face, with such distinctive features
as lightly cupped serifs and an oblique horizontal bar
on the lower case "e."